The Sewerside
Chronicles

Tim Lay

A first novel by Tim Lay, Undiscovered Authors
National Fiction Winner 2007

Available from Discovered Authors Online –
All major online retailers and available to order through all UK bookshops

Or contact:

Books
Discovered Authors
Roslin Road, London
W3 8DH

0844 800 5214
books@discoveredauthors.co.uk
www.discoveredauthors.co.uk

Printed in the UK by BookForce Distribution
BookForce Distribution policy is to use papers that are natural, renewable
and recyclable products and made from wood grown in sustainable forests
wherever possible

BookForce Distribution.
Roslin Road, London
W3 8DH

www.bookforce.co.uk

Chapter One

You want to know about fashion? Let me tell you about fashion. It's expensive, it's time consuming, and it's almost impossible to get it right.

Take a pair of trousers, for instance. It takes two and a half metres of material to make your average pair. Before they even get made you need to get yourself a pattern, and pattern cutters' fees don't come cheap. Add in the cost of your trimmings: labels (washing instructions on the back of the waistband, folded logo labels stitched into the seams), buttons, velcro, shock chord, eyelets, and don't forget about the zips.

All this has to be factored into the price even before you start manufacturing your samples, and believe me, getting the sample right is a time-consuming process. How much your garment costs to make depends on how long it takes your manufacturer to make it. He or she does this by working out how many pieces there are in your pattern and how long it will take to put them together.

To be a player, you're required to produce two collections per year, one winter and one summer, and one year ahead of the market. It's a non-stop conveyor belt of production, consumption and redundancy – for after all, today's fashion is tomorrow's rags.

The cliché that you hear the most in the rag trade is: 'If I knew then what I knew now, I probably wouldn't have bothered.' Now if I'd known all that shit I know now, back then, back at the beginning, maybe things would have been different, but that's someone else's story…

It was cold in the yard. High ceilings, big windows and no heating, the building was old, and the walls were thick. The 'yard', our office, was a huge loft space at the top of three long flights of stairs. It was often colder up here than it was outside, and on a Monday morning in January it was as depressing as a prefabricated farmhouse in Siberia.

I was sitting at my desk wearing thermal underwear I'd bought from the army surplus store – two pairs of socks, two T-shirts, a sweatshirt, a heavy hooded fleece and a woollen hat pulled low to cover my ears, and still the damp chill gnawed through to my bones.

My computer didn't like the cold, and the internal motor was growling so much I thought the Millennium Bug had finally kicked in. There was a pile of letters in front of me and each one of them was red. I sifted through the envelopes and reluctantly picked them open. Winter was biting and the creditors wanted their money. The phone rang.

'Hello. Is that Che?'

'Speaking.'

'John Pinfold.' The bank manager. 'Just thought I'd give you a little call regarding your account.'

'Oh?'

'Did you realise you'd gone over your overdraft limit?'

Course I did, but I feigned surprise. 'There should be some money coming in later this week,' I told him. It was a lie, of course, there was no money coming in at all.

'Right,' said Pinfold. He started to clear his throat. It was a bad sign, and I knew I had to improve my act.

'Yeah, we've got a big shipment going out to a shop in Iceland,' I said, digging deep for some false enthusiasm.

'Iceland?' he repeated with interest.

'Yes. Have you been?'

'No. The wife's not too keen on the cold. We tend to take our holidays in Spain.'

'Apparently, it's not that cold.' Talk about the weather and divert his attention from the dire state of our bank account. 'In Reykjavik the temperature isn't much different to this country.' I could hear a phone going off in the background.

'Is that so?' he said with no interest whatsoever.

'Of course, they have 24-hour night-times in the winter, seeing as they're so close to the Arctic Circle...'

'Right,' he said, his tone implying he wanted to pick up his other phone.

'...And then in the summer you get 24 hours of sunlight a day. I know someone who got so confused about what day it was he actually missed his plane.'

'Right,' he repeated.

'So anyway, this shop in Iceland...' I threw him the hook.

'Yes.' He sounded relieved to be getting back to the point.

'...Wants to put in a big order later this week, for immediate delivery.' I started reeling him in.

'That's good news,' he enthused.

'We're pleased,' I responded. 'We've been trying to crack the Scandinavian market for a while now. They're well known for being good payers. Should take care of the overdraft and leave us with a nice bit of spare change.'

'Sounds encouraging,' he said, his tone warming.

'So about this overdraft?'

'Well, to be honest with you, it sounds like you've probably got it under control.' It was the answer I'd been hoping for. 'I think we can wait a while before we review the situation. Will the order be cash on delivery or...'

'Bank transfer, before the goods leave.'

'Excellent,' he murmured. I could almost hear the scratch of the pen as he marked a tick in the right box.

There was no shop in Iceland, but Pinfold didn't have to know that. If I'd learnt anything from running a business it was that the truth could be avoided so long as you told people what they wanted to hear.

'Now, while I've got you on the phone,' Pinfold continued, 'I thought you might be interested in our new internet banking facility...'

The danger had passed.

'Good news, mate?' asked Travis. He looked up from his computer and blew into cupped hands to warm his fingers. Travis was my business partner. He did the designing, and I did the business. We'd known each other for years, and had been in business together for four.

'Bank manager chasing up funds for the missus's new swimming pool.'

He laughed. 'What's wrong with the last one we paid for?'

'She says it's not big enough.'

The phone rang again.

'Hello, could I speak to someone in your accounts department please.' The voice whined with urgency.

'Hang on, I'm putting you on hold.' I left it for ten seconds. 'Accounts,' I said, dropping my voice an octave.

'Hello, it's Charlotte from Privit Supplies. I'm chasing up an invoice from you.'

'I'm afraid I can't help you. I'm just minding the phone, but I can take a message.'

'We've got an unpaid invoice dating back three months. It needs to be settled this week.'

'If you tell me the amount, I'll get it sorted out for you.'

'A hundred and forty-eight. Plus VAT.'

'Consider that done,' I said, sounding as if it had shot to the top of the priority list.

There were some days when the action flowed, and there were others when it was all you could do to push pieces of paper round your desk. And then there were days like today, when you should have stayed in bed. The vultures were circling. Maybe they could smell the rot...

I quit the yard to do some errands, dumping a wad of 'Happy 2000' junk mail envelopes in the bin on my way. Today, grim layers of grey brought the oppressive worst out of Liddleton, and made me wish that I were somewhere else. I called into the post office in search of stamps but only found a long queue of pensioners, clutching their pension books, which snaked its way almost to the front door. I waited for ten minutes before losing patience. Besides, the blast of the central heating was making me sweat in my thermals.

On my way back to the yard, I bumped into a face I knew from the past. Back then she'd been bubbly and vivacious and always up for a laugh. Now she had a smack habit. Clusters of acne jumped out from the needle thin lines etched on her prematurely aged face. Her eyes had a cold lifelessness to them, and as she talked they seemed to look through me even though I was standing only a step away. She spoke in an empty monotone, like a bad actress reading from a script. She told me she was off the gear, but she was lying. Her pupils were pinned – no bigger than the full stops at the end of her sentences – and mottled saliva drew at the corners of her mouth as her lips moved. She had a bump on her forehead the size of a large pebble. She told me she was having a bad day. She'd just had a fight with another addict who'd stolen her stereo and sold it for 20 quid – two bags of brown.

'Five hundred quid that stereo's worth!' she cried. 'That's all I had. I was going to sell it and start a clean life. Go abroad or something.'

I didn't believe her, but I felt sorry for her even though I knew what was coming next.

'You couldn't lend us a tenner till next week?' she asked. There was no change of expression, just a pitiful look in her eyes. I told her I didn't have any money, and instantly she was no longer interested in talking to me.

And that was the kind of Sewerside world we lived in. A world made up of very different layers to Tokyo, Milan, Paris, London and the other fashion centres of the world. Layers beneath layers, like the silt at the bottom of the lake, where life is harsh and desperate despite the pretty picture on the postcard. If you didn't come from a place like this, then why else would you choose a name like Sewerside? Try and explain that concept to the doyens of style who peddled the concept of heroin as chic. And Liddleton? Who's heard of Liddleton? Sewerside from Liddleton. We couldn't have written a less marketable strap line if we'd tried. Unfortunately, we could never have been anything else…

Large droplets began to fall from blackening skies. I found enough coins in my pocket to buy a small jar of coffee, and ran through the rain back to the yard. The phone was ringing when I came through the door.

'Hello, could I speak to Che please.'

'Speaking.'

'It's Brian McTafferty at the Sixty Million Dollar Show.' He was in sales and marketing. Worked for the Rustcombe Corporation, a multinational, multimedia conglomerate with fingers in a plethora of pies. Whenever he called he adopted the manner of a long-time best mate, but he only ever called if he was trying to sell something.

The Sixty Million Dollar Show was a bi-annual fashion trade show, where designers and labels brought their collections to the corporate marketplace. If you were a rag trade mover and shaker, you'd be there. High fashion, low fashion, street fashion, sports fashion, it was all catered for under the same roof… It was a trade show where the likes of ourselves – small independent labels struggling for a piece of any pie – jostled for buyers' attentions side by side with the big name clothing brands. Have a good Sixty Million Dollar Show and it could set you on your way. Overnight, your two-bit fashion operation could turn into a multinational brand bonanza – or at least that's what it said in the marketing brochure.

In the fashion trade, the Sixty Million Dollar Show was somewhere between Piccadilly and Mayfair on the Monopoly board, and it was the major league if you had the money to play. We'd played the game before and were still waiting for the Get Out of Jail card. It had been the Sixty Million Dollar Show that had set us on the downward slope. We'd gambled money we didn't have on presenting our collection there the year before. It wasn't a bad collection, but it wasn't good enough or cheap enough to bring in the orders that would have guaranteed our financial survival.

'How are you, Che?'

'OK.'

'I was just giving you a call really to see how things are going.'

'They're fine,' I replied, waiting for the pitch.

'You sound a bit bunged up.'

'Thanks. I've got a cold.'

'Tried wrapping a hot towel round your head?' he asked.

'No, actually.'

Even his chuckle was supercilious. 'Just wondering if you had any thoughts on the Sixty Million Dollar Show?'

'It's expensive?' I yawned.

'Ahem…' McTafferty had an irritating habit of deflecting criticism with a conscious clearing of the throat, like a teacher faced with a student's impudence.

'It's in February?'

'Yes it is.' He was growing bored of my sarcasm. 'We were wondering if you had any plans for it?'

'Like?'

'Well, I suppose what I'm really trying to get at is that we've had a couple of companies pull out due to other commitments (substitute with 'unsold space') which means we've got a couple of stands left. Wondered if you might be interested in taking one.'

'Not unless you take payment in buttons.'

His laugh was hollow. He was undeterred and launched into his script. 'We've got a really strong show this year, and if you're looking to reach out to new markets, I would seriously recommend you consider us. There's a lot of interest in Sports Fashion at the moment and we've got a really tight exhibit this year...'

That's what we were. Lumped in a box called 'Sports Fashion', a generic term which didn't really mean anything at all. Sports Fashion covered everything from lycra aerobic-wear to Italian tracksuits, and the current vogue, extreme sportswear.

I held the phone away from my ear and picked my nose while waiting for him to finish.

'Thanks Brian, but we really can't afford it.'

'You exhibited last February. Must've been worth your while.'

'Not really.'

'That surprises me. Most of the brands I talked to had an excellent show.' If I'd learnt anything about the rag trade it was that everyone was so paranoid about losing face in the company of their peers that the spoken truth was rarely the actual reality. It was a cardinal sin to admit that business was anything but booming, thus spawning a self-perpetuating spiral of deception. 'Do you think your range was strong enough?' McTafferty added. He was making a play to my wounded pride, goading me in to proving him wrong. I wasn't swallowing it though.

'The range was fine. I seem to remember you were pretty interested in a pair of our trousers.'

'Ahem.'

'The trouble with your show, Brian, is there are a lot of buyers with eyes bigger than their budgets, and when push comes to shove, they'd rather bump the smaller orders than risk offending the big boys.'

'Oh really? That's a shame. I'm sorry about that.' He wasn't at all. He didn't give a fuck so long as he sold his quota of floor space. 'Well, I can't mend broken orders, but I can help to make amends by giving you a really good deal on a stand at next month's show...'

He had the skin of a rhino and wasn't going to be deterred, but I'd had enough. 'Brian,' I cut in, 'I've got to go. There's somebody at the door.'

'OK. Look, I'll put you down as a "maybe", that way if you change your mind…'

He had no sale, but he couldn't bring himself to give up the chase.

'Whatever,' I said disinterestedly.

'And just before you do go, we've got something else we're working on for the end of the year. It's not trade. It's a retail show we've taken over. You've heard of Off The Peg?'

'Of course. We've done it a couple of times.'

'Interested?'

'The end of the year's a long way off.'

'I'll call you closer to the time maybe?'

'You do that, Brian.' I hung up before he could say any more.

Chapter Two

January: A Brief History of time

If you're thinking that this is a story about the fashion business, well you're only part of the way there. That's certainly the way it started out, but for you to understand Sewerside, it's probably best if I take you back to the beginning…

Truth be known, I always wanted to be in a rock band, so it was most unfortunate that I didn't have a musical bone in my body. The only option left therefore was to take a management role – it was the one job that nobody else wanted to do. My first break came at school, when I was appointed (or rather appointed myself) the manager of a not-very-slick four-piece called 'Missing in Action'. The first gig I arranged was a success though I never got to see it, banned as I was from the Queen's Head pub, on account of being underage. I was forced to watch my finest hour through the window, standing on a beer crate.

Unfortunately it was my first and last gig in charge, on account of my mother deciding to uproot the family and relocate from the Home Counties to Devon. I was 16 and didn't expect to like the place. I had preconceptions of smock-wearing locals, who crunched carrots between their cream teas, and said 'ooh ar.' Of course, I was surprised to discover that nobody wore smocks any more, and there really weren't that many more carrots than I'd seen elsewhere.

Things were different in Devon. The pace of life was slower and the rest of the world, referred to as 'upcountry' by the locals, really did seem to be a long way away. We settled in Liddleton, a seaside town with a history of trading with the former colonies of the New World. More recently, it had been a bustling fishing port, but those days had long gone by the time we moved there, and tourism had become the lynchpin of the local economy now.

In my old life, seasons came and went, and the world on my doorstep didn't seem to change significantly. But in Liddleton, when the seasons changed, so did the town. Each spring heralded the start of the annual migration westwards by flocks of holiday-making tourists, known locally as 'grockels' or 'grocks' for short. The grocks would start to appear around Easter time, pursuing the 'wild' and 'unspoilt' views quoted in the tourist brochures. By the time of the school summer holidays, the streets heaved under the weight of blubber and cheap souvenirs.

On a sunny day, the light danced over whitewashed house walls and reflected off the top of tiled roofs, creating the kind of picture that graced the front of postcards. Tanned locals in shirt-sleeves went about their business with a laid-back sense of purpose, the cobbled streets chattering to the sound of a lazy Devonian drawl and the shriek of seagulls overhead. From the fish-man selling the morning's catch on the quayside, to the narrow streets lined with cafés, fudge shops and cosy pubs with crooked angles, Liddleton had holiday town written all over it.

To the locals, the summer season was a time of mixed blessings. Yes, there were the crowds and the inherent unpleasantness that tourists anywhere in the world brought with them, but the grockels also brought the sweet sound of music to local ears – the ringing of cash tills. Summer high season was a six-week window for making money – the equivalent of the rainy season in a drought-prone area of Africa. No rain and you're fucked. No tourists and you're fucked. Year after year, the summer season was make or break, and for every local businessman rubbing his hands in glee at the end of it, there were three more staring down the line and wondering how they were going to survive the winter.

At 16, however, my understanding of seasonal economics extended little further than the patio garden of the hotel I was working in. I had a summer job washing pots in the kitchen. With a beaten-up wreck of a car affording me the freedom to roam, I steered clear of the frying flesh on the main tourist beaches and discovered deserted rocky coves where the water was so clear it could pass for the Mediterranean. Every day felt like it was part of one never-ending holiday, and during my first summer in Devon I fell under a spell cast by my surroundings, a coastal habit that I would find impossible to kick.

As the last of the summer sun disappeared it was replaced by autumn winds that stripped trees bare, followed by a winter that was made up of seven parts rain, two parts sea mist, and the occasional clear day. It was during my first winter that I discovered that my shiny new coin had a flip side to it. Liddleton sat on an exposed hump of land jutting out to sea, and was in the firing line of every weather-front rolling in from the Atlantic. More often than not, that meant rain; heavy rain that fell as razor-edged raindrops that didn't fall but scythed down from the sky, soaking you through to the skin in minutes. I had never seen so much rain before, and with it came the all-permeating damp that chilled the bone despite the relatively mild climate. That first winter was a succession of streaming colds and hacking coughs.

Nevertheless, I continued to explore my new environment and discovered that the beach in winter could be just as magical. When it was stormy, the sky would darken with banks of black cloud that smothered the sea like the fall-out of a nuclear bomb. Gale force winds whipped the top of the waves so that they reared like white horses of the Light Brigade, spitting up rocks and stones and hurling them onto the beach as they charged onto the shore. At times the wind was so strong that the lids of your eyes felt like they were being blown inside out. On other days the coast would be enveloped in a grisly greyness that blurred the lines between the sea and the sky so that there was no such discernible thing as a horizon. The sea becalmed, the air would be filled with the smell of salt and a pervading clamminess that clung close and coated your clothes like early morning dew.

Liddleton was different in the winter too. It wasn't just the lack of tourists, it was something else – a depression that seemed to descend over the white-washed walls and the tiled roofs, like an invisible veil. The same streets so bustling in summertime became lined with boarded shop fronts and those cosy pubs were now filled with alcoholic in-patients viewing their world through the bottom of a glass. If you scratched the surface and looked beneath the postcard views, you found a desperate poverty that few tourists could ever imagine existed.

I left Devon when I was 19 and spent three years at university, where I developed a healthy dislike for students and discovered the evil joys of ecstasy and dance music, the two combined giving me the sense of rhythm that had eluded me throughout my wannabe rock star period. It was also during this time that I adopted the pseudonym, Che Capri. Let's just say it began as a joke and I used to think it gave me an air of mystery, but by the time I'd changed my mind, it had stuck. I got a degree and returned to Liddleton to contemplate my future. I was only supposed to stay in Devon for the summer but I got involved in the free party scene. I had a mate with a small system and that summer we forged ties with DJs, travellers and a pack of hardcore local boys and started putting on wild parties in forest clearings and hidden valleys secreted between Devon's rolling hills.

It was during this time that I first met Travis. We had a mutual friend, a surfer, and the two of them took me out for my first surfing lesson, although all I managed to do that day was get wet and paddle around like a wounded seal. I remember Travis looked distinctly conspicuous in his pink wetsuit, dreadlocks tied up on his head so they resembled the tuft of a pineapple. He was thin as a stick and brown from an unemployed summer lapping up the sunshine.

I didn't see him again until I got back from a month in America – the antidote to an unhealthy autumn of putting on parties at the weekends and spending the week on a come down. My old man lived in the States. He'd left England when I was a kid, to chase a dream of owning a ranch. He'd never got further than New York, however, and the ranch had since become a theatre.

On my return, I managed to wangle myself a job as a promoter at a new club that had been opened by a Londoner with big ambitions and seemingly a budget to make them happen. Travis, it turned out, was the in-house artist. We hit it off from the start. He had a real fluid style with his artwork, and he was always able to take an idea, sneak up behind it, twist it round and throw it back with his mark stamped all over it. The club was a cavernous place, a converted cinema that had been lying dormant since the days of Pathe newsreels and an old geezer belting out tunes on an organ down at the front. I was putting on raves and for a while we were caning it, but it didn't take long before the money ran out and once things started to go downhill they did so very quickly. Within a year the owner had done a runner back 'upcountry' and the club was shut down and boarded up.

I went off to the States and ended up staying for three years. Meanwhile Travis stuck around in Devon, had a couple of kids, and survived on scraps of freelance work. One time I was on a visit home when he showed me a handful of designs that he had printed up on T-shirts and started knocking out to mates. Travis's designs proved popular – so popular in fact that it wasn't long before he was stepping up his operations. He began selling to shops out of the boot of his battered old motor, and was looking to extend his T-shirt designs into a clothing range.

He'd called the label Sewerside. The name was taken from a reef break, a surf spot zealously defended by territorial Liddleton locals, that ran parallel to a sewage pipe (which brought a new meaning to the phrase 'dirty brown barrels'). Like the break, Sewerside designs were hardcore and uncompromising, and so anti-fashion that they soon picked up a cult following. Inevitably he could only hold it together for so long before demand got too great for him to keep handling everything on his own. Besides, he was an artist who liked smoking weed and didn't have the aptitude or desire to handle the business side of things. He desperately needed a partner and called me up to sound me out.

On the face of it, I was doing OK in New York. I'd gone there on holiday, met a girl, and ended up staying. I spent the first summer sweating in the kitchen of Antonio's Spanish restaurant as a kitchen porter, my sole responsibility being to wash pots. My Devon experience had prepared me well and I'd soon been nicknamed Máquina (machine) by my Mexican and Guatemalan co-workers. In our breaks we played cards and sniffed cheap Colombian cocaine. If there's one thing I took away from Antonio's it was the knowledge that you should never, ever, send food back to the kitchen in a restaurant... After six months, I did the first of many hops back and forth across the Atlantic to get my visa stamped, each time running the gauntlet with officious immigration officers who could have sent me back on the next plane for breach of visa terms.

Working at Antonio's had done a great deal to motivate me into getting my arse into gear when I got back. With my British accent, a doctored CV, and a phoney social security number, I managed to blag my way into one of those hip advertising agencies that had cottoned onto the fact that MTV wasn't just the channel but a byword for the next generation. It was glamorous for about six months. The money was good – too good – but as time went on I felt like I was missing something. I began to question why I should be giving so much of myself for someone else to take all the credit, and for someone higher than that to make all the money. I could also see what we were doing to the 'next generation', feeding them shit they never knew they wanted through slick advertising messages that were getting ever shorter, faster, more freaky in order to stand out against all the other adverts that plastered the world. My own world had become very hollow, and I one day realised that I had become bored with the life I had. This boredom set me thinking, and my thoughts became occupied by idealistic dreams. I was 26 and aware that my life was disappearing up the arse of a work-money-work system in which I was a small cog in a machine that served no real purpose. Those old wannabe pop star tendencies started to stir again, and the creative urge began to tug. At the back of my mind I'd been nurturing a desire to be part of something creative, and here was Travis giving me the opportunity to fulfil this dream of being boss of my own destiny.

So it was, on a gut feeling, that I agreed to become Travis's partner and move back to Britain. My circle of friends in New York thought I was crazy. Swap the Big Apple for the small potato, why would I want to do that? Of course, it was a line I'd been playing over in my mind too, but I was determined. I knew fuck-all about the rag trade, but I knew a bit about the day-to-day running of a business, and I had an unquestioned faith in Travis's talent as a designer. I took what savings I had managed to scrape together and bought into the business. I remember arriving at Heathrow on a cold and damp October morning, and actually being pleased to see the drizzle, as I stood waiting for the bus. 'Fack me guv'nor,' said the bus driver who unceremoniously threw my bag into the baggage hold, 'what you got in there? A dead body?' After the 'Have a Nice Day' mentality of America it was as refreshing as taking a piss under the stars.

Within a week of being home, I was surfing deserted reef breaks with Travis, drinking in the fresh air and the majesty of the landscape around me. I was broke, of course, but that didn't seem to matter. I had moved back into my old room at home, and once my savings started to dwindle, I signed on at the Job Centre, in the belief that it would only be a matter of time before wages started rolling in.

I reasoned that destiny lay in our own hands and that with hard work and our combined talents we could carve ourselves our own niche. Travis didn't have any training as a fashion designer, but he had an intuitive feel for what might work and the learning curve, although steep, was an exciting ride into the unknown. In those early days, everything was an adventure, and anything was possible. Enthusiasm overrode our inexperience, and we took each setback in our stride and placed all our faith in the little steps forward.

Sewerside clothes were designed as a reflection of our environment. They needed to be hard-wearing, practical and weatherproofed against the Atlantic weather fronts that battered our backyard. Travis took inspiration from the kind of designs used by the military. He used bio-chemical warfare jackets as templates, and adapted the details found on parachute pants and snipers' trousers that we picked up from army surplus stores.

With scant practical knowledge of the manufacturing process, we picked our materials from tiny swatches sent by the fabric warehouses, which, when they arrived, seemed nothing like we'd anticipated. We were naïve and inexperienced, so we didn't know that the fabrics we were choosing weren't intended for the type of garments we were producing. With little money for manoeuvre, we had no choice but to work with what we got sent. We made trousers out of stiff waterproof material meant for jackets, and jackets out of even stiffer material that was meant for making bags.

Yet, strangely enough, people liked the stuff we were making. It was dramatically different to what anyone else was doing at the time, and that gave us a lick that got people interested. More by luck than judgement, the five shops became ten, and then 15. For some reason better known to the bank manager, we were granted a loan of 25 grand, even though our assets were negligible. At the time it seemed like a lot of money. The loan enabled us to jump another rung up the ladder, and as well as selling on the road, we could now afford to do the odd trade show. By our third year in business, we were supplying 35 shops, as far afield as Sweden, Greece and Italy, and turning over 50 grand. I was no Richard Branson, but I was tight-fisted enough to make sure that the money wasn't gobbled up in one go. In the meantime, every penny we made got put right back into the business. We'd been working without wages for so long that we rarely thought about it anymore.

With only the two of us, it was hard work, and the business roles we had to play were many. For a while we enjoyed a modest notoriety. Our clothes ended up on the backs of rising stars in the music industry, graced fashion shoot pages of magazines, and on obscure cable TV channels in the early hours of the morning. But the loan didn't last long, and once it had gone, we were at the mercy of the marketplace. With hindsight, even back then we weren't swimming with the big fish, just drowning slowly. The thing about the fashion business is that you're only ever as good as your last collection. While a particularly successful range could earn you a reputation, you couldn't just carry on reproducing it. You had to be constantly moving, constantly looking towards the horizon in order to predict what was coming next. It was true that if your reputation was established enough you could dictate what was coming next, but your only chance as a small brand was to keep creating, keep innovating, and it was only if your designs struck a chord with the popular culture bubbling around you at the time that your creativity produced significant sales.

In our 'street fashion' world, the Holy Grail was getting a foothold in the Japanese market, where style, not price, governed consumer purchase. We'd had some success in Scandanavia and our T-shirts had picked up some decent shops in Mediterranean destinations, but unfortunately our search for a mythical Japanese 'Mr Yakomoto' figure to patronise us had proved fruitless. Consequently, the bulk of our sales came through independent shops within the British Isles, and on every selling campaign we had to scrap hard for a piece of the action as independents rarely had the money or the inclination to order big.

Compounding the whole sales issues was the fact that while companies like us pushed the boundaries and innovated, we were always being monitored by the High Street chains, ready to pounce on the next trend. They had the infrastructure and the financial clout to clone whatever was new, fresh and exciting and mass produce it in their Far East sweatshops so that even before the season was out you'd spot variations on your fashion theme dressing up mannequins in High Street shop – and costing a fraction of the price we could afford to sell at. With our inexperience, it had taken a while to realise this fact, and even when we had there was very little we could do about it. Piracy doesn't just run from the bottom up – the biggest pirates in the game are often those sitting at the top. Even as we were scaling the ladder it often felt like we were the ones creating in order for others to make the money from it. I guess that's what business is all about, but that fact isn't much of a comfort when you're counting out coppers to raise the price of a jar of coffee.

All these factors had conspired against us in the years since we'd been operating. In the end, all it took was a shift in currency rates, a couple of cancelled orders and one fucked-up production run, before our ascent up the ladder halted and, slowly but surely, we started to slip back down again. It's funny, you set out with a dream and it seems like a straight road that lies between your starting point and it's conclusion. In the four years since Travis and I set out on our journey though, that road had bended and kinked so many times that it was easy to forget just where we'd set out to go.

They don't give you a handbook when you start your own business and unless you're extremely lucky or extremely talented you have to learn by your own mistakes. Unfortunately, they don't come cheap. And there's your Catch-22 right there; in order to compete in the major leagues, you had to have the money to do it. If you didn't have the money you were forced to hustle. And if you hustled, you were never in control of your destiny.

Consequently Sewerside had ceased to be just about the clothes. That four-year journey by road I was talking about had never been about putting the peddle to the metal in a racing red Ferrari. Instead, it had been a rambling drive in a rickety old bus that was prone to stopping for every hitchhiker on the long and winding way. I use this analogy, because Sewerside had never been an orthodox small business. From the start we had never thought to ape ourselves on the corporate model that brought success in the marketplace. In the early days we were convinced that creativity would breed financial success. Maybe it had something to do with where we came from. Perhaps if we'd been living in London, we wouldn't have been allowed the luxury of thinking that way. But we didn't live in London. We lived in an isolated corner of the world that was far detached from the incestuous circles and competitive influences that our fashion-label peers moved in.

As such, we weren't the product of an industry where ideas were battery-farmed on the basis of fear of what our competitors were doing. I guess the plain truth was, we never really had a business plan, just lurched from one side of the business road to the other, running on blind faith. Hence the rickety old bus analogy. How else could I explain how a fashion label suddenly acquired a 30-foot skate ramp, became almost as well known for putting on parties and club nights, and how Travis and I had managed to pick up a rag-tag crew of creative misfits and miscreants along the way?

The thing is, the crew thing somehow worked. In my mind I'd like to think it was a little bit like the Magnificent Seven. You remember that film? Each person does the thing they do best. The knife thrower doesn't tell the sharp shooter how to shoot, because the sharp shooter knows what he's doing. And that's what we were like, a collective posse, a membership of exclusive skills. Each person that came seemed to bring with them with them a different skill, and for this reason the whole thing kind of became this one big collective posse of dysfunctional talent, fiercely loyal to each other and the Sewerside cause.

Chapter Three

There was no point even talking to the Pig when he was in this mood. As the name suggests, his skin was thick, and even thicker when he was working. He looked through me with small eyes that stared down his snout. I tried to tell him that the puddle was actually a river that had broken its banks and was swelling by the raindrop, that I'd just had to wade through two feet of dirty brown water to get to my car. He gave the impression he was listening to me, but really his mind was on the numbers coming through the door of the club, and he wasn't having any of it at all.

'It'll take more than a fucking puddle to stop the party. Don't you worry about that.'

The way he said it made me feel inadequate and small, like the schoolboy humbled in front of the class by the teacher. The fact that I'd had to abandon my car in the 'puddle,' and that I'd seen the waters rise to the point where they were starting to lap at the car door; the fact that I really wasn't exaggerating, and that the rain was heavier now than it was half an hour ago, didn't phase him at all. These were problems that didn't stress the Pig – he'd seen it all before and he'd seen it worse before.

That's what they said about the Pig. Nothing got in his way when it came to putting on a party... The sound man, he had an IQ of 142 and a 30k custom-built rig at his command. He'd made his name in free parties and over the years his sound systems had wreaked havoc across the county, keeping many a copper up late on a Saturday night chasing down and trying to put a stop to his illegal raves.

He was older now, more selective with his choice of venues. We'd first hooked up with him a couple of years ago on a crazy mission to build a skate ramp for a warehouse rave he was putting on. We'd been stiffed on the cash we were promised and the Pig had been indebted to us as a result. He'd put his sound system at our disposal and one party had become another and another, until eventually the rig was flying the Sewerside banner. The Pig was a safe pair of hands who'd learnt his craft in muddy fields and tumbledown barns. He was practical, logical, and possessed an innate ability to operate against the odds.

I was left feeling awkward, standing in the warm foyer of the club, steam rising from my wet shoes.

'Just make sure you've got enough bodies here at one,' he said. 'Tell Glyn to bring the van round to the side door. The minute the lights go on, we've got to get the speakers out of here. I don't want to be hanging around and I don't want to be doing all the donkey work myself.'

I gave a placid nod of compliance and a raindrop fell from my brow and started rolling down my cheek like a tear drop.

'Cheer up, mate, it may never happen,' said a gurning jerk in a jester's hat as I squelched through the foyer and down the dimly lit corridor lined with shady dealings and dance floor casualties.

'It already has,' I snarled through gritted teeth, moving to dodge his sweaty hug.

My trail of wet footsteps meandered its way to the end of the corridor and side stepped the throngs massing at the entrance to our room. It was packed, and clearly entranced by the twisted drum and bass Haze had growling through the speaker stacks.

Haze was one of our secret weapons, one of the big guns in the Sewerside sound division. I'd been around long enough to know a good DJ when I heard one, and Haze was one of the best. Each gig was a personal mission to captivate the dance floor. 'Che,' he used to say to me, in his Colchester accent, 'when I'm on the decks I don't play records, I'm telling the dance floor a story.'

Haze was loud, and often obnoxious, and many people found him intimidating, not because he was physically imposing but because he was a loose cannon. He had a mad dog look in his eyes – the kind of kid who'd have ten tons of shit kicked out of him at school but would still come back for more. We'd met him on a drunken Friday night in Hackney, and on the Saturday he'd been playing at one of our club nights.

Haze's speciality was driving bass lines and twisted tempos. He had a presence behind the decks that was sometimes frightening to witness. His face had a touch of the ghoul about it anyway, but as soon as he got behind the decks the colour would drain right out of his cheeks, his eyes would glaze over and he had this stare that seemed to look right through the dance floor. With the ability to turn out a set that was half-macabre, half-evangelical and completely bewitching, he could take three tunes that had been played a million times before and somehow mould them into something new.

It was a squeeze getting down to the front, the dance floor broken down in the colours of the lights, strobes cutting up people's movements and faces, dissecting the frenetic forms and shapes and throwing them back as twisted fractions. I misjudged my passage through an opening on the dance floor and watched a pint of beer stutter its way from the glass, in the strobe-light, and down my arm in slow motion. 'Sorry bud,' mumbled its shirtless owner, clasping my shoulder. I pushed through his grip and clocked Cas standing by the side of the speaker, head crooked close to the brow of a brunette half his size.

Cas was my brother. Younger than me by eight years, we had different fathers and couldn't have looked less alike. He stood a foot taller than me, was thickset and broad. He'd been rolling with me since a kid of 12 when I had him running the tea stall at parties I was organising. At 22 he could still be a walking box of itching powder with the ability to wind up a saint, but he was good with his hands and fast with his fists, and as near to a minder as I had. He was also the architect of the skate ramp.

'Where's Travis?' I asked. He jacked a thumb in the general direction and I pushed on past the bass freaks hugging the speaker cabs that popped like a bad case of hyperventilation.

There was no such thing as a VIP section at the Buccaneer Leisure Complex, not that there'd ever been a VIP to warrant a room. The crew had done their best to stake out a territory though. Camouflage netting screened off a patch of the dance floor, slung between the speaker stack and the DJ booth to create a narrow bottleneck that was policed by nothing more than brooding atmosphere.

Dark shapes were sitting low in rancid couches, horseshoed around a couple of small tables that had been liberated from an old people's home too many years ago. Each Saturday night they became that bit more rancid. Weed smoke hung heavy in the air, and practically everyone in this corner of the room was smoking or rolling. Occasionally club security would amble by, but seeing as they were smoking themselves they didn't bother anyone. Nods and handshakes as I passed through the gathered bodies, my feet still dragging like Gollum's.

I was aware of someone calling my name. The call was persistent, like the bleep of an alarm clock reaching out to you as you slumbered until it became so urgent you couldn't ignore it anymore. 'Che... Che... CHE.' Someone was yanking at my trouser leg, and suddenly, through the gloom, I could make out Stig, sitting with the other skaters.

Stig, Ginger Gaz, Grubby, Little Johnny. There were other skaters that came and went, other skate tribes that had an affiliation with Sewerside, but these four formed the nucleus of our skate team. Sewerside may have had its origins in the sea but it was the skateboarding that had made it a name in the clothing market. This was one of those bends in the Sewerside road. Why? Because I'd never ridden on a skateboard in my life.

Nevertheless, Travis skated, and over time I had become educated to skater culture and had come to respect it. I liked the way they really didn't give a shit. Skaters were a breed of their own; they were anti-authoritarian, predominantly deviant, and because they spent their lives sweating it up on their skateboards, rarely travelled without a cheap can of deodorant at hand.

The Grubby was the oldest of the bunch. He was in his late twenties and had learnt his art in concrete precincts 'upcountry' back in the days when he should have been at school. There was little to separate him from the new generation except for an untidy growth of stubble and a hairline that was starting to recede. Unreliable, sloppy and totally untrustworthy as he was, the Grubby, with his eye on the skate scene at street level, was the self-styled 'team manager'.

The other three were local boys, grommets, ranging in age between 16 and 19. They were, all three, rippers on the street, and had they come from one of the big cities they would have been sponsored for sure. As it was, they came from Liddleton, and Sewerside had given them the opportunity for occasional escape to the wider world. As a result, they were dog-pack loyal.

Grinning like a highwayman from the couch below, Stig motioned for me to sit and offered me a line. I'd been running around since 9 o'clock that morning, and all I'd eaten was a chocolate bar and 20 cigarettes. 'Go on then. I'll have a little one.'

He chopped out two thick lines of coke in the space between glasses and beer bottles on the table, and snorted the bigger one. He handed me a dog-eared five pound note and I hoovered up the other. 'I've got some pills too if you want one,' he grinned, pushing a wrap of cellophane under my nose.

'I'm OK, thanks. I'm still working.'

'You work too hard,' he said, popping a pill in his mouth.

'Have you seen Glyn?' I asked him.

'Are you blind?' he howled. 'He's sitting right next to you.' And sure enough, so he was.

Glyn, the Pig's younger brother, was busy rolling a spliff. I gave him a prod.

'Glyn, the Pig says you've got to bring the van round to the side doors at 1 o'clock.'

He nodded, balancing his skinned joint between two grubby fingers. 'That's the good thing about these couches,' he drawled, as if he'd spent a while in contemplation. He dragged a furry tongue across the sticky gum of the papers. 'They're so deep that when people lean back they lose stuff out of their pockets. Do you know what I've found tonight?'

I shook my head.

'Three quid and a lump of hash. Look, I'm smoking it now.'

'That's a result!' I beamed. I wasn't patronising him. The charlie had kicked in and, for now, my enthusiasm was genuine.

'I know,' he replied in the manner of someone who knew he was onto a good thing. 'Wait until the club shuts. I reckon my pockets will be bulging.'

Looking around, I spied Travis. I hauled myself out of the couch and wound my way through bodies. I put my hand on his shoulder and he turned round, blowing a cloud of smoke into my face.

'Hello, mate,' he said. You look like you could do with a spliff.'

I shook my head. 'I'm all right.'

'How's the weather?' he asked.

'Worse. There's a fucking river running through the fish yard, and the car's stuck in the middle of it. My feet are still fucking wet. Had to wade through it. Water came up to my knees.'

'Shit. What's the Pig say?'

'It'll take more than a fucking puddle to stop us.'

'Well,' he said, affecting the Pig's stance. 'Do-you-know-what-I-mean, it's not a problem then.'

Travis laughed and for the first time that day, I laughed too.

Numbers were filling up nicely in the club considering the state of the weather. It was still raining, but the droplets were getting smaller. A few bedraggled stragglers continued to pass through the door. The Pig was standing with the bouncers, rocking back and forward on his heels.

'How are we doing?' I asked.

'Four hundred,' he replied, showing me the clicker. 'Did you see Glyn?'

'One o'clock,' I nodded.

'Good,' he said as a dickie-bowed bouncer came up to us and feigned a left hook at him. The Pig toppled and tipped into the cigarette machine.

'I'll see you later,' I said as the bouncer grabbed the Pig in a friendly headlock. There was no crowd trouble to sort out and he was getting bored.

The foyer floor was slippery underfoot, and occupied by wide-eyed punters blinking in the stark light. I pushed past the bodies congregating by the double doors and the heat hit me hard as I passed into the bar. Tekno rumbled from the dance floor, making the bottles behind the bar shake. The bar was lined with red faced and sweaty punters jostling for eye contact with the girls serving drinks. One of the girls who knew my face came over and I ordered a grapefruit and soda. She returned with a pint, the contents looking like they'd been strained off from the gents' toilet.

'What's that?' I asked her.

'Grapefruit and cider,' she replied.

'No, grapefruit and soda.'

She tutted and corrected the order. She nodded at the pint. 'You can keep that,' she said as if she was doing me a favour. I spied the most out-of-it person at the bar and handed it to them.

The drugs were working on the dance floor, although the full madness was concealed within the thick mist kicked up by the smoke machine. The tekno thumped methodically, monotonous in delivery, relentless in its drive. I lingered for a while just watching the shuddering shapes skipping to the music's direction, until it became too hot, too hectic, too loud. I quit and made my way back to our room. The urgent atmosphere of the drum and bass had given way to laid back hip hop beats, and Natty was working the floor, launching a freestyle assault from the microphone.

Natty was the other musical missile in the Sewerside armoury. We'd first met him at a trade show. Back then he'd been just another ligger on the lookout for free clothes. He told us that he was going to be a rap superstar, and of course we hadn't believed him. But we were wrong, because Natty was indeed an exceptional talent and proved his point. 'Show me what you've got in your pockets,' he demanded of Travis, and proceeded to conjure a rhyme for every item.

He wore a constant growth of untidy stubble, and a baseball cap that he'd worn for so long his hair beneath it had moulded to the shape. Subtlety and discretion were characteristics that were alien to him and he was constantly in your face, babbling and postulating with a mischievous cackle.

He'd hooked up with us again at a festival we were doing in Cornwall. It was the usual story, us supplying the skate ramp and the sound system in return for a free stall. He'd never been to a festival before and turned up in the whitest pair of sneakers money could buy. The festival was a long one, five days and one eclipse, and the clientele was distinctly on the crusty tekno side.

Against my expectations, Natty took to festival life like a lurcher pup to a traveller site. He charmed the pants off the crowds that turned up at the system each night and by the end of the week he had booked himself a place on the crew whether he liked it or not.

I stood for a while, nodding my head, drinking my drink, revelling in the buzz of another successful club night. I checked my watch, one eye closed to focus properly on the hands, and realized there wasn't long left. I'd managed to chill for precisely two minutes, but there was work to be done. Closing time was looming, but phase two beckoned and I was suddenly aware that, apart from the Pig who only ever drank Coke while working, I was the only sober person in the place...

In our part of the world licensed events rarely ran past 1 o'clock, so 'phase two' as the Pig had referred to it was an after-club do, a chance to carry the party on through the night. Our parties had earned a bit of a reputation over time, and they worked because they were something a little bit different. When we first started doing them, the

West Country scene had been dominated by tekno sound systems, but we had broken the mould by playing the bass-heavy sounds of reggae, hip hop and drum and bass, with the added ingredient of decent live MCs.

In the cities, these styles of music had distinct crowds and their own designated events, but out in the sticks there was no precedent for this and so what had been born as an experiment had developed into a new scene all of its own. Slowly but surely, we had recruited converts from within the tekno crowd, and they'd brought with them their up-for-it attitude and penchant for hedonistic pursuit. Hip hop and pills shouldn't have worked together, but because of where we were, there were no purist cliques to get in the way and our crowds tended to have this crossover element that gave our parties a great vibe. It helped, of course, that we had a sound division core of exceedingly talented DJs and MCs who knew how to play for the crowd instead of to them...

The venue had only come together late that afternoon – a deserted fish yard that sat close to the seafront, just out of town. The Pig had sorted it out, done some deal with its owner, Micky Vendell, a gangster with a past and a name that got things done in Liddleton. He'd bought the place with the intention of constructing a marina development. On a cold afternoon in February, however, it had looked every bit the fish yard – cold, damp, and stinking of yesteryear's fish. The Pig had unlocked the heavy steel door, flicking on the lights to reveal a large box-shaped room, tiled from floor to ceiling, the off-white stained the colour of blood and guts.

'Christ, it stinks,' I'd said, pushing my nose into the material of my jacket.

'I can't smell anything,' the Pig had replied, like the guilty kid who'd just farted.

'You're joking?'

'Nah. Got a fag?' The Pig liked to smoke while talking the turkey, and that was what we were doing. He'd lit up, exhaling a cloud of smoke that just hung in the air.

'This is the small room. As you can see, there's running water.' He'd pointed in the direction of dripping taps, like an estate agent showing me round the property. I'd checked his face for signs of irony but there were none.

'Electric.' He'd stuck his snout into the fuse box, and started rummaging. 'Not a problem. We've got fucking loads of it.'

We'd passed through a curtain of heavy rubber strips and into another room, with no windows. The walls and the ceiling were made of metal. Along one wall sat concrete cleaning pools, and heavy grooved work surfaces where the fish would have been washed and gutted. The room was big enough to hold around two hundred people. 'It's cold,' I'd said.

'Course it fucking is. It's a fucking freezer.' The words had flown like insults, but he hadn't meant anything by them. That was just the way the Pig talked. We'd stood in silence for a while before the Pig broke it. 'We'll have a speaker stack in the corner there, another where that drain is, and I reckon the best place for the decks is on that surface behind.' I'd nodded. 'Well then,' he'd said, obviously pleased with himself, 'what do you think?'

'I think its OK,' I'd replied.

'OK?' The Pig had retorted. 'I think it's fucking wicked.'

I'd spent the rest of the afternoon sorting shit out. We were going to be running the bar. It was an opportunity to make some petty cash. February was always a quiet time for the business. I'd hit Nice Price to stock up on booze. The supermarket, a former cowshed lurking on the fringes of town, had its floor space piled high with generic brands and fresh goods that were a nice price because they were on the turn. But the grog was cheap and the tills were still operated manually. I'd chosen my cashier carefully, steering my trolley full of booze towards a woman with a squint and a tongue that looked too big for her mouth. I'd flirted with her unashamedly, and she'd become giggly and confused, not realising that I'd changed the price labels so that a crate of beer cost the same as a six-pack of Coke.

I'd arranged for Travis to get to the club early and sort things out before the doors opened, while I'd shuttled back to the fish yard, chasing the clock, with a car full of alcohol, lights and a few bits of décor. I'd had Haze riding shotgun with me. It had been raining hard all day and there were high winds that whipped treetops back and forth and made lamp posts wobble. By the time we'd reached the fish yard, there was a small river running across the track that hadn't been there earlier in the day. I'd stopped the car, staring into the murky waters in the hope that a safe passage through the torrent would present itself.

'Don't tell me this is where the party is,' Haze had said. I'd nodded. 'You boys are fuckin' crazy,' he'd replied, swigging from a bottle of Martell. 'You're not goin' to drive through it, are ya?' I'd nodded again. 'There's probably a proper fucking Sewerside fish living in there ready to eat us!' he'd shrieked.

I'd driven through on an act of faith. Plumes of spray had arced over the bonnet, causing steam to rise from the engine, but it didn't cut out, and we'd made it to the other side. It had taken us a while to unload the car and sort things out. Haze had left to get his records, taking a lift with one of the Pig's cronies, but I stayed on to add some finishing touches to the makeshift bar. ' I'll be right behind you' , I'd promised…

However, by the time I'd emerged, the river running through the fish yard had swelled. I'd taken another act of faith and plunged the car through what I'd hoped had been the shallowest point. It hadn't. The engine had spluttered as the exhaust dipped below the waterline, letting out one final cough before it died…

Now I was driving that same stretch of track again, only in a different car. The Pig was right about the puddle. The rain had stopped and the river had disappeared. I passed my car, abandoned earlier, a dirty brown tidemark round the car's chassis the only evidence that the river had ever been there.

We approached the fish yard slowly, riding the potholes, the exhaust occasionally grating on the ground below with the weight of the six people inside the car. It was my fourth and final shuttle run from the club. Haze was in the passenger seat, cradling the last third of the Martell bottle on his lap, and lamenting that his set hadn't quite gone how he'd wanted it to, the way he always did.

There were about 50 cars parked up along the track and in the small parking lot besides the building. The wind had blown itself out and the skies had cleared to reveal a half-moon that looked bleached it was so bright. The temperature had dropped too and the air was fresh enough to pinch at the lungs with each breath. A preponderance of bass permeated the thick walls of the freezer room inside the fish yard, making loose tiles on the roof rattle.

Glyn accosted me on the way in. He looked pleased. 'Eh Che, you'll never guess what I found down the side of one of the couches when the lights went up.' I shook my head. He pulled a mouth organ out of his pocket, and swiped his lips back and forth a couple of times to produce a sound like the hee-haw of a donkey. 'Told you there was more to be found,' he grinned.

I caught sight of Cas standing just inside the door, and left Glyn to speak to him. The body heat of the post club crowd had warmed the place, although the smell of fish still lingered. 'How's the bar doing?' I shouted over the noise of the music.

'Good, mate. Selling well.'

There was a shout behind us and I recognised the voice. It was Ginger Gaz, calling from the doorway. 'Che!' he yelled. 'You'd better check this out.'

'What is it?' I retraced my footsteps to where he was.

'Old Bill.' He pointed in the direction of the track. I saw the blue lights first, flashing through the gaps in the hedgerow, and then the first of the squad cars came round the bend and towards us, bouncing over the potholes of the track…

Chapter Four

<u>March: Button Up</u>

I was in the yard sitting at my desk and working through a list of things that needed doing. We were in pre-production. Translated, that meant we were getting our sample range together so that we could get out and start taking orders. There was no money left in the account to pay for another Sixty Million Dollar trade show, and so all our sales for the coming season would have to be generated by good old-fashioned legwork. I was a reluctant rep at the best of times, and the thought of having to hit the road with a sample bag wasn't one that filled me with great enthusiasm. This year, the state of our finances dictated the size of our range, and this year's range was going to be limited to safe bets (although in the rag trade, there's rarely a safe bet); a couple of jackets, a couple of pairs of trousers and ten designs that would be printed onto tees and sweats.

At our peak, we'd run a 20-piece range, with two seasonal collections; three jackets, three pairs of trousers, two pairs of shorts, a couple of fleeces, two types of sweatshirt, T-shirts. Back then we'd even run a women's range too, although the logic behind it had been questionable. It was hard enough designing for blokes, but at least you didn't have to worry about proportions. One pair of baggy trousers, in three sizes, pretty much covered the entire male population. Designing for women was a

business stinks..

different story. Waist, hip and leg measurements had to be precise, and the finished garment had to flatter curves, not accentuate them. It didn't help either that with just the two of us blokes it was more often than not me who served as the model for these designs. In retrospect, the women's range had been another contributory factor in the slippery slide into our currently dire financial straits. It was one of those costly learning curves I was talking about. At the time, it had seemed like a necessary diversification that would allow us to further compete with the big brands. In reality, it had caused nothing but headaches, and we still had four boxes filled with an ill-fated trouser/skirt combination (referred to as a 'sk-ouser') that had gone from vogue to vague in the blink of an eye.

Travis wasn't in the yard. He'd spent the last week working the peace and quiet of the night shift and smoking his weight in weed in the search of inspiration for the new T-shirt designs. Already, he was a week over deadline, but that was Travis for you. No matter how much advance warning he had, he always left it to the last possible minute. He was the kid who would be doing his history homework in the French lesson before it had to be handed in. It used to bug the shit out of me, but there was no way he was ever going to change, so I'd come to accept that was how things were. He was cutting it fine, but if he could crack the designs by the end of the week then I could be out on the road with a good three weeks to push the range before Easter, the traditional start to the selling season.

We did all our manufacturing in England. It was expensive and that's why the big brands used sweatshops in the Third World. They could produce complicated garments with intricate features for peanuts, seeing as that was all the local workforce got paid. But that wasn't our style. It was bad enough we exploited ourselves for no money without having the guilt of exploiting a factory full of kids chained to their sewing machines. We may have had a clear conscience from doing our business like that, but in the marketplace it meant we were getting killed.

We used two British manufacturers for our outwork, and I had been pulling every sympathy trick in the book to coax them into action. The sample work was something they didn't like doing. It was time consuming, bitty and a pain in the arse if they already had work on. There was little incentive for them to pull off a couple of machinists from a run of five hundred jackets or eight hundred trousers for another client just to have them knock up a sample for us, even if it did mean more work for them down the line. They knew from experience that our runs were more like 50–100 pieces a go, and in manufacturing terms that was big hassle for small change.

Nevertheless, I had managed to lock them into a timetable, and Travis and I had spent the past month reviewing fabric swatches. We had our patterns ready, materials ordered, and were now waiting for the garments to be made. Samples were your prototypes, and translating them from the designer's dream to the wearable reality rarely went without a hitch, so the sooner they got made and checked the better.

The manufacturers were supposed to be starting work this week, so I decided to give them a call to make sure that was what they were doing.

First on the list was Frank. Frank Masker had been in the manufacturing trade since he'd left school at 12 years old to support his mother and eight siblings – a fact he told us every time we went to see him. Originally from Manchester, he now lived in Cornwall, running out of a faceless industrial unit crammed with a cutting table and machines operated by a team of frightening-looking ladies whose talk was anything but ladylike. He was a thickset Northerner with a taste for king-sized cigarettes and gold jewellery, and only smiled at his own sarcasm. He wasn't cheap, but he was good.

'I s'pose you're calling about them bloody jackets of yours,' he said gruffly when I told him who it was. He was caustic at the best of times, but today he seemed particularly so.

'That's right,' I replied.

'Well, 'ow the bloody 'ell do you think I'm going to do that if I 'aven't got the material to do it with?'

My heart stopped. 'But you should've had it delivered.'

'Well, I 'aven't. And if you want 'em by the weekend, then my girls need to start on them this afternoon.'

'Christ. I don't know, Frank,' I said, trying to think, 'I mean, you should've had it sent out to you middle of last week.'

'Well, I 'aven't. And if you want 'em by the weekend, then my girls need to start on them this afternoon.' Frank had a habit of repeating things unnecessarily. 'I've got that much bloody work on at the minute, I'm 'ard pushed as it is.'

'Let me call the warehouse and find out,' I told him.

'Well, you tell 'em this. You tell 'em that if I 'aven't got the material, 'ow am I s'posed to make your jackets?'

'OK, Frank,' I said, holding the phone away from my ear, 'I've got the point. You could've let me know you hadn't had the delivery.'

'I just have. Bloody 'ell, you want me to be a messenger service as well now, do you?', he barked and hung up.

I swore out loud, threw some things around my desk and found the number of the fabric suppliers. They were based up north. Everyone involved in the manufacturing game, it seemed, was either up north or came from up there.

'Hello, Canterbury Textiles…'

'Sales plea…' My line was drowned out by the receptionist's refusal to abandon her scripted phone greeting.

'…Sandra speaking. How may Canterbury Textiles help you today?'

'Sales please.'

'Certainly. Hold the line. I'm transferring you,' she said with no urgency at all. Soft rock played in the background. 'Line's busy. Can you hold?' The soft rock returned before I could even answer. I threw some more stuff around my desk and muttered.

'Sales,' a voice said finally.

'Hello,' I said. 'It's…' I had a sudden sense of something that I had to do today and then the realisation dawned. 'It's… I'm going to have to call you back,' I garbled and hung up. It was gone 11 and I was already ten minutes late for my interview at the Job Centre.

I had to sign on every two weeks at an appointed hour. It was different for Travis. He had kids, and the business really wasn't making any money so he was aided by benefits. As a single, able-bodied male, however, I didn't qualify for any of that so I was forced to lie through my teeth in order to get 'Jobseeker's Allowance'. Sewerside couldn't pay any wages (every penny we made, Sewerside swallowed again), and I spent so many hours working on trying to make the business pay that I had no time for a part-time job. As a consequence, I was dependent on these Social Security handouts. Out of the 52 pounds and 43 pence a week granted by Saint Giro, 25 went to my mother for food and rent, and the rest got eaten up on living.

Money's a funny old thing. I've had money, and I've had no money, and to tell the truth, neither financial situation has greatly changed my quality of life. If you have no money, you spend your time wishing that you had it. If you have money, you spend your time wishing you had more. You can survive on very little and you can blow a great deal… and you always spend what you've got.

I had come to regard my fortnightly trip to the Job Centre as wage day. It was just unfortunate that in order to earn my 'wages' I had to lie through my teeth. I didn't particularly like doing it, but the way the system was set up honesty really didn't pay. I justified my fraudulent activities through the fact that while I may have been taking taxpayers' money, through the business I was at least keeping people in employment. I also knew that if the business ever did take off the taxman would be the first in line to grab his pound of flesh.

Most of the time I could get away with a signature and a few fictional answers to the stock question: 'What have you been doing to find work?' Today was different though. It was my six-monthly 'Back to Work' interview, with my very own personal adviser, and there was always the chance that it could get a little sticky. Most of the time the Job Centre staff were happy just to put ticks in the right boxes, but every now and again there would be a Government shake up followed by a department drive to slash unemployment statistics.

When this happened they'd try their hardest to shoehorn you into any job they could.

The Job Centre was housed in one of those government buildings that was permanent, but had a depressingly temporary feel to it. All glass and faux wood, it was hot and stuffy regardless of the season; the kind of place where someone sneezed and the whole building got infected.

I signed myself in at the front desk, and the receptionist told me to wait until my name was called. I was always nervous when I was in there, paranoid I'd bump into someone I knew who'd start asking me about the business. While I waited I kept one eye over my shoulder, pretending to browse through the vacancies on the board that had been dressed up to appeal (for supermarket shelf stacker read 'Ambient Replenishment Technician'). My name was eventually called and I was directed to one of the small plastic office cubicles down the hall. My personal adviser, Tina, introduced herself by pointing to the name tag pinned to the front of her blouse, and told me to take a seat. I hadn't seen her before.

'Do you mind if I call you Che?' She smiled.

'Not at all,' I said, 'it is my name after all.'

She found that funny. 'Some people can get a bit shirty if you're too familiar,' she smiled.

'What happened to Cherie?' I asked.

'She got moved upstairs. We've had a bit of a staff shuffle round, so I'll be your new PA. That doesn't bother you, does it?' Her smile was pure saccharine.

'No.'

'Good. Now let's see what we have here.' She brought up my details on the computer. The screen was turned in her favour, but I lent over the desk in such a way that I could read what it said. There was nothing on it to indicate that this was anything other than a routine interview.

'Oh, I see you worked in New York.'

'Yes.'

'I'd love to go to America.' She said it like it was the moon.

'Maybe you should, then.'

'I'd love to, but I've just taken a mortgage out on a new house.'

'That's nice.'

'It is, actually,' she beamed 'It's not that big but it's got a nice garden. My cats like it anyway.' She was sweet but that smile was starting to annoy me.

'So you're looking for work as a journalist. Hmmm, not much call for one of those round here is there?' Exactly the reason I'd picked it. If you said 'waiter', they'd find you a job before you could say 'soup of the day.'

'No,' I said, reverting to the well-worn script, 'I've been applying for jobs upcountry mainly.'

'And you've been unemployed for four years now.'

'I've been unlucky, I think,' I said in a way that suggested so. 'I've had quite a few interviews, but they never seem to go anywhere.'

'I know,' she said sympathetically. 'It's hard.'

'But the good news is, I've got a call back next week so I'm hoping that something might come out of it.'

'Oh good!' she said enthusiastically entering the data into the computer. 'Where's that?'

'London.'

'OK.' More tapping at the keyboard.

'And if that doesn't work, I'm thinking of starting my own business.'

'Oh really. Doing what?'

Damn. Shouldn't have pushed it. 'Setting up a multimedia agency,' I replied, plumping for the first thing that came into my head.

'Gosh,' she said, 'that sounds technical. What would that involve?'

I didn't know. 'Websites mainly.'

'Ooh. I'll stop you there. I don't know the first thing about computers. I only learnt how to check my e-mail last week and that was hard enough.'

Bingo. I gave her a smile. 'It's not that hard.'

'I'll take your word for it,' she giggled. 'OK, it seems to me like you're doing all you can to help yourself. If you don't have any luck with this interview and want to make a go of your business idea then I suggest you come back and we'll see if we can't get you on one of our programmes. I'm told they're very useful, even if people do complain that it's a little bit like going back to school.'

'Sounds interesting,' I said with an expression I hoped looked enthusiastic.

'I think that's about it. Any questions?'

I gave a sincere shake of the head.

'OK,' she said with a final flourish on her keyboard. 'Just give me a second and I'll print out your new Jobseeker's Agreement.'

The 'Jobseeker's Agreement' was the Department of Social Security's equivalent to an Alcoholics Anonymous ten-step programme – a bond between me and them written in the language of mantra along the lines of 'In order to find employment, I will… check the local and national press for job vacancies/visit the Job Centre twice a week to check the vacancy boards/ask friends and relatives if they know of any job vacancies.' I was supposed to keep it on me at all times. Unfortunately, the last one they'd given me had been used to clear up something nasty the dog had yacked up after it had been scavenging through next door's bins.

She disappeared in the direction of the printer, and I took a quick snoop at the framed photograph facing towards her side of the desk. It was of two fat hairy cats.

'Here we go then. One for you, and one for us. If you could sign them both, we're all finished.'

I signed them both.

'OK then,' she said in a tone I could imagine her using to coax one of her cats in from the rain, 'good luck with the interview, and remember, you can always call.'

I smiled.

'For help with your job search I mean,' she added with a blush.

For some reason, the material intended for our jackets had been sent to Blackburn instead of Cornwall. They were sending out a new batch, but it wouldn't be with Frank until Friday. Obviously, he wasn't pleased.

'I told you I was going to start on 'em today,' he scolded me down the phone.

'I know you did, Frank. But to be honest you did tell me that an hour ago.'

'Well, you should be better organised than that.'

'Honestly, Frank, it's not my fault. The warehouse sent it to Blackburn instead.'

'Blackburn?' he thundered, choking on a lungful of cigarette smoke. 'That's bloody miles away.'

'I know. But like I told you, you'll have it by Friday. Will you still be able to do them?'

'My girls won't be pleased.'

'Please, Frank. I'm desperate.'

'You're always bloody desperate, Travis.'

'It's Che.' Even after all this time he confused the two of us.

'What?'

'It's Che, not Travis.'

'Course it is. Like I told you, I'll do my best.' His voice crackled with irritation. He'd get them done. He was professional like that. He might moan and gripe, but he would do them. 'You know we close early on Fridays, don't you?'

'Yes, it's coming to you on a morning delivery.'

'Well, tell the driver not to call round between ten and 11, because that's when I go to the bank.' As if the driver gave a monkey's.

In light of the supply hiccup with Frank's material, I was keen to call Kevin, who was making up our trousers. I liked Kevin, probably because he was the least professional manufacturer I'd ever come across. He actually made me feel knowledgeable. His handiwork wasn't in the same league as Frank's, but he was pretty good at making trousers and he was also very cheap.

'Hello Kevin.'

'Can you hang on a minute?' I could hear him talking in the background. 'No, not a problem,' he was saying to someone. 'Not a problem at all… I'll have them for Friday, I promise… Super… Yep, thanks… Not a problem. I'll see you then… Hello?'

'Hello Kevin, it's Che. Just giving you a call about the trousers. How are they coming along?'

'Fine,' he said.

'I was hoping to come and pick them up on Monday.'

'Monday?' he stuttered.

'Yes, Monday. You did say last week they'd be ready for then.'

'Yes. That's right. I did. Only I thought you meant a week on Monday.'

'I did, Kev. I said a week on Monday, last week.'

'Right.' He was confused. 'OK. That's not a problem. Not a problem at all. I'll have to check with the girls though.' I knew this meant that nothing had been done yet. 'Can I call you back?'

'OK,' I said. 'We need them for Monday, though.'

'Yep, I haven't forgotten.'

'And you'll call me back?'

'Yep, that's not a problem. I'll call you back in five minutes. Let me take your number again.'

I told him the number and hung up. He didn't call me back. I knew he wouldn't. He never did.

Chapter Five

I was on the road with a bag of samples in the back of the car, hopping from town to town on a sales rep mission. We both were. Travis had gone east and I'd gone north. I'd been away for five days, staying on people's floors by night and turning up for appointments in the day, fuelling myself on junk food and cigarettes, and was starting to feel the worse for wear.

I'd been hoping to return with my order books filled and a clear idea of what we were going to be running this season. It was the way things worked. You showed your sample range, tried to determine which pieces were the runners, concentrated on them and discarded the rest. Healthy advance orders would mean that we could launch a low risk production run – get it in, bang it out again and cover our costs without having money tied up in stock sitting around the yard. Unfortunately, things hadn't been going according to plan. The Great British Shopkeeper was a cautious beast at the best of times and confidence on the High Street was low even though Easter, the traditional start to the selling season, was just around the corner. The sales orders I'd taken on my mission to date had been bitty at best and had so far failed to provide clear 'runners' from the sample range.

I was standing in the Hofbrauhaus (what possessed Andy to name his shop after a beer hall, I never knew), wishing I was anywhere else but here. The last thing I needed to hear right now was that the trousers were too expensive. I knew they were fucking expensive, but it was the cheapest we could do them for without giving them away. That was another thing I'd learnt about our nation of shopkeepers. They were rarely happy, and always complaining. Whatever they took off us would be marked up to a retail price that they thought they could get away with. If they sold their orders, then they'd be back for more and complain if there was no more stock to be had. If they didn't sell, they'd be on the phone complaining and asking me to take the order back. Admittedly Andy, a paunchy middle aged retailer who thought dressing like a teenager and a dash of aftershave made him the trendiest thing in town, was more bitter than most. The Hofbrauhaus was always a blood-out-of-a-stone call, and every garment was a fight to sell.

'I don't know,' said Andy, screwing his nose up like I'd just taken a dump on the floor. He held the trousers up to himself. 'They're a bit expensive, aren't they?'

'I don't know,' I replied. 'Are they?'

'Well, they are compared to these.' He plucked a trouser leg from a swinging hanger on the rail. It was a garment made by a competitor whose office coffee budget was probably the same as our annual operational fund.

'But Andy, ours aren't knocked up by kids chained to sewing machines in the Third World.'

'Well, maybe you should think about it,' he replied, with no hint of irony. 'I've always said you make great clothes, Che, but you've got to think of the margins. Your prices are uncompetitive. Your bottom line's too high.'

I could have risen to the bait, but I couldn't be bothered. Instead, I made a show of taking the pair of trousers he was talking about and kneading the material between my fingers

'They're nothing special are they?' I noted, wrinkling my own nose for effect. 'Fabric's a bit thin. And look at the stitching. Hardly built for wear, are they? It's the kind of crap that only gets editorial coverage because the company runs full page ads in the magazine.'

Like the majority of shopkeepers we dealt with, Andy spent six days a week sitting in his shop, planning his orders around what the style magazines were touting as the next best thing. Thus, Andy assumed this qualified him as something of a trend expert, and my comment had hit him where it hurt.

He let the trouser leg fall, recoiling like he'd been up on the sewing machine all night making them himself. 'I think you're wrong. Check out the detail.'

'Like?'

'Like the reflective piping on the pocket tabs,' he said, pulling the fabric so that the piping caught the glare of the shop spotlights.

I gave an unimpressed shrug.

'Like I said, to you, it's about the margins,' sniffed Andy. 'These come in to me at tens, and I can get the full two point three five on the mark up. I can't get them in quick enough.'

Oh really.

'It's up to you,' I said stifling a yawn. 'You know our stuff sells. But if you don't want them, that's OK.'

'What about if I take a couple of pairs on sale or return? They're quite baggy, I don't know how well they'll go down.'

'Can't do it Andy,' I said, shaking my head and starting to fold up the trouser sample. 'We've got a small quantity for short order. Besides, our shops in London can't get enough of them.' I was lying, of course, but the trousers had polled well amongst our Liddleton focus group (Cas, the Pig, the skaters, Travis's missus) and we'd taken a gamble, committing ourselves to a production run with Kevin to take advantage of a manufacturing lull.

Andy licked his lips and looked at me, trying to work out if I was bluffing or not. 'OK. I'll take 12 pairs,' he finally said. If we didn't need the money, I'd tell him to shove it up his arse, but instead I calmly passed him the folded pair and took out my order book. 'What other colours have you got apart from the grey?' he asked.

'Navy.'

'And?'

At four hundred quid for the smallest roll of material the fabric warehouses were willing to sell us, the answer was no, but I wasn't going to tell him that. 'Maybe on the next run.'

'So you haven't got anything in green?'

'No. Like I say, probably on the next run.'

'OK then, change that. I'll take eight pairs now, and wait. Green always sells well for me.'

Shit. 'Could be a while, though. Are you sure you don't want to take the lot now?'

'No.' He shook his head and I knew the sale was lost for good. What else have you got?'

'Jackets?'

He wrinkled his nose again. 'Don't know about jackets. Look at these.' He led me to another rack. The jackets he showed me were over-priced and looked like they'd been made for the Siberian winter. 'They're from America. Lovely jackets they are. Look at the work in them. Good price too. I don't believe people round here. I'd have thought they'd have sold like hot cakes, but they've been sitting there since I unpacked the boxes.'

'I suppose it is almost summer,' I said. 'Maybe you'd have more joy with these.' I crossed back to the sample bag and pulled out one of ours. It was a pullover cagoule with a deep hood, fleece-lined pockets, windproof, waterproof, and breathable, with a profit margin that would make our bank manager weep. 'Got them in green too,' I winked holding it up for him to check.

He shook it brusquely, as if he was shaking crumbs from a picnic blanket. 'Mmmm, don't know about green. Don't sell many green jackets. How much?'

'Thirty,' I replied, 'and they're selling out fast.'

'A bit expensive, aren't they?'

'Look at the quality, Andy. They're made in this country, built to last.'

'Better not last too long. That's no good for my sales, is it? I'm one step away from the liquidators as it is. I don't know what's going on at the moment. It's dead. You know how much I took last week?'

I shook my head wearily. 'Hundred and fifty quid. Didn't take anything from Monday to Friday. Not a frigging sausage. I don't know why I bother sometimes, I really don't.' He stood for a good long while, shaking his head until he realised what he was doing. 'Anyway, what's it like for you at the moment?' He was digging, and his eyes looked shifty.

'Not bad,' I said, returning to the jacket and changing the subject. 'These are our best seller at the moment.'

He rubbed his chin as he flicked his eyes from me to the jacket. 'I'll take two, one in each colour. Sizes?'

'Medium and large.'

'No XL?'

'Maybe next run.' I had to stop saying that.

'OK. One of each size. You choose. Let's see what else you've got… Oh shit, I've forgotten about the coffee. How do you take it?'

'Milk, one sugar.'

'Back in a tick.' He disappeared through a curtain and into the stock room.

'Can I use your toilet, Andy?' I shouted after him. My bladder always took a hammering when I was on the road.

'It's on the blink. Ask in the charity shop next door,' he shouted back.

It took a while for the old ladies knitting behind the counter to understand what I was after. 'Did you see it in the window?' one of them asked.

'Your coffee's on the counter,' said Andy when I came back, 'I'll be with you in a second – customer,' he mouthed. A small girl with a bag slung over her shoulder moved methodically down the rails, her boyfriend in tow. Andy hovered in the background.

'What do you think of these?' she asked the boyfriend about a pair of trousers.

'I dunno,' he shrugged disinterestedly. 'How much?'

'Forty-five pounds,' said Andy who'd sidled up behind them. 'Try them on if you like. There's a changing room out the back.'

'No,' said the girlfriend, any interest she may have had vanishing at the whiff of Andy's aftershave. 'I'm just looking.'

'What about this?' said the boyfriend, who'd picked one of the jackets I'd been showing Andy minutes before. He removed his cap and pulled it on. 'Tasty,' he said to his reflection in the mirror. 'How much?'

'Seventy,' said Andy, looking in my direction for guidance.

'Sixty-five,' I corrected.

Andy frowned. 'Do you want it?'

'Would do, but I'm skint, mate,' said the boyfriend, patting his pockets for emphasis. It was the story of our business life…

'I can hold it back for you,' said Andy, desperately chasing the sale.

'Nah, you're all right.' The boyfriend slid the jacket off and re-placed his baseball cap. 'Done yet?' he asked his girlfriend.

'Yeah. Let's try up the road. There's nothing in here.'

The two had to circumnavigate Andy on their way out. I could see he was quietly fuming. 'Fuck you very much,' he called after them before they'd even closed the door. 'That's right, just walk away, waste my time, you bastards.'

The boyfriend looked over his shoulder, wondering who Andy was talking to.

'Can you believe it?' huffed Andy. 'The cheek of some people.'

No, I couldn't believe it. Andy was almost certainly in the wrong business, and quite possibly deranged.

'He liked our jacket,' I replied, trying to take the edge off the atmosphere.

'I wouldn't bet on it,' spat Andy. 'I'm sure people like them just come in here to wind me up. Him up the road probably sent them down here to check up on my prices.'

'So, just two of those then?' I asked pointing at the jackets, desperate to avoid another of his retail conspiracy diatribes. He nodded morosely, and I wrote it down in my order book.

'Sweatshirts?' I offered, pulling a bundle out of my sample bag. I leafed through the various colours and designs but Andy was looking without seeing, his thoughts clouded by red mist.

'I'll take six. You choose the designs. Different colours, different sizes – nothing too small.'

'T-shirts?'

'Same again. And don't give me the brown, because I always get left with it. Never sells.'

The bell above the shop door rang as an overweight woman came in, a small kid sucking on a lollipop trailing behind. 'Do you sell wallets?' she asked. In a flash Andy had rediscovered his salesman's smile.

While he dealt with the customer, I totted up the order and prepared my excuses for a quick getaway. I'd had enough of Andy for one day. As I packed the samples away I watched the kid leave his mother's side and glide along a rail running a sticky hand along a row of jeans. He looked around, waiting for his mother to tell him not to, but she was preoccupied. He looked at me and flashed a cheeky grin as he took the lollipop out of his mouth and popped it into one of the pockets…

I left the shop. It was a poxy order. It hardly covered my petrol. Andy had the habit of finding a cloud in every silver lining and an hour in his presence had sucked the life right out of me. I was pissed off, depressed, and ready to jack in the whole rep mission and head back home. The last few days had throttled away what little glimmer of hope I'd held for digging us out of our financial hole. We were one skipped bank loan repayment away from financial disaster and it was becoming almost impossible for us to function as a business anymore.

Andy may have set me slipping on my way into depression, but he wasn't the cause, just a symptom. The truth was the past four years were starting to catch up with me, and as I walked back to the car I chewed on my negative thoughts. I was sick of playing the salesman. I was sick of being told that our clothes were good but too expensive. I was sick of having to compete with corporate brands that had a stranglehold on the market. I was sick of spending every working hour busting my balls to make money that always went into someone else's pocket and never into ours. But most of all I felt sick that I had been so naïve as to assume that it could have been anything different.

In frustration at our dire straits, I kicked the car door so hard that I attracted the 'oh-no-another-nutter' gaze of an elderly couple in the multi storey car park. I flashed them a smile that was meant to say 'having-a-bad-day', but they had their eyes fixed straight ahead and quickened their pace. I started the engine, and was about to drive off when my phone started ringing. It was Scottish Jack.

'Hello, boy!' he bellowed. Jack was actually Welsh, but he owned a string of five shops in Scotland.

'Hey Jack. How's things?'

'Fantastic. We've got a mini-heatwave up here. Blue skies and 13 degrees.'

'That's not a heatwave,' I laughed.

'Maybe not for you, English boy, but up here you'd better believe 13 degrees is a fuckin' heatwave.' I liked Jack. He was one of the few shopkeepers I actually did like. 'Will I be getting a visit from you before Easter?' he asked.

'Not before Easter, I'm afraid. Bit tied up down here at the moment.' The truth was I couldn't afford the petrol to make it that far north.

'That's a shame,' he said. 'Never mind. I've just been looking at your website, and I like the look of those trousers you've got posted up there. The baggy ones. Do you have any in stock?'

'Yeah. Want me to send you up a sample?'

'I tell you what, fuck the sample. I've just kicked one of my bastard suppliers into touch up 'ere and got some space to fill, pronto like. So just send me up 50 pairs, ten for each shop, mix of sizes and colours. I know they'll sell, your stuff always does. Come to think of it, I need jackets and tees too, boyo, and lots of 'em.'

Chapter Six

<u>April: The Truth Hurts</u>

Stock was always a problem. You either had too much of it, or too little. Right now we had too much and none of it had been paid for. Boxes of fresh stock worth in the region of eight grand were gathering dust in the yard. Everything had been bought on 30 days' credit, and the 30 days were just about up. I was chasing up shops to settle their accounts so we could pay for it all but I'd had few cheques through the post. Seemed like everyone was feeling the pinch. Today, though, we had a different type of stock problem on our hands. I was on my way to see Kevin and I wasn't happy. In fact, I'd go so far to say that I was fuming. We'd had a crisis. A trouser crisis.

Easter was a week away and I'd been packing up an order when I'd made the discovery. It was lucky really. I'd been in a bad mood and tried on a pair of trousers with the intention of taking them for myself. When I put them on, my feet didn't even come out the end of them. The legs were cut a good four inches longer than they were supposed to be. I'd cursed Kevin for mixing up the size labels, and tried on another pair. To my horror, they were no different. Within minutes, Travis and I were frantically tearing through stock boxes of trousers, holding each pair up against the original only to discover they'd all been cut the same way.

As I've said, the manufacturing process is studded with pitfalls and in translating designs from the drawing board to the sewing machine there was always a huge margin for error. For instance, if you made your sample in denim and then decided to switch your fabric to cotton, you had to account for the additional 'play' in the fabric. This would make the finished garment hang differently, meaning you had to tease your hip, waist and leg measurements accordingly. As we had already made that expensive mistake before, I knew that the fault didn't lie with us (you only made those kind of mistakes once). Kevin had used the same cotton fabric that he'd used on the sample to complete this run of trousers, and the sample had been precise.

I was at a loss for an explanation, so I'd rung Kevin, only to get his answer phone. During the course of the afternoon I'd made at least ten more calls, but still he wouldn't pick up. Eventually, I'd left a growled message that I would be down to see him first thing in the morning.

The English Riviera was looking decidedly Baltic when I arrived at Kevin's factory, situated in a small industrial estate in one of its less fashionable corners. The factory consisted of two storeys. A cutting table took up most of the room downstairs, and Kevin's 'girls' (his sewing machinists) worked upstairs. How Kevin came to be in the manufacturing business was a mystery, as he'd sold washing machines for ten years before jumping into the rag trade. Kevin had none of the old-boy-of-the-rag-trade traditionalism that Frank had. A spade was a spade with Frank, and there was no messing around. Kevin by contrast wouldn't know a spade if it hit him on the head, and messing around was part and parcel of his working process. Kevin's problem was that he couldn't say no and always said 'not a problem at all'.

I rang the bell and walked inside. Kevin poked his head out of his office at the end of the room, saw who it was and flashed a nervous grin. Before I could launch into a tirade he started shaking his head. 'Just 'ad the accountant in and he's not very happy with me,' he said in his soft Devonian burr.

Despite the cold he was wearing a T-shirt, revealing arms covered with dodgy home-etched tattoos. 'I 'ad all my windows smashed by vandals over the weekend. That's why it's a bit dark in 'ere. Had to board 'em up. Forgot to send off my bloody insurance forms. It's gonna cost me an arm and a leg.'

That was the trouble with Kevin. He was terminally unlucky and giving him a bollocking was never easy – you just ended up feeling sorry for him.

'Kevin,' I said, when I could get a word in edgeways.

'I know,' he held his hand up to his heart. 'I got your message on the answer machine. Sorry about that. I was here yesterday, but it must have got switched on by mistake.'

'Happens all the time,' I said.

Kevin appeared not to notice my sarcasm. 'Thanks for coming anyway. Got a couple of things to straighten out with you.'

I inhaled, ready to deliver my verbal blows. 'That box of trousers…'

'Yep. I've just been through the figures again,' said Kevin, thrusting me a piece of paper.

'What's this?' I said, scanning his spidery scrawl.

'New invoice'

'For marble bags?'

'Wrong one.' He gave me another. 'I quoted you wrong. Them trousers wasn't ten pounds a pair. It's nine pounds, though don't tell the girls, 'cause they say they're well fiddly to do and I should be charging you more.'

See what I mean?

'Oh thanks,' I found myself muttering.

'Not a problem,' he said re-folding a football shirt on top of the cutting table for the third time. 'Like I say, I thought those figures were right, but…'

He'd taken the sting out of my intention, but there was a reason for me being here and I had to get down to it. 'Kevin,' I interrupted, 'I wasn't calling about the price yesterday.' I spoke fast, tone growing harsher with each word. 'I've got 80 pairs of trousers in the back of my car that look like they've been made for fucking basketball players. The legs are four inches too long.'

Kevin stopped folding the shirt and looked at me like a man trying to remember his name.

'That can't be right. I done you a sample and everything.'

'The sample's fine. It's the other 80 pairs that aren't.'

We brought the boxes in from my car and placed them on his cutting table. Kevin took a pair of trousers, and laid them up against the sample pair. He took another pair and did the same. Painstakingly slowly, he repeated the exercise five times before giving me his prognosis.

'Yep,' he said, 'the legs are definitely longer.'

'I know they're fucking longer!' I exploded. 'And they should be on a carrier to Scotland tomorrow. If I don't get them there by Easter, I can kiss goodbye to five shops.'

'It's not a problem,' he said calmly.

'But it is a problem Kevin.'

'Well, yeah, it is, but it's not a problem that can't be fixed.'

'Really?' I said, barely able to contain my surprise.

'Yeah,' he said, holding a trouser leg up. He nodded his head as though if he did this for long enough he'd make the problem go away. 'OK. Let me find your pattern and we'll work it out from there.'

Now a pattern bears little resemblance to the finished product. It's just a bundle of cut-out pieces of card, with a nick here and a scribbled dimension there, which corresponds to the components of the finished garment. The pattern pieces are placed over the fabric on the cutting table, traced round, cut out, individually bundled up and sent upstairs to the girls on the sewing machines, where they're stitched together like a cloth jigsaw. If the pattern's right, the finished product should be right. As Kevin laid the pattern against the pair of trousers, it was obvious that the trouser leg he held bore little resemblance to the trouser leg on the pattern. In fact, looking closer, I realised the leg pieces weren't from our pattern at all. I didn't recognise the handwritten dimensions, but I knew for a fact that they hadn't been written by Travis.

'Oh shit,' said Kevin after I pointed that fact out, 'I think you're right.' He winced as he returned to the pattern hooks and began to rummage. 'Got it,' he said eventually, hauling another off the hook.

'Is it a problem?' I heard myself say. His assurances that our trouser crisis was fixable had taken the edge off my anxiety, and I was now able to assess the situation rationally. Loosely translated, this meant the trousers had stopped being my problem to sort out (for the time being) and had become Kevin's.

'Not a problem for you,' he replied, placing the patterns together. I recognised Travis's handwriting on the leg pieces. 'Big problem for me though,' he said, his eyes growing wider. 'There's five hundred trousers on a container to Sweden that have got your legs on them. Oh bollocks,' he added softly. That was the thing about Kevin. He never lost it. Never started ranting and raging. It was almost as if he accepted the inevitability of his mishaps. 'I cut them out the same day I cut yours. I don't know how they got mixed up. I mean the other trousers were a tartan fabric…' His sentence tailed away with his concentration.

'Oh shit.'

'Oh shit,' he echoed.

'What are you going to do?' I asked.

'Cross my fingers and hope they don't realise,' he shrugged. He was putting on a smile, but I noticed a bead of sweat on his forehead. 'Oh well, nothing I can do about it now.'

'And what about our trousers?'

'Oh, they won't be a problem. I'll just have to get the girls to take them up. It's lucky really,' he added a little too optimistically. 'The width of the leg is almost bang-on the same as yours.'

'Apart from the trousers and your smashed windows, how's things?' I asked, tactlessly, trying to fill the silence that had lasted for at least a minute.

Coming out of his trance, his mood appeared to lighten. 'Oh, you know. They could be worse. I've got quite a lot of work on at the moment. I've got three thousand marble bags to make. Oh, and this is something that'll make you laugh…'

He told me he'd had a call from one of our business peers, a company a few rungs further up the ladder. They'd got a shipment of two thousand long-sleeve shirts made up in India that had come back with the left arm shorter than the right.

'Can't do a thing with 'em,' chuckled Kevin. 'They wanted to know if I could chop the arms down and make them into short sleeve shirts instead. I told them it was impossible.'

'Two thousand?'

'Yep. Two thousand, and they're only good for dusters.'

Our trouser crisis suddenly paled in comparison. Every season we'd hear the latest batch of manufacturing horror stories. My favourite concerned a clothing label that had ordered five thousand pairs of trousers from a factory in the Far East. The factory had made a sample that had been sent to England for checking. It had been inspected, cleared and sent back eastwards with instructions to copy exactly. Weeks later, back came the shipment – five thousand pairs of trousers, each with an identical hole in the left trouser leg. Turned out the sample had left England with a cigarette burn on it and the factory, as per the client's directions, had copied the trousers exactly.

Whether the story was true or one of those rag trade myths I didn't know, but it served to illustrate a point. Unless you were totally on top of your manufacturing (and I mean literally standing over the sewing machine), fuck-ups like that happened all the time.

I went up to say hello to Kevin's girls before I left. I knew they thought I was 'a nice boy', and with a need to get the job done I wanted to be in their good books. 'Best if you don't tell them about the trousers,' said Kevin, 'I'll break the news when you've gone…'

As I drove back to Liddleton I knew that even though it was late afternoon, my working day had only just begun. After winter months at the drawing board, manufacturing was in full swing for the summer and with the trouser crisis out of our hands for now, my mind turned to the three hundred and fifty T-shirts and two hundred sweats that needed printing to meet Easter orders.

Tees and sweats were our bread and butter, being the only things we produced that turned a decent profit. We could knock out a T-shirt, printed and labelled, and double our money. We kept the costs low by printing them up ourselves and had the use of a print shop down the road where we had an agreement with the owner. When the day shift finished, he'd let us come in and print through the night.

The whole screen printing process revolved around the use of noxious substances. Once you got used to the smell you hardly noticed it, but by the end of a night session your head throbbed and your throat rasped. The job was frustratingly labour intensive as we were working on a carousel that was the junk side of antique. It took time to set up the screens, meaning we could usually do four or five prints per night. With 12 designs to print, that meant that we were looking at three nights of burning the midnight oil.

Travis was in a sullen mood to match my own when I got back to the yard. It was the usual story. The last thing either of us wanted to do after a day's work was to put in a 12-hour night shift. Nevertheless, the thought of a print run was always worse than the actual session itself and once we started getting into it, it wasn't so bad. We had the place to ourselves, a couple of beers, the music as loud as we wanted and we could take frequent spliff breaks.

We'd been working for nearly four hours. The first design had proved tricky to line up and had taken longer than expected. We'd just finished our fish and chips – the grease helped to line our stomachs against the chemicals – and had smoked a spliff on the stoop outside. Back in the print room we shot the breeze while finishing our coffee, discussing Easter and the start of the selling season.

'It'll be shit,' said Travis.

'How do you know?'

'It's always shit! When was the last time we had good weather at Easter? It'll be the same old story – shit Easter, ages for anyone to pay us, and we'll all be looking at May bank holiday to bail us out. It's always the same.'

'I hope not,' I said, rolling a cigarette even though I'd already smoked far more than I should've done that day. 'I don't know if we can make it to bank holiday.'

'It's that bad?' he asked.

I nodded grimly. The fresh stock still hadn't been paid for, and I'd been banking on swift sales to settle the costs. Travis never looked at the books. Figures scared him and I handled all the office crap. Of course I kept him informed what was going on, but it usually went in one ear and out of the other.

'We need a sideline that's going to make us money,' I said at length.

'Same old, same old,' said Travis. We were always looking for a sideline to make us money.

'Who knows?' I said, thinking out loud. 'Maybe Madonna will be on the bog, reading one of those mags we've got a shoot in, order a jacket and hail you as the best designer since Leonardo Da Vinci.'

'Yeah, right!' Travis laughed. 'Great thought, though.'

'Being hailed as the greatest designer or Madonna on the crapper?'

'Take your pick.'

'Do you ever think that maybe our destiny is to be one of those overnight successes that in reality comes off the back of many years of struggling?' It was a stoned thought that had forgotten that was all it was and popped out of my mouth instead.

'I used to think like that,' said Travis. 'But as time goes on, I can't help thinking that it might just be wishful thinking.'

The conversation petered off, and we sat in silence listening to the sound of the print shop water pipes gurgling, neither of us daring to say what we knew the other was thinking. The past year had been all about survival, but both of us knew that we couldn't go on just surviving forever.

'You know what I'm scared of?' Travis said eventually.

'What?'

'Slogging my guts out for the best part of my life and still not getting anywhere. Being so convinced that I'm on the right track, then waking up one day and realising that it's come to a dead end and it's too late to do anything else but make the best of a bad job.'

'That's dark.'

'Yeah, I know it's dark. It's not a thought I have that often but...' He paused. 'I just have this fear of time passing me by, and suddenly it'll be too late. I'll be pushing middle age and have to accept the fact that I'll be working until I physically can't do it anymore, and all of it just to survive.' He shook his head.

'That's still quite far off,' I tried to sound assuring. Both of us had dark thoughts, bleak moments, times when our faith was challenged. When one was down, the other naturally moved in to provide a counterbalance.

Travis shrugged. 'Thing is, the longer time goes on, the closer it gets. It's different for you. You haven't got kids.'

He was right, of course. I struggled enough with only myself to look after but for him it was a different story altogether.

'We'll make it,' I said. Maybe it was the spliff talking, or the chemicals of the print shop addling my brain, but at that moment I really did believe it. 'Maybe it's time to rally the Magnificent Seven.'

'What for? A bank job? 'Cause all I keep thinking about at the moment is money. Seems like we spend our lives working our arses off and someone else always gets the break.'

'It'll come. We just have to keep the faith.'

'I don't know about that, mate,' said Travis, his voice tinged with scepticism. 'All I know is that I'm getting older and everyone I'm hanging around with is getting younger. Most people my age have got jobs and houses and pensions and cars that start first time.'

'Except for me.'

'Of course.' He forced a thin smile.

'Think of the positives, though. At least we're in charge of our lives,' I countered. 'How many of those people you talk about are actually happy with what they're doing? Most of them are in jobs they hate, because they bought into the dream of two point five kids, mortgages, new cars, a hundred crap TV channels... How many of those people can say they're really happy? Take that fabric rep that comes around every couple of months. Good job, nice house, smashing car. He's the same age as us, but how old does he look? He's got his life mapped out, but it's empty. Spends his life chasing a dream to move to Australia, but he can't do it because his life is devoted to dealing with all that other shit.'

Travis nodded. 'You've made your point.'

'Our problem is we've always wanted to do it on our own terms and the system just isn't set up to give us an easy ride. But at least we're doing something because we want to be doing it. At least we won't look back on what might have been.'

'Like working a 24-hour shift for no money?' His laugh was hollow.

I didn't stop. The spliff was firing my thoughts off on a tangent. 'It's all about getting the combination right.'

'What?' He was understandably confused.

I laughed. 'Sorry, mate! Thinking out loud… It's like a safe door. It'll only open if you get all the numbers right, and all in the right sequence.'

'I understood that part.'

'OK, so say that success lies behind the locked door. Sometimes you have two of the numbers, sometimes you have three, but you need all five to make the door open. That's what it's been like with Sewerside. We've had the numbers, we just haven't had them in the right place at the right time.'

'I like that theory,' said Travis, draining his coffee and standing up. 'So maybe we should look into getting a safe cracker on the firm.'

'Or just blow the bloody door off,' I replied. It would have been a good pun but Travis was the one person in the world who hadn't seen The Italian Job…

The night shift had a funny habit of warping time. Sometimes minutes seemed like hours and you were half-asleep, sometimes the hours felt like minutes and you were wide awake. Always at about two in the morning, things became a bit twisted for half an hour or so as the body did its best to convince the mind to send it to bed. Survive that, and you got your second wind. A line of charlie helped, but we couldn't afford charlie. Instead, we drank strong cups of coffee until our tongues grew so furry we had to switch to tea.

Our hard day's night finished at 7am the next morning, exactly 24 hours after I'd set out to see Kevin. I should have gone to bed but there was office stuff I had to do and I knew that when I woke later that day, my mind would be in no fit state to do any of it. I returned to the yard, boxed up the printed garments ready for labelling, fired up the computer, and put another four hours of work in.

Chapter Seven

May: To the Barricades

Easter had come and gone, along with my uncelebrated 31st birthday. The weather, as Travis had predicted, had been shit. My own holiday had been a family affair. My sister was down for the weekend with her husband and two kids. It was a bittersweet experience. Sweet because I hadn't seen them for a while, bitter because I found myself unable to resist cocking a snoop over the other side of the fence and pondering on what might have been. My brother-in-law was a sound chap, same age as me, and had his own business too – except his business revolved around corporate clients with fat cheque books. I didn't know how much he earned, but I did know they'd just bought themselves a new car, looked tanned from a two-week holiday, and were about to buy a new house.

Over a large Easter Sunday roast and too much wine, I went into a decline. As the evening progressed, a feeling of dread gnawed away at my bloated belly. My trials, tribulations and achievements suddenly seemed very small and insignificant compared to their material success. I lurched through dinner, block-nosed from a cold, drunk and feeling like the down-and-out brother-in-law in the Rocky movies. I went to bed feeling depressed, empty, and remembering my conversation with Travis in the print shop. In my state of decline, I saw it for the musings of a stoned monkey, trying to convince himself he was swinging

FEAR MAKES THE WOLF LOOK BIGGER

in the jungle when really he was messing around on a rope swing in a cage.

I lay in bed unable to sleep, kept awake by a hacking cough and an overactive mind that churned the same thought over and over again in my head: my sister and her husband were upwardly mobile, successful and reaping the rewards of playing the system. They didn't have to worry about money, they had their own house, they had two kids and another one on the way, and they were happy. More than that they were really happy…

And what did I have? Fuck-all.

Sorry. Fuck-all, and a cold.

The other big news to come out of the Easter weekend was the little bombshell my younger sister dropped into our dessert bowls as we sat around the dinner table. She'd started dating a copper. Not just any old copper, but CID. I raised an eyebrow but didn't say anything. Cas called it a 'breach of security' and branded her irresponsible, and the inevitable sibling slanging match ensued. If the relationship hadn't been serious before, I knew it would be now…

The Easter bunny hadn't delivered any nice surprises. It had ravaged the vegetable garden and pissed off back to its burrow leaving the rest of us to pick up the pieces. Easter had been as dire on the sales front as it had on the weather front as it had been on my domestic front. Even Scottish Jack, the eternal voice of retail optimism, was downbeat. 'I tell you, man,' he told me on the phone, 'I've never seen an Easter like it.' Pete in Sheffield blamed it on the lack of disposable income floating around the economy. 'Everyone's too fuckin' busy buying their DVDs and video games, which means there's nowt left for the rest of us.' Andy at the Hofbrauhaus blamed the Easter egg industry. 'Look at all the fat kids you see around these days,' he'd sneered. 'It's obvious. They're too busy stuffing chocolate to be interested in buying clothes.'

Poor shop sales meant that we wouldn't get any re-orders before May. It also meant that we'd battle to get paid, and would struggle to pay even half our manufacturing bills. The bank didn't deal in excuses, and would extract the monthly loan payments from our account whether there was money in there or not. If our overdraft slipped further into the red, there'd be running charges, and then, of course, interest payments on top of all of that. The letters that arrived to clog up my desk were of the red variety, and we were collecting enough final demands to paper the walls of a small outhouse. It was looking more and more like we were heading for a hard fall. What we needed was a distraction, a glimmer of hope in the darkness, something to take our mind off the doom and gloom which hung over the yard like the black clouds suffocating the sky outside.

So it was that I'd been in the yard when I got a call from the Party Porpoise, an environmental awareness group, that was putting on a fashion show in London and desperately looking for brands that had the right profile. Travis's designs had always had a pro-environment slant to them and went down well with London trendies who enjoyed a rant about the dirty air they breathed while throwing their litter in the street. We also had our environmentally friendly skate ramp (i.e., cobbled together on the cheap with salvaged timber and safety/fishing netting that had been washed up on the beach), and as such we'd fitted the Party Porpoise bill perfectly.

The point of contact was Felicity, an excitable Sloane who told me three times during the course of the conversation that she was 'absolutely loopy, darling'. I reasoned that she probably had more money than sense, but gave her the benefit of the doubt. A London fashion show might revive our flagging fortunes and she'd told me there'd already been considerable press interest.

It was May Day, and we were up in town, enjoying the first of the summer sunshine after too many bleak months. We'd left Devon early and driven up to London in the latest company car, a bright orange Vauxhall Chevette that was at least 20 years old. It had been re-christened The Shove-it (in homage to a skating move) and it had a top speed of 65 miles an hour. On our arrival we dumped it in west London and jumped the tube.

As it happened, our trip coincided with an anti-globalisation demonstration being held in the Capital, and the weekend papers had carried ominous warnings of anarchy and rioting on the streets. The movement had first grabbed the headlines when protestors clashed with police in Seattle during a meeting of the World Trade Organisation in 1999, and had become an international rallying call for the disaffected. Having been mauled by the corporate market place ourselves it was a theme we could relate to, and we decided to go along.

By the time we got to the City of London it was awash in a wave of blue. Side-streets were crammed with police vans, shop fronts were boarded, and the streets were empty except for coppers, booted and suited up and giving the evil to every civilian that passed them by. The police had promised a 'ring of steel' to guard against potential troublemakers and the eerie silence within it was punctuated only by the whine shudder of police helicopters above. The sun was out but a chill wind blew, rustling plastic bags and sending empty cans scuttling.

Crowds of demonstrators had begun to gather in Parliament Square, a curious mixture of anarchists, trade unionists, yoghurt weavers, students, media sections spoiling for fight coverage, and bods like us, tagging along in sympathy or curiosity. For a couple of hours nothing really happened, and Travis and I sat and smoked grass on the grass, people-watching. The media had made a lot of noise about the sophisticated organisation behind the demonstration but now we were here it seemed as if nobody really knew what was going on. The crowd was a couple of thousand strong, maybe more, and noisy but hardly menacing. As time went on, I had my suspicions that the whole thing was nothing but a set-up – a cunning ploy designed to trick the authorities into believing their own hype, and send them barking off on a futile exercise in wasting taxpayers' money. The most subversive act we had seen so far was a naked man shinning up a lamppost to hang a home-made poster urging the world to go naked. It had indeed caused a mini riot, but only amongst the attendant media crews.

By 3 o'clock the sense of boredom receded, replaced by a sudden surge of expectation as a rag tag samba band that had been circling the square peeled off down Whitehall. In true Pied Piper fashion, the crowd followed. The pace was slow and the atmosphere carnival-like. Buoyed by the confidence of its own momentum the crowd continued to push towards Trafalgar Square. As lines of police looked on the whistles, horns and yells increased in volume, the demonstrators clearly coming up on the first wave of adrenalin, and I could feel the mood begin to change.

Around us, people pulled hoods over their heads and covered their faces with scarves and bandanas. I could make out the chattering of Spanish and Italian voices, amidst the war cries of anarcho-crusties cradling tins of strong lager, as they bayed at the increasingly thick lines of riot police that had formed a human shield around the gates of Downing Street. While the main body of the crowd surged on towards Trafalgar Square, a small group gathered outside the gates of the Prime Minister's residence and threw insults that inevitably turned to bottles and stones. The policemen dodged the missiles and held their ground, peering through the plastic visors of their helmets with eyes that stared a fine line between fear and fight. Travis and I couldn't see what was going on, but there was enough noise coming from the front of the demonstration to know that something was. We broke ranks and moved towards the front, arriving in time to see numbers pressing around a McDonalds outlet.

Urged on by the crowd, a small group started to attack the windows with baseball bats and pieces of wood until there was the sound of breaking glass and resounding cheers. The biggest cheer of all went up when the golden arch came crashing down. In the attackers poured, teeming like black rats into a grain store, throwing chairs and anything that wasn't fixed to the ground out onto the street. I saw someone rip his jacket on broken glass as he came back out again, his arms filled with hamburgers looted from behind the counter. He lobbed them into the cheering crowd, and raised his arms in triumph.

'Stupid twat,' said Travis behind me, 'I thought we were protesting against them, not giving them free advertising.'

'Maybe he's the Ham-Burglar,' I joked, but he didn't hear me because my words had been drowned out by the sudden surge of the crowd. With McDonalds in tatters, attentions had turned to a souvenir shop next door. The windows of the souvenir shop gave way, and the T-shirts that hung in the windows showing cartoon Beefeaters and sights from the city, were ripped out and thrown in the air.

Someone crashed into the back of me as the crowd shifted and I almost went over. I regained my balance in time to see an overweight thug in black swing a piece of wood at one of the windows of a pub next door. It splintered but didn't smash, and he went for it a second time.

'Oi!' came a shout from behind him. 'What the fuck you doing? Leave the boozer alone.'

'Oh shit,' said Travis, grabbing my arm. I turned and followed his gaze down a side street.

Up to this point there had been little sign of a police response but that was about to change. We watched as columns of riot cops moved briskly in our direction. Even above the noise of the protestors I thought I could hear their boots drumming the tarmac. Others in the crowd had noticed too and we got caught up in the scramble to get away, finding ourselves being squeezed up against the wall of a building on the other side of the road.

Those either watching or doing the ransacking were oblivious to what was happening until their ranks buckled under the surge of a police charge from the rear that scattered all before them and sent everyone running for cover. Batons swung through the air and cracked any limb that got in the way as a line of policemen took up positions in front of the McDonalds, trapping a few of the black rats inside, and creating a space between them and those in the crowd who'd stood their ground. In between them, it seemed, the press corps jostled for the best positions to train cameras and fire off rolls of film. There followed a stand-off which lasted a few minutes, the tension mounting with each second that ticked by. You could feel the tangibility to the atmosphere; like a high pitch that got higher and higher and higher until you felt it couldn't go any further, until the point where the pressure seemed to 'POP.'

In a few seconds that seemed to last like minutes, the world around us froze. It was as if everyone, cops and demonstrators, realised in that tiny window of clarity, that a line had been crossed and there was no going back.

And then WHOOSH!

The effect was like an explosion of gas, a surge of adrenalin as powerful as any drug I'd ever done in my life, and the whole thing just kicked off. The Old Bill moved fast, the ranks of blue armour sweeping across the road, shoulder to shoulder and charging the demonstrators down. There was nowhere for the crowd to escape except towards Trafalgar Square or back down Whitehall, the way they'd come. Within seconds I was staring at my reflection in the helmet visor of a large riot policeman. He had his baton raised and I put my arms out to protect my head. 'Over there or over here!' he screamed to no one in particular, motioning up and down the street. 'Fucking move it!' he bawled, splattering the inside of his visor with saliva.

I made for a gap and joined the masses running back down the street towards Parliament Square. I looked back in time to see Travis's dreadlocks bobbing off in the other direction towards Trafalgar Square. It was too late to follow because the thick blue column had driven a wedge through the crowd and split the demonstration in two.

I was shaking, my heartbeat knocking holes in my head. All around me, people stared with eyes that were busting out of their lids, as they tried to anticipate what was going to happen next. Off to the left, a woman was crying, blood streaming down her face. I could hear someone else on a mobile. 'Yeah, that's right. Get your arse down here now. It's gonna kick off big style.' Agitators were beginning to regain their confidence, occupying new ground and facing the police square on. 'Don't back down from these cunts!' someone yelled. 'We can take them if we stick together!'

Eventually I got hold of Travis on the mobile. He'd been penned into Trafalgar Square. 'You wouldn't believe how many coppers there are up here,' he said.

'Likewise down here,' I told him, 'I'm going to see if I can get round the roadblock and come up there.' He told me he'd wait by the ice cream van... if the mob didn't trash it first.

It wasn't easy to get into Trafalgar Square, but I pretended I'd been split up from my girlfriend, and eventually blagged it through the police ranks. Sure enough, Travis was by the ice cream van. Rather than falling under attack from the anarchist hordes, it was doing a roaring trade selling them ice creams and cold drinks. Mr Whippy, it seemed, like the boozer, had been granted special immunity.

We decided to get out of there, only to discover that we couldn't. The cops policing the roads that funnelled into the Square were refusing to let anyone out. We could see more reinforcements swarming behind the fixed lines they'd drawn. A journalist trying to get past them was being physically removed. An older man with the appearance of a university lecturer, was remonstrating with one of the cops. He demanded to be allowed to leave.

'I'm not authorised to let you leave,' came the reply from a burly copper with stripes on his arm.

'On what grounds?'

'On the grounds that you are being detained under section 60 of the Public Order Act.'

'This is ridiculous!' implored the lecturer.

'Those are my orders,' replied the policeman.

'Are we living in a democracy or under the sword of a dictatorship?' he demanded.

'You tell him, mate,' sneered a crusty over the lip of his cider bottle.

Travis and I walked back down into Trafalgar Square. The ring of steel had us surrounded on all sides. Line after line of policemen stood firm, stoic behind the plastic shields they held across their chests like Roman legionnaires. Looking around at the motley collection of protestors, I was suddenly scared. Nowhere to run to, nowhere to hide, and still the agitators barracked the cops with insults and the occasional tossed missile.

'Shit,' said Travis quietly, 'we're going to get a kicking.'

Two hours later, we were still being held. The police were maintaining their 'no exit' policy and with reinforcements in place they were tightening the noose. Periodically, their massed ranks moved forward from all sides, a few metres at a time, establishing a new front line and pushing the crowd into a space that grew ever smaller. Psychological screws were being turned and the bravado of the pack was beginning to dissipate as it realised it was hemmed in with nowhere else to go. People looked worried, some burning up their mobile phone lines to the outside world. Denied the right to leave, rivulets of piss ran down the flagstones beneath our feet, as people couldn't hold their bladders any longer. There were no directions, no indication of what to do next, only the pulsing ebb of fear. And still the noose pulled tighter, another line of policemen filing down the steps into the square and forming a second front at crowd level.

Nelson's Column had become a position of strategic importance for both sides, and the police marched forward in an organised offensive. Tussles broke out as they used force to gain a foothold on the raised concrete plinth holding the famous lion statues at its corners.

Those protestors who tried to make a last stand were pushed to the ground with shields and batons, and dragged away. A handful of protestors climbed onto the back of the lion statues in an effort to postpone the inevitable, but they too were dragged off. A cheer went up as a policeman shuffled along the spine of a lion's back in an effort to extricate a lone protestor who'd been sitting on the statue's head since I'd arrived.

The crowd had become muted and docile, the fight ground out of them after three hours of captivity. There had been no major exchange of blows, no running battles, just a slow process of suffocation that had smothered the fire and snuffed out the intent. There were few revolutionaries now, just a thousand citizens watching the clock and thinking of getting home, or work tomorrow, or relieving themselves in private. I had to take my hat off to the rozzers, they'd run a slick operation, and had won the day hands down.

After four hours, we were told, over loud speakers, that we were allowed to leave, in groups of four and five. Jeers greeted the announcement, but they were desperate and half-hearted, and belied a sense of relief. I felt like a vanquished prisoner of war as we shuffled closer to the front. Word had filtered back that those leaving were being stopped and searched. Beside me a man with a scarred face who told us he was Kurdish asked in broken English if we thought there would be any more fighting today.

'I don't think so, mate,' said Travis sarcastically.

'No more need for this then,' he said, dropping an axe handle on the floor, making sure to wipe his fingerprints off it first. He turned to me. 'Today they win, but we will come back stronger, better prepared. All the police in the world will not be able to stop us because truth is on our side, no?'

There was something both prophetic and pathetic to the Kurd's words.

Prophetic because I'd met people when I was travelling through India who were convinced the world was going to end within 50 years because it had been destroyed by the human race. I'd laughed at the time, but in retrospect, perhaps I'd missed the signs that had started to appear. Sleepy little villages where people had been living their lives the same way they had done for hundreds and thousands of years before, were already hurtling towards a future where there would be McDonalds franchises knocking out Veggie Macs to kids in Levi jeans and Nike trainers. Colonialism didn't die with the 'Wind of Change', it just had a makeover. Consumerism, not religion, was the opiate of the people in this new century. Spend, spend, spend and always aspire, because it didn't matter whether you were white, black, yellow or brown, we were all consumers living in the same global village now. The Kurd's words were prophetic too because there was a feeling that, after Seattle, people were getting it together to challenge the power of the multinational corporations, and that was the banner that had rallied the likes of Travis and me to the anti-globalisation cause.

But what the Kurd had said was pathetic too. I knew even before I saw tomorrow's papers that today's demonstration had done nothing to put the message across, and done everything to paint this movement as little more than another radical loony cause for thuggery to hide behind. The pictures would be used to fill news space and respectable householders around the country would be incensed and outraged, and totally miss the fucking point. The Kurd unnerved me. We were on the same side, had the same view of the world, and the same belief that the system was corrupt and spiralling out of control. Yet it was like looking in the mirror and seeing a reflection that didn't agree with me. I needed to get away from him and his axe handle, and his belief that wearing a ski mask and fighting with coppers was going to change anything. I turned my back on him and took the gap that presented itself with the next lurch of the crowd towards the exit point.

They had the biggest coppers they could find overseeing the stop and search operation. They loomed tall and barked at us to turn our pockets out as they frisked us with heavy hands. They gave me a quick sweep, and I waited for them to finish with Travis. Predictably, his dreadlocks earned him a thorough shakedown.

'Fuck me,' said Travis, as we headed towards the tube station, past yet more ranks of booted and suited riot cops. 'That was all a bit heavy.'

'I know,' I said, yawning. It had been a long day, and my adrenalin levels had been shooting up and down for most of it.

'All that excitement has knackered me out,' added Travis as if reading my thoughts.

I was about to answer when there was a shout behind us, followed by the sound of breaking glass as a bottle exploded on the ground not far away. We both turned in time to see a heavily tattooed crusty take a swing at a policeman, who hit back with a baton swipe to his attacker's knees. The crusty buckled and went sprawling on the floor, three more cops jumping on top of him as he fell. There was more shouting and a scuffle broke out as a handful of protestors jumped in, only to be jumped on themselves by more policemen in riot gear.

'Come on, let's get the fuck out of here!' Travis said to me. We walked briskly and turned the corner, but the melee seemed to be following us. I glanced behind and saw the crusty come barrelling round the corner in full flight. His eyes were wide and a trail of salivary foam hung from his open mouth. He had a cut on his forehead and his black T-shirt, ripped down one side, flapped with each sprinting footstep. I saw him soon enough to jump out the way, but too late to warn Travis. The crusty hit him with a full force which sent both of them flying, and they landed heavily on the pavement.

'Get out of the fucking way!' the crusty yelled, struggling to get back on his feet, but he couldn't because his foot was caught in the strap of Travis's bag.

It happened fast; one moment I was gawping at the sprawling tangle of bodies and the next at the handful of cops rushing headlong towards us, and then it was me who was being bundled onto the floor before a sound even came from my mouth. A gloved fist smashed into the side of my head and a boot in my belly knocked the wind out of me. Reeling, I threw my hands over my head and rolled into a ball. I didn't have the air to do anything, even if I'd had the inclination to and I took the pummelling that came to me. It only stopped when my hands were yanked behind my back and cuffed.

I was grabbed by the throat, hauled up and slammed against the wall. 'Right, you cunt,' a copper breathed all over my face. 'You move and I'll break your fucking head open!'

'I didn't do anything!' I shouted. He punched me in the stomach and I was on the ground again.

Chapter Eight

There were four other people in the van with us, all in various states of disrepair. Travis had a deep gash over his left eye, which was beginning to swell. I was aware that my forehead had crinkled into an anxious frown, and I felt sick with dread. Conversation was impossible above the noise of the siren. We were taken to a police station in Bow and frogmarched to the cells by uniformed policemen who would only say we were being held under Section 60 of the Public Order Act. The crusty kicked off again as we got into the reception, and it took five cops to haul him off to a cell. Travis and I were placed in another with five other people, none of whom had been in the van with us.

I didn't see the owner of the voice that greeted us from the corner. I was having my cuffs taken off at the time. 'Not you carrot crunchers?' it mocked light-heartedly.

'Fuck me!' said Travis, once the door had been slammed shut. 'It's Dennis.'

Leering over the top of a pair of Lou Reed shades and dragging on a cigarette was Dennis 'The Menace'. A graffiti terrorist and a legend in a spray can, I didn't know his real name, but it certainly wasn't Dennis, or Menace. He didn't just write his name on walls or trains, but used his sprays and stencils far more subversively. Eccentric, sarcastic to the point of obnoxious, The Menace didn't give a fuck. His forte was hit-and-run jobs on high-profile targets, and he planned his raids with military precision. The Metropolitan Police were still after him for a piece he'd done on the walls of the Ministry of Defence. 'Weapons of Mass Destruction. Apply Within.' The accompanying graphic depicted a civil servant in a bowler hat, astride a phallic warhead. We'd known him for a couple of years – one of those faces on the scene.

'I might have known you bumpkins would have hitched a tractor ride for the occasion,' he drawled. A couple of nervous looking teenagers pressed themselves into the wall, clearly misinterpreting the exchange as a prelude to violence.

'Who are you calling a bumpkin?' said Travis. 'You've got as much mud on your boots as we have.'

'I'll have you know I'm a respectable city boy. Never seen a cow before in my life,' retorted Menace, in his West Country drawl.

'Maybe not the front end.'

After the fear and concern about what might happen to us, I suddenly felt more optimistic, the banter with a familiar face cutting through the tension.

Menace laughed. 'Make yourselves comfortable, boys, and have a seat.' He pointed to the gash on Travis's head. 'How'd you get that?'

'Got jumped by pigs as we were leaving Trafalgar Square.'

'You country boys. You should have been jumped in the Square. It was all over by the time they were letting you out.'

'Case of mistaken identity,' grimaced Travis.

'Looks like they got the right men to me,' Menace grinned. 'It's riff-raff like you that give the rest of us a bad name.'

'What about you? What's your crime?'

'Bottle of cider and half a gram of MDMA,' he said with a sniff. 'I was too fucking loved up to move my arse when they told me to. Had a nice little spot on top of one of the lion's heads. Smashing view.'

'Do you reckon we'll be charged?' I asked, after we'd swapped a few riot experiences.

'Did you smash up McDonalds or beat up a copper?'

I shook my head.

'In that case it'll probably be an all-nighter and they'll kick us out in the morning. They've already got a few crusties to throw to the

dogs and some public school anarchists for the Daily Mail readers.'
The three of us looked in the direction of the teenagers. 'Then again, natty dread here looks like a crusty to me.'

'Cheers,' said Travis grimly.

'What about you?' I asked.

'What about me?'

'I thought you were a wanted man?'

'Do you think I came in here with a name tag saying "Nick me, I'm Dennis the Menace, scourge of the Metropolitan, Greater Manchester and West Midlands police forces"?' He snorted indignantly.

'I wouldn't put it past you,' said Travis sarcastically.

'Yeah right,' said the Menace, taking it as something of a compliment. 'They're barking up the riot tree today. You've seen them. They're in 'bovver boy' mode. Hardly going to call in Poirot, are they?'

'Sounds like you've been here before.'

'Been here, seen it and had away the fucking blanket. Still it's not all bad, we get fed. Could get a bit boring though. Might have to take me a bitch...'

The spottiest of the teenagers looked as if he was about to start crying.

We passed our time smoking and shooting the shit. Of our other cellmates, two were Italian, their knowledge of English limited to political rhetoric that sounded like it had come from a listen and learn language tape for anarchists. Menace took the piss out of them mercilessly, but did so smiling, and they smiled back. The two teenagers, it turned out, were Oxford university students who had been caught spraying up a war memorial.

'Someone passed me a can,' one of them added apologetically.

'And if they'd jumped into the Thames would you have followed?' mocked Menace. He turned to us and made a slit throat signal that the student couldn't see.

As the hours drifted by, one by one the cellmates went to sleep until it was just the Menace and I who weren't. 'So what do you reckon about today?' I asked him.

He was quieter now, the effects of his Trafalgar Square cocktail had worn off and he was sitting hunched up, hands dug deep in the pockets of his leather jacket, legs stretched out in front of him.

'Not bad for May.'

'You know what I mean.'

He sat up. 'Yeah, I know what you mean. Why, what do you think?'

'I think it was a mess.'

He nodded. 'You know there were five thousand coppers out there today.'

'Doesn't surprise me.'

'Couldn't fart without being caught on camera. Helicopters, cameras on the ground, CCTV on every fucking corner. They were organised, more organised than I've ever seen them before. You know they have a central surveillance unit at Scotland Yard. Fifty people target spotting. That's all they fucking do. Watch the whole thing on TV and decide who's worth nicking. In the old days you threw a bottle and it was just another bottle in the crowd. Now you throw a bottle, they've got a picture of your mug on film, a one-to-one on the radio to make sure it's you they nick and not one of your sorry-arsed mates, and they can even get your fucking DNA off the broken glass.'

I nodded, 'It's all a bit pointless now.'

'What?'

'Rioting. It's too predictable. Seemed like most people were there today just to kick off.'

'Course they were,' said Menace incredulously. 'Not every day you get to row with the coppers. What do you want? Peace, love and daisy chains? Who are you, fucking Jesus?'

He said it with such vehemence that I couldn't help laughing. 'No, course not. It's just that there was nothing spontaneous about it. It was a pre-arranged row, and it played into their hands. It won't do anything but push people further away from the wider issue.'

'Which is?'

'You know, anti-globalisation.'

'Oh that,' he yawned.

'I mean, we're all getting fucked over by the system. The corporates have got everything sewn up.'

'Ah, so that's your real beef is it?' said Menace with a cynical sneer. 'You're concerned about your bottom line.'

'No – well, maybe – but no, I'm not saying it like that. I just don't want the world to become one big bland shopping mall in which corporations are bigger than fucking governments.'

'I thought they already were,' he said disinterestedly.

'Maybe. But they'll get bigger if nobody stands up to them.'

'So what do you propose to do about it?' he challenged.

'I don't know. I suppose the same as all of us are doing now. Subverting in our own little way, but trying to do it creatively, bringing a bit of colour to the world. Not scrapping in the streets. That's just a waste of time.'

'Yeah, but we're insignificant,' hissed Menace. 'What makes you think we can make a difference? We've got no clout. At least when there's people revolting in the streets it gets noticed.'

'I suppose what I'm trying to get at is…' I paused for thought. 'Have you seen The Magnificent Seven?'

'Course. I've seen The Seven Samurai too. So what?'

'So… Of course, it's just a film, but there's a lesson in there.'

'Which is?'

'Which is, that you can make a stand with not very many people. You just have to have the right people. If you're organised, you can make a difference.'

'I can see it now,' leered Menace. "Magnificent Sevenism". Nice one, Charlie, I can see that one catching on.'

'It's just a metaphor.'

He gave a dismissive tut. 'And didn't the Magnificent Seven fight in the streets?'

'They did.' I was starting to feel exasperated. 'Like I said though, it's only a metaphor. The important thing is they were an inferior force but they beat the odds because they played to their strengths. It's all about creating movement.'

'I know,' said the Menace sarcastically, 'let's call it "The Magnificent Seven", shall we?'

'No, not a movement. Movement,' I said, pushing my hand slowly forward to illustrate the point.

'Meaning?'

'Meaning forcing the pace. Not sitting back and being content with the crap they're feeding us. Nurturing something that eventually moves from its own momentum, because once it does, anything can happen.'

'You're talking shit,' shot the Menace. 'That's idealist bullshit. "The system" (he said affecting the nasal tone of a BBC presenter) "and how I'm going to change it by a bloke who makes T-shirts in Devon."

'A bit harsh,' I said, beginning to regret I'd even started the conversation. I knew what I meant, but even I had to admit it sounded naïve when thrown back at me like that.

'Nobody gives a shit about what you, I or anyone else has to say because you're not the president of the World Bank or Mr Coca Cola, or even a fucking Spice Girl,' snapped Menace. 'So you can talk all you like about how bad the system is but nothing will ever change. You can't disinvent money. And you can't do the same with greed. It's what makes us human. You have to accept the world for the confidence trick it really is.'

'And?'

'Once you've accepted that, you realise that the only thing you can do is make life difficult for those fuckers. That's why fighting coppers in the streets might not change anything but it rattles the cage and pisses a lot of people off. Scare the fuck out of them, that's what I say. Maybe then they'll take notice.'

'Yeah, but they won't. You saw what it was like today. Kicking off doesn't prove or change, anything. It's like head-butting a brick wall.'

'So? Why should it have to change anything? It's fucking direct action.' He said it with a smile but his sarcasm stung.

'But that's my point. You can't fight them through brute force. It doesn't scare them. In their eyes they can see the dirt and they have the resources to sweep it away. Divide and rule. They know their enemy, they know what to expect, and they're ready for it.'

'So go on then. Tell me what does work.'

I thought for a while, but had to admit I didn't have the answer. 'I can't. But I'll tell you what really scared the shit out of them. Do you remember Castlemorton?'

Castlemorton had been a watershed for the rave scene. It was one of those moments where everything came together and the police and local authorities could do nothing but stand to one side and let it happen. It was the summer of 1992 and sound systems like DiY, Spiral Tribe and Circus Warp were kicking off illegal parties all over the country. The authorities had been trying to stop them from linking up and throwing a free festival but they got caught on the hop as a number of small convoys slipped through their fingers and rolled to a halt on a patch of common ground in Worcestershire. What followed was a festival that drew fifty thousand people over the course of the weekend while the police stood by, their numbers too insignificant to intervene. It was like an independent state had bloomed in a pocket of middle England. The main strip resembled the street of a busy town, with cafés and stalls, and the whole place shook to the sound of a hundred different sound systems. Self-running, self-policing, self-expressing, it wasn't just another traveller party. The crowd at Castlemorton criss-crossed the cultural spectrum and music was its rallying cause.

Menace smiled. 'Fucking right I do.'

'And don't you remember how much that panicked the authorities?'

'Yeah. That really was a fucking riot.'

'Exactly. But it was a riot without violence. There was no kicking off on the front line. We beat them, and the only weapons we had were sound systems, music and the weight of numbers. I just remember being at the top of the hill and looking down over the site and knowing that we were in control. The authorities didn't understand it, and they didn't know how to deal with it. We didn't give them anything to push against so they couldn't break it. The authorities like a row. It makes them look tough on law and order and they look good in the pages of the Daily Mail. They couldn't handle Castlemorton. That's why they had to legislate to stop it all from happening again. The Criminal Justice Act came quicker than a Peer in a schoolboy outfit, that's how scared they were.'

'I like your style,' said the Menace, 'but you're chasing ghosts. You just said it yourself. They simply changed the law and all of a sudden you could get nicked for dancing to repetitive beats with three mates round a stereo in the park. So it didn't really work, did it?'

'OK, if you look at it like that… but yeah, it worked. At that time we were a powerful force because we were united behind one cause. All I'm trying to say is that it was positive. For just a weekend, it really did seem like all our ideals had become real. Anything seemed possible. And you're wrong. It did work because Castlemorton inspired me to do what I'm doing now rather than get myself a nice safe job behind a desk and mark time. I'm not the only one either. Don't you see? The wave may have been short-lived, but the ripples of that weekend are still being felt.'

'It's easier to think that way when you're E'ed up in the middle of a field. Drugs tend to make sense of the world while you're on them,' said Menace. 'It may have looked like the ungovernable force was coming, but in reality we were just a lot of fucked-up people lunching it out on drugs.'

'Maybe.'

'Nobody stopped to think it could have been the start of something. Most of those munters just thought of it as another party. You can't build a movement on drugs, especially when the happy pills don't work no more and smack becomes the short cut to getting off your head.'

'Shame.'

'It wasn't at the time though,' smirked the Menace.

'True.' I agreed, the atmosphere lightening.

'I sniffed so much K that weekend I ended up going blind.'

'Won't ask you to lead the revolution then.'

'What kind of comrade are you?'

'A Devon one.'

'Animal Farm and all that. Jesus, I'm banged up with fucking farmyard Reds.'

'Fuck that shit. We're just a couple of Devon boys…'

'Who've been smoking too much of that fucking weed you spend your lives growing down there.'

'Who see through the bullshit,' I corrected. 'The same as you do.'

The Menace had been right. At 8 o'clock the next morning, while the students were bundled off for a court appearance, the Italians and ourselves were released without charge. Menace said goodbye and began to walk away, but turned back again.

'Hey, Yul Brynner,' he called after me. 'What you were talking about last night… You're assuming that what you saw yesterday was the whole thing. When it comes down to it, all this street fighting's just a distraction. Black Flags get the headlines, but it'll be the Grey Man who makes the difference.'

'What Grey Man?'

'Like those spies. What did they call them?'

'Sleepers?' I offered.

'No,' he said. 'Office mice.'

'Office mice?' I laughed.

'Yeah, that's it – office mice. It's like them. The Grey Man's been there so long he's just part of the building. Then one day, bang, he'll achieve more with a keyboard than the rest of us street fighters could ever hope to do. Didn't you learn anything at school? It's always the quiet ones.' With that, he zipped up his jacket and put on his shades. 'I'll see you boys around. Give us a shout when the barricades go up on Animal Farm.'

Chapter Nine

May: Change the World

The temperature had risen dramatically overnight and the early morning rain soon became mid-morning sunshine. The concrete trapped in the heat but it wasn't the fresh open heat of Devon. It was a claustrophobic, dirty, hazy heat that bubbled with pollution and made your sweat smell of the city. Or maybe that was just the lingering scent of the jail cell. We went to pick up the car and blagged the use of a shower at one of our west London bolt-holes, a flat belonging to a photographer we knew called Richard. The car had been given a parking ticket – another bill to pay – which kind of put all the talk of revolutions into perspective. It was back to the real world.

Travis went to sort out some weed. He had a new connection in town with a container full of prime Amsterdam bud to turn over. It was real mash up stuff, proper Monster-weed, and a good price too. It was so strong I couldn't really smoke it. Turned you into a zombie. Nevertheless, it was exactly the kind of shit we could sell bushels of in Devon. I didn't like selling so much weed, but we had rent to pay and bills to pay off and right now it was the only money-spinning option available.

We met up later in the day at the fashion show venue, a bar called Double S, tacked onto the side of a nightclub in the West End that had a snooty air about it. A big banner with 'Party Porpoise – The World is Ours' written in large letters, hung cock-eyed from the balcony. Dancers and models lounged around on the various sofas, some dressed in Sewerside clothes taken from the sample bag I'd sent up a few days before. They were waiting for the sound people to finish setting up so that they could have their dress rehearsal. The sound crew were waiting for the décor to be put up so they could get on with their sound check. It was the usual pre-gig chaos, and amongst it all, I found Felicity, talking loudly into her phone.

'Well, it is a problem, sweetie. Because if you can't make it then I'm going to be fucked for a twelve-to-one slot – no, not literally, you cheeky monkey – and I'm going to have to set something else up… What was that?… Yes I'm sure that would get press coverage, but not the kind of coverage we want. People can go to Ibiza to see that kind of thing… It's really not an option, darling. I'd much prefer it if you could play the DJ slot. You did promise me after all… OK, OK, give me a call soonest. Yah? OK that's great. Speak to you later.'

'Felicity?'

She turned and peered at me through a pair of spectacles with violet lenses. She was about 30, slim and plain, but had that well-groomed look only money could buy which projected an illusion of attractiveness.

'And you are?'

'Che.'

'Che. Course you are. My eco fashion boy.'

She kissed me on both cheeks with a loud 'mwa' sound.

'This is Travis, my partner,' I said.

'Hello Tris. Love your hair,' she mewed, shaking his hand. 'What happened to your eye?'

'I had an accident,' mumbled Travis.

'Poor dear.' Her tone was patronising. 'Oh well, never mind, you're here now so welcome to the party!' She said it over dramatically, stretching her arms out wide.

'How's it all going?' I asked.

'Fine, darling, fine. And how's Cornwall?'

For Londoners, everything west of Bristol was classed as Cornwall.

'Cornwall's OK,' I said with a wry smile.

'I'm a country girl too, you know. My daddy's got a spread in

Surrey. Can't stand the place personally. Smelly animals, cows, aren't they?'

I couldn't really think of a reply, so I asked her a question. 'So what's the purpose of tonight?'

She looked at me dumbfounded. 'Silly Che,' she scolded, stroking my arm. 'The planet's dying and it needs our help. Tonight we're launching our mission to save the world.'

'Oh,' I said. 'Silly me. Are you a charity?'

'No, darling,' she replied, looking wounded.

'A pressure group?'

'I don't like the sound of pressure group,' she said. 'I don't like putting pressure on people, and besides, that would only confuse people. They might think we had something to do with those beasts that ran riot yesterday.'

I didn't tell her we'd been among the beasts. 'What then?'

'We're the Party Porpoise,' she declared, as if it was explanation enough. She launched into a brief monologue that could be abbreviated to: rich girl on far-away beach hatches scheme to save world, has the money and the time to waste doing it. Glossy brochures, empty statements and a space in a rich relative's office building. There was much to be done to save the world but for now Party Porpoise was profile-raising.

'What a spinner,' said Travis as we walked away.

I'd secured Travis a DJ set later in the evening, and we'd roped Natty in to MC. He could work a crowd like a ringmaster worked a circus. Natty was in a good mood when he arrived and his mouth was motoring more than usual. He cackled when I told him about our brush with the law. I gave him a couple of T-shirts I'd brought along.

'Wicked. I meant to call you. I gave all my other ones away.'

'What have you been up to?' I asked.

'Usual shit,' he said, pulling at the peak of his cap. 'Living on people's floors, eating out of dustbins, writing beats and rhymes.' He pulled a record out of his bag for Travis. 'Test pressing of the new tune.'

Natty had been running his own hip hop record label for the past two years along with a couple of mates. They had a studio that tended to move from one flat eviction to the next. It was called Default and bubbled somewhere on the periphery of the music industry a little like we bubbled on the periphery of the fashion business. In name he was a record executive, in reality he was in the same boat as Travis and I – permanently in debt and living hand to mouth while trying to keep the vessel afloat.

The fashion show started at seven with the main event scheduled for ten. I'd clocked the prices in the Double S bar and bought a bottle of vodka to smuggle back in. The crowd, like the venue, was trendy. Coloured spotlights trawled lazily across the empty dance floor. The three of us sipped overpriced soft drinks, topped up with our contraband liquor, and watched the after-work crowd drift in with superimposed airs and graces and an air kiss for every occasion. People checked us out with the kind of glances that suggested we were at the wrong party while nodding their heads to the supermarket muzak-style tunes the trendily indulgent DJ was playing.

Travis returned from a reconnaissance mission with news that he'd found an unlocked door leading into the empty club next door. The club was lit by emergency lighting and without a crowd in there to make it sweat it was pretty cold, but it was a convenient place to smoke a few joints and wait for the fashion show to start. We were strictly red eye by the time we went back upstairs and the place had filled up since we'd been away. We took a plot on one of the deep couches near the decks and observed our surroundings like a family on a daytrip to a safari park. Travis was busy selling Monster-weed deals from our new plot and it wasn't long before our couch was overrun with trendies and model types who were suddenly Travis's best friends.

At 10 o'clock, Felicity took centre stage to announce the fashion show was about to start. She was wearing one of the costumes that had been made especially for the party. The theme was recycling, and it looked like someone had made holes in a dustbin liner and presented it to her as a slip-on dress. She slurred her way through a speech that was made up of pro-environmental soundbites and a tearful anecdote about finding a dead porpoise on the beach.

There was no catwalk, just the faint traces of chalk lines left over from the dress rehearsal on the bar floor, and bouncers shepherding people to the sidelines. The lights faded then re-emerged to half-hearted cheers. The fashion show had begun. The models made the best of a bad job. They flounced their way up and down the chalk line catwalk dressed in more of the same recycled haute couture that Felicity was wearing. Most of the outfits looked like they'd been knocked up by down-and-outs on acid as a cruel joke. There was a lot of plastic sheeting and jewellery cobbled together from recycled cans. With all the grace in the world, the models couldn't help looking like they'd rolled off the nearest council dump, and we weren't the only ones sniggering quietly into our drinks.

An over-the-top operatic soundtrack had been chosen to give the whole thing a sense of drama but it only served to expose the pretentiousness of the whole display. It was made worse by the fact that Felicity couldn't help herself jumping in at every available moment to make unscripted twirls on the catwalk. It hadn't taken her long to forget about her poor little porpoise and she was behaving like the five-year-old who needed to remind everyone that she was the one having the party. It was clear she was ruffling a few plastic feathers.

The garbage segment came to an end and the opera music gave way to a hip hop soundtrack. After a quick change the same models re-emerged wearing our clothes and launched into a choreographed streetwear routine that involved vigorous activity and exaggerated posturing. They jumped around a lot, and a couple of them threw in some breakdance moves for dramatic effect, but it was obvious that none of them had been to a hip hop gig. When they stopped jumping around they left to a round of polite applause and the fashion show was over. It had lasted no longer than 15 minutes, and had clearly been just an excuse to have a party.

The soundman had told Travis to be ready with his records.

He was eager to please, having sampled Travis's greens, but the self important DJ who'd been spinning through the show didn't seem to want to get off. Natty prowled around in the tight space behind the decks like a tiger in a cage. It was a familiar routine. He'd stopped jabbering and wore a frown of concentration, the calm before the storm.

I could see the soundman was getting pissed off. The DJ was ignoring his requests to wrap it up and was pulling another record out of his bag. 'You got your records ready?' he yelled at Travis. 'I'm going to pull the plug on this plonker.' The DJ stooped to pick another tune from his record box, and the soundman made his move. He flicked a switch somewhere and the system went dead. People stopped and stared over, confused by the sudden silence.

Natty put the mic to his mouth and the sound crackled back on again. 'Evenin', evenin', evenin',' he roared. The DJ looked miffed, but while he'd been dithering Travis had already slipped in behind him and slapped a record on the turntable. Natty continued. 'You've seen the clothes. Now we're going to bring you a taste of the Sewerside sound. Are you ready?' As he finished the line, the beat kicked in and Natty exploded into life, reading from the script that was unfolding in his head. The rhymes fell thick and fast in a freestyle onslaught that caught the room unawares:

'Life's a struggle to survive – juggle the hustle,
Pay attention to graphic detail – wrap it and tussle,
Open you're eyes – see past the end of your nose,
Keep it true whatever you do, or you're getting exposed,
Who gives a shit about the sticks and the stones?
Cause I've been around in this industry,
Forever educate the whole world with the vision I see,
Banish ignorance like battleships in the depths of the sea…'

Natty was good, every bit the secret weapon we had him billed as. People looked up from their drinks and when they did Natty turned them into subject fodder for his next line. He was bawdy, cheeky and at times downright insulting but the crowd couldn't resist his charms and it wasn't long before he was marshalling the place like a holiday camp host running a twisted game of 'Simon says'.

If Natty yelled 'It-Girls throw your hands in the air,' the hands would go up. If he yelled 'Everyone say 'yo',' then everyone did as they were told.

'Isn't he good?' shouted Felicity, spitting into my ear. I smiled and nodded. 'I've got someone who wants to meet you. A journalist. Come and find me in a minute and I'll introduce her. I'm just off to powder my nose,' she said with an exaggerated wink. I nodded and waved her off.

The journalist was a tired old hack in her mid-30s, with a fleshy belly and an arse that sagged from years of sitting on it – either writing stories, or waiting for them to break. She was squeezed into a mini skirt and the smoke from her cigarette filtered through the cracks in her make up so her face look older than it really was. She looked like she could do with a decent night's sleep but ordered a vodka and tonic instead while asking the usual questions, reacting indifferently to my answers until I mentioned surfing. When she told me the paper she wrote for it was my turn to be disinterested.

'So what's it like? Surfing.'

I thought I'd string her along a bit. It's a real hang ten experience,' I told her with a faux Californian twang.

'Really?' she said, running her lips over the top of her glass and inadvertently tipping it so that a splash went up her nose.

'Really. Once you're in the green room that's it. It's like dying and being re-born.'

'Wow,' she said, 'I suppose with all those gales we had in March the surf was really good.'

A popular misconception amongst landlubbers, high up there on the list with putting on a wetsuit back to front. I told her that gales were no good when they came over the shore. It blew out the surf and churned the sea to shit.

She looked disappointed. 'Fascinating,' she said unconvincingly. 'Can I ask you a question. Do you get many girls, being a surfer?'

'Babes?' I said.

'Yeah babes,' she echoed, falling in love with the word.

'Course. Why do you ask?'

'Oh you know, I'm just looking for an angle. Listen, I'm interested in doing a feature.'

'On the clothes.'

'Mmm, not exactly. I'm more interested in doing a piece on what it's really like to be a surfer in the UK. You know, the lifestyle, the music, the clothes – and the babes, of course.'

She was so predictable. I could see where this conversation was going. She was after a Baywatch-style feature filled with strapping surfers and blonde beach bunnies running around on English beaches but she'd have to find herself another lead. I'd got my free drink and was bored of playing this game. I spied Natty sauntering over, faking the lopsided walk of a street thug.

'I tell you what,' I said. I caught Natty by the arm. 'You should talk to this man. We call him the Duke. He's the only man to surf the Liddleton Shipyard and survive. Natty,' I said, 'meet Caroline.'

'You awright, luv?' said Natty, still playing the role. That was the thing about Natty. He was a flawless impersonator, and whatever mood Natty was in for the night, a character would emerge from his wardrobe of personas to fit the bill. Tonight, he was playing the B-boy.

I saw the look in her eyes. It said double page feature.

'Hello,' said Caroline holding out a hand. 'Che tells me they call you the Duke.'

'What about it?'

'Do you mind if I ask you a question?' she asked, sidling closer. 'Are you Asian?'

God she was predictable.

I left Natty telling tall tales of large waves and went off to seek Travis. I couldn't see him in the bar and went downstairs. The club was no longer a secret, and various nefarious activities were going on within its four walls. Happy to cool down after the heat of upstairs I pulled up a chair and started to roll a joint. I knew Natty would be down soon enough. This journalist wasn't the greatest in the world but it wouldn't be long before she smelt the bullshit.

I started putting together the papers, aware of the shrieks of wild laughter and the slur of drunken voices around me.

'Would you mind if I sat down?' asked a woman's voice.

I looked up expecting to see Caroline, but instead caught the smile of a demure looking woman with kind eyes and a face that seemed kind of familiar. I couldn't put an age to her but she was probably in her late forties. She wore what I believe we'd call in the rag trade a trouser suit. She had a simple white T-shirt underneath and wore her jacket buttoned so that it cut a grey V on the white background. She had a small purse in her hand.

'Go ahead,' I said, fumbling to conceal the joint I was putting together.

'Don't mind me,' she said, motioning to the mess of tobacco and weed in my lap. 'I've seen it all before.' She laughed. It was a warm laugh.

'I felt like I'd been caught smoking behind the bike sheds,' I said, adding, 'I didn't mean that to sound like I thought you looked like a teacher.'

She laughed politely. 'No offence taken, I just needed to get out of there for a bit. It was getting too hot.' She lightly fanned her face with her hand.

'Are you a DJ?' she said after a few moments.

'No,' I laughed. 'I make clothes. They were in the fashion show.'

'Great. Which ones?'

'Not the ones that looked like they'd been found on the rubbish dump.'

'I've got you,' she laughed. 'Are those yours?' she pointed at my trousers. I nodded. She took out a cigarette from her purse and lit it with a silver lighter. 'I like them,' she said, inhaling. She told me she used to be a designer and we talked for a while about fashion.

'Where are you from?' she asked.

'Devon.'

'I love Devon.'

'You know it?'

'I lived there for a while.'

'Whereabouts?'

'In the north.'

'That's where I'm from.'

'Uh-huh,' she said gracefully pulling on her cigarette. I liked the way she didn't ask where. Despite her age there was something about her that was kind of sexy. She was talking, but I wasn't really listening. I was watching her face, watching the way she drew on her cigarette and the shape of her lips as she blew the smoke out again. I was so busy watching her that I was suddenly aware that she was aware that I was doing so. Embarrassed, I gave a crooked smile and turned my attentions back to the joint I'd lost interest in making.

'Where did you live?' I asked, trying to conceal my embarrassment.

She told me the name and I recognised it as being one of those villages that had a reputation for being a strange place.

'Did you live there long?' I continued.

'About 18 months, actually.'

'Were you working?'

She laughed. 'Not really, I was living on a commune.'

'No shit.'

'I was a bit of a hippy in those days,' she said, throwing her head back so her bobbed hair swished. 'It was the Sixties,' she added almost apologetically.

'And how was it?' I asked her.

'Great fun,' she said, crushing half the cigarette under her heel, 'but I was ready to leave. Things had started to get a little political.

Hippies make great idealists but aren't too good at putting their ideals into practice. Besides, I was very young and free love didn't agree with me.'

'Oh?'

'I got pregnant,' she said.

'Oh, I see.'

I liked her. 'Must have been quite a crazy time.'

'Living on a commune?'

'No, the Sixties.'

'Yes, sometimes it was,' she laughed. 'But I'm sure it would have all seemed rather tame compared to what goes on now.' She motioned to the joint. 'The grass certainly wasn't as good.'

'How come you're here?' I said.

'Oh, a promise I made.' She didn't elaborate.

She took another cigarette and lit it. 'Do you come up to London often?'

'Once a month or so,' I said. 'That's the trouble with living in Devon, you're kind of out of the loop. Have to keep showing your face so people don't forget about you.'

'What's your name by the way?' she asked, lightly pressing her hand on my knee.

'Che.'

'I'm Susan.' We shook hands. 'I was thinking of leaving...'

'Right,' I said, jumping the gun. 'I should be finding my...'

'...Until I ran in to you.' She finished the sentence and my words faded into a mumble. She smiled. 'It's nice to talk to someone here who doesn't think the sun shines out of their backside.'

I didn't know what to say so I put the spliff I'd been twirling between my fingers into my mouth and lit it. It wasn't long before the weed was starting to work its wicked way in to my head, filling it with larger than life thoughts that consumed large chunks of my present thinking. Was she making a pass? I thought so loudly that I wondered if I'd actually said it. Did she think I was making a pass at her? came the paranoid thought that bounced back, and all the time, a chorus of tiny voices were singing the same line in my head, over and over, like a terrace football chant. 'She's old enough to be your mother,' the voice sang, and it was getting louder.

'Where do you live?' I said. It was a dumb question but I couldn't think of anything else to say.

'It depends on what I'm doing,' she said. 'Sometimes I'm in London, sometimes in the country.'

'Which do you prefer?'

'I like both,' she smiled.

I was really struggling now.

'Listen,' she said, looking me in the eye, a mischievous smile gracing her lips, 'I'm not one for beating about the bush, and you're obviously too shy to ask yourself. Would you like to come home with me?'

I hadn't seen that one coming. The abruptness struck me dumb. A sudden spasm jerked my leg and breathed the life back into me as I felt my foot knock my drink over. I'd been in the fashion game for four years and, despite the hype, I'd never had a wild fling with a scantily clad model or a loose party girl. Perhaps it had something to do with coming from Devon. Perhaps it had something to do with me.

'I'd love to,' I stammered. The little voice in my head berated me. 'You sad fuck,' it said, 'don't sound too desperate will you.' 'I mean, yes, that would be very nice,' I added.

'Good,' she said, holding that smile, 'I'll get my coat. I have to say goodbye to someone but I'll see you by the front door in five minutes.' I nodded. She rose from the couch and I stumbled to my feet, remembering my manners.

I found Travis. He was in a small bar at the back of the balcony that I hadn't even realised was there. He was sitting on a table with Natty and Turnist, a magazine writer who'd done a story on us before, and Carlos, another record exec we knew who ran a successful drum and bass label.

'Hello, mate,' said Travis, 'where have you been?'

'Downstairs.'

'Oy,' said Natty, 'that woman you set me up with.'

'The journalist?'

'Yeah. I think I've dropped myself in it this time. She only wants to do a fucking article on me, and the Asian surf scene. I swear, mate. I gave her the biggest pile of bullshit I could think of, and she swallowed every bit.'

'You're joking?'

'No. I've got to give her a call tomorrow. Man,' he cackled, 'you boys are going to have to teach me to surf before I make a right tit out of myself.'

'You're not going to do it are you?'

'Course I am. It'll be free publicity for Default.'

'I can't wait,' I laughed, quietly wondering if the journalist was too pissed to see sense or just a very bad journalist. I turned to Travis. 'I'm going to chip. I'll see you later.'

'Off already?' said Travis. 'It's early.'

'I know. I'm knackered though.' I didn't tell him the truth. I couldn't handle all the granny jokes. 'We need to sort out what to do about the clothes.'

'Let's just leave them here and pick them up tomorrow,' he suggested.

I nodded, said my goodbyes and hit the stairs. Susan was waiting by the door. 'I've just got to find someone,' I said, meaning Felicity. She nodded and told me she'd be waiting in a cab outside. I scanned the crowd for signs of the Party Porpoise hostess but she found me instead. Or rather knocked into me. She was hammered.

'I know you,' she said, waggling a finger and looking through me with bottle top eyes.

'Felicity. I'm glad I found you. Listen I'm off now, but I was wondering if I could leave the clothes here for the night and I'll pick them up in the morning.'

'Leave your clothes?' she slurred.

'The ones from the fashion show.'

'Oh those clothes. Of course you can, sweetie.' She put her arms around my neck and planted a sloppy kiss in the direction of my lips but her aim was out and caught them only half on.

'I'll give you a call tomorrow,' I told her.

'OK,' she said, taking a drunken stumble backwards and throwing me a salute. I turned towards the door, and bumped into Felicity again. She was going in the same direction. 'Whoops. Scuse me,' she squeaked.

'Are you leaving too?' I asked her.

'No, darling, it's my party. I can't leave until everyone else has gone. I'm just saying goodbye to my mummy. Where's she gone? She was there a minute ago.'

'Right,' I said, seconds before the sledgehammer of realisation fell. Jesus Christ! Of course Susan had looked familiar. She was fucking Porpoise Girl's mother.

I hopped into the back of the cab anyway and carried on the conversation with Susan as if I hadn't rumbled who she was, quietly plotting a quick get away for when we got to wherever we were going. Then I changed my mind. What the fuck? I thought to myself. So what if she was Porpoise Girl's mother? So what if she was old enough to be my mother? As long as she wasn't my mother, what difference did it make? She was far better looking than Porpoise Girl who, I surmised, obviously took after her father. Besides, we were just a couple of ships passing in the night, and it had been a long time since I'd done any docking...

The flat was near Marble Arch. It was tastefully decorated and everything seemed to have its place, tidy in a way that made me wonder if she really did live there. She poured us drinks and sat beside me on a couch that wasn't made for comfort. I finished my drink very quickly while she hardly touched hers. Conversation was animated and I felt like a boxer feeling his way round the ring with jabs that were going nowhere, looking for an opening to make my move. God I was useless.

'Shall we get it over with?' she asked eventually, removing an earring. I failed to follow the lead, cursed my cowardice, and gripped my glass tighter. 'You're not very good at this,' she said, throwing back her head and letting out a warm laugh. I went to answer, but her lips were already on mine, her tongue pushing into my mouth. I squirmed for a moment before recovering my composure and kissing her back. For some reason she tasted like strawberry.

Chapter Ten

We'd been booked to do Glastonbury Festival, but unfortunately, we were going in on someone else's ticket. It was a moot point as I'd been chasing the festival organisers myself, but their original enthusiasm had cooled and for the past month my phone calls had been unreturned. For some reason they'd decided to go with a student, by the name of Robert Rustcombe, who'd told me on the phone that the 'Create Collective' (as his package was called) was registered as a charity and part of his final university project. However, he was missing a couple of components and was desperate to get his hands on a sound system and a skate ramp, and the organisers had passed on our number.

Our skate ramp was one of those freak but serendipitous accidents that sometimes come out of nowhere. A couple of years back, the Pig had been involved in putting on a party and had suggested we build a skate ramp to fill a hole in the cavernous warehouse space. Back then it was practically unheard of for skate ramps to be anything other than solid structures, permanently fixed to one spot. However, as this was just a night deal we decided to build a mobile skate ramp that was portable enough to transport in the back of a Transit van. Between the Grubby and the skate crews' skating knowledge and Cas's two years at engineering college, plans were drawn up for a mini ramp that could be put up and broken down quickly and skated by almost anyone.

Using borrowed tools, they built it out of recycled timber

that was bought off a dodgy salvage crew foreman, and after infinite fuck-ups and extra costs they managed to produce something that did the job we were after. The party had been a disaster, and the skate ramp hadn't fitted in the back of a Transit, but it had showed us the way ahead. Stick a skate ramp together with a sound system and throw in the right music, and you had the recipe for a party that was different to anything else that was going on. A few more events, now with our own DJ and MC crew and a bit of graffiti on the side, bought us a notoriety that began to creep beyond the Devon frontier. Our travelling circus had also started to pick up that kind of underground kudos that also helped to sell the clothes.

I'd been against the ramp idea at the start, deeming it a waste of precious time and financial resources, but I was wrong because building that thing was one of the best business moves we ever made. Skating had been enjoying a second wind in popularity and everyone, it seemed, wanted to inject a bit of extreme sports action into their events. At the time skate ramps had tended to be huge vert ramps that could only be skated by the best of the best. Vert ramps were also expensive to hire. We were cheap in comparison and the flexibility our mini ramp afforded started to get us bookings, each appearance gaining us more. Since it had been built, the skate ramp had proved to be the ultimate Trojan Horse that had seen us breeze into shows and festivals, the Sewerside rabble bundled up inside it. Each time I wondered how our inexperience hadn't been rumbled, and yet each event we did we managed to bring a vibe that was totally chaotic and unruly but that people seemed to be into. Perhaps it had something to do with those laid back West Country roots of ours.

However, every year, the health and safety noose had been tightening around our necks and the insurance premiums climbed higher. Meanwhile, the bigger brands were realising the potential marketing power of having their own extreme sports attractions. Nevertheless, our skate ramp was a veteran of numerous festivals and was perfect for what Robert was looking for (although I did wonder why the Glastonbury people hadn't just contracted us directly). Logic dictated that we should steer well clear as there was no cash in it, but then again Glastonbury wasn't about the money. It didn't matter whether you were headlining on the main stage or running a burger van, it was something of a privilege to appear at Europe's biggest music festival. Besides, doing Glastonbury was a little bit like performing in our own backyard and for Sewerside it represented the chance to roll out the whole crew for three days of West Country mayhem. It was also the first time that we wouldn't have to jump the fence to do so.

Monster-weed would fund the skate ramp costs and we were allowed to set up a stall to sell clothes, but there were the Pig's sound system expenses on top of that and there was no way we could afford them too. I'd had a meet with him and told him the score, and he was still up for coming. I had to take my hat off to him for offering to front the expenses for his end of the operation. I didn't really want to know how, but he told me anyway. He was taking a thousand pills to sell.

It was a couple of days before kickoff and we were on our way to buy essential supplies from the cash and carry. The Pig had a passenger along for the ride, one of the crew he'd be taking with him. I knew the face, but not his name. Stick-thin, he had wispy hair that had probably been a mane in days gone by but now looked distinctly mangy, and a greying moustache, styled like the Marlboro Man. His conversation was littered with sentences that ended in 'brother' and 'man'. Clothes that belonged to an era long gone by marked him out as a breed I thought had been hunted into extinction. Psychedelic Steve, as he liked to call himself, was an original hippy.

As the Pig drove, he ran through sound crew logistics. He was intending to take 14 kilowatts of sound system, three vehicles to transport our combined load, two caravans to accommodate crew, and a marquee.

'Are you sure about the marquee?' I asked, mindful that I only had a limited allocation of passes, and his marquee man wanted four. 'It probably won't rain.'

'Fuck the rain,' he snorted. 'Look at me.' He held up a pasty freckled forearm. 'I need shade.'

'OK, get the marquee,' I relented. If it made the Pig happy then I was happy.

The Pig began to dial a number on his mobile, and narrowly missed an oncoming truck in the process.

'Does the seatbelt work?' I asked from the backseat, although it clearly didn't.

'Fuck off,' he replied distastefully.

We had to do a detour before the cash and carry, in order to pick up some amplifiers. I was a little surprised when we rolled into a quiet lay-by, but I knew it was better not to ask. It was early morning but it was already getting hot. The sun had the blue sky all to itself, and Devon was a lush patchwork of green fields and blossoming trees. After waiting around for half an hour, the Pig's man turned up (without amps), and the Pig announced he had to take a quick ride. The hippy and I were left to laze on the grassy verge and catch some rays.

'So where are you from?' I asked Steve.

'All over, brother. I'm a travelling man.'

I thought he was about to burst into song. 'Have you known the Pig long?'

He nodded. 'We shared a cell at Her Majesty's pleasure.'

'What were you in for?'

'The brown sugar, baby,' he replied wistfully.

'Smack?'

He nodded. 'I never met a lover who could taste so good yet hurt so bad.'

'Dealing?'

He put his hand on his heart. 'No, brother, I was just selling enough to keep my own fire burning. Unfortunately the judge didn't see it that way.'

The Pig returned with no amplifiers, but whistling in a way that implied the detour had been a success (I didn't want to know) and we carried on to the cash and carry. I bought bulk: pasta, rice noodles, tins of beans, coffee, tea, eggs, longlife milk, cheap biscuits and three bottles of Napoleon brandy. The crew was going to be on site for the best part of a week, and while the menu was short on frills, it would at least keep us from starving. Mindful of scurvy, I made a note to pick up some fruit before we left.

The Pig was upbeat in the car on the way back, conversation soon turning to memories of Glastonburys gone by. While puffing away on a cigarette, he told us that he'd taken his first sound system to the festival many years before. 'We played punk at full volume for three days and nights. Fucking lost it we did.'

'Many people turn up?' I asked.

'No, just me, my mates and five hundred tins of extra-strong Belgian lager.'

I had the picture in my head. I could see the Pig reeling on the grass in DMs and a pair of skin tight black jeans slipping down his builder's arse. It was the kind of scene I'd stumbled into many a time at Glastonbury and wondered to myself, 'Who are these people?' before quickly moving on.

Now I knew.

'Yeah, brother,' said Steve, not wishing to be outdone, 'I was there at the beginning, man. I remember when Michael – Eavis – used to come round in the morning giving out free milk. I love him to bits for giving the world the festival, but I can't forgive him for chasing the money and forgetting about the people that made the festival what it was. The festival wasn't about money back then. It was all about love and brotherhood. It's a crime I have to pay for it now.'

'You're not paying, you've got a fucking pass,' said the Pig dismissively.

Steve nodded. 'True, but what about my brothers who aren't fortunate enough to have a benevolent soul like yourself to give an old dog another opportunity?'

'I wouldn't worry about it,' sniffed the Pig, 'half of them are probably dead by now anyway.'

'Oh thanks a lot man,' said the hippy, sinking into a melancholic mood that lasted until we got back to the yard.

The Pig dropped me off and I went in to check the mail. There was only a letter from the bank informing us our overdraft was 'critical'. As for the 20 people and four vehicle passes I'd been promised by Robert Rustcombe, they still hadn't arrived. The kid was already annoying me and I hadn't even met him. He'd told me he'd never done anything like this before and it showed. All the information he'd provided so far had been useless. A typical example was an envelope he'd sent containing photocopies of a hand drawn map marked with different coloured pens declaring, 'We are here!!! 'Create Collective Café' (subheading: i.e, 'Robert's mum!!!'). The whole thing smacked of a Famous Five adventure and already he'd been re-christened 'Nobit'.

I gave him a call and left yet another message. 'Robert, it's Che. Still waiting for passes. If they're not here by tomorrow, you'll be having a lonely Glastonbury.'

On Site: Day One

'You're going to have to pull up over there,' said the girl with the day-glo waistcoat and a Glastonbury Festival laminate round her neck.

'How come?' I asked trying to act the innocent.

'There's a problem with your pass.'

'You're kidding?'

'I'm not. We think it's a forgery.' She was searching my face for my reaction.

'You're kidding?' I said again, wearing the fixed grin of disbelief, like a tourist who's been told his train ticket isn't valid. 'How did that happen?'

She shrugged. 'Pull up over there please.' She pointed to the side of the dusty track.

'Shit,' said Cas, his eye on the wing mirror. 'They're pulling Glyn over too.'

Two vehicles from our convoy had made it through, but our van with stock, supplies and skaters, and Glyn's big green army truck with the skate ramp inside, had failed to breach the gate. We jumped out of the van to look as natural as possible. We waved our arms around and stretched our backs and talked in overly loud voices about the journey. There was little point. We'd been caught red-handed. Nevertheless, we ambled over to Glyn's truck and made some more happy-go-lucky gestures for the benefit of the gate stewards, while getting stories straight. We knew we had some serious blagging to do.

The passes had finally arrived that morning. I'd opened the package to find only ten passes, two vehicle passes, and a handwritten note: 'Yo homies! Can't wait to meet you guys. It's going to be a slammin' session!!!! Unfortunately, I couldn't get all the passes you asked for, as I need most of them for my own team. Hope it's not a problem… Respects. Robert.'

It was a problem. We had four vehicles and a crew of 20 all ready to roll. Even as I was opening the parcel, the vans were being loaded down at the abandoned fish yard. The Pig had three vehicles; two vans carrying speakers, amps and cables, and the army truck with the ramp inside. The truck and one of the vans had caravans attached. We had the fourth vehicle, a beaten up old transit we'd bought during better cash flow days, which we used for festivals, skate events and general stock schlepping.

Nobit, the little bastard, had stitched us up. This had left us with no choice but to wing it, and after a heated debate Glyn's suggestion of photocopying the passes had seemed like the only option available. I'd given the Pig the two genuine passes – best to get the sound system in with no questions – especially as there were a thousand 'little fellas' stashed inside one of the vans.

This left the Sewerside van and Glyn's army truck with the copies. Rolling up there with forged passes was a risky move, I knew that, but in that moment we really hadn't had a choice – passes, especially this close to the festival, were like Wonka's golden tickets and there'd be no way of getting any more. Besides, we reasoned, we could sort it all out once we got on site…

That good idea at the time now appeared to have been a very bad one. Travis and I strolled around like a couple of prisoners in the yard discussing our options, the gate stewards eyeing us suspiciously. As far as we saw it, there was only one shot at getting through this. We'd have to blame it on Nobit.

It wasn't long before the head steward came marching towards us with a clipboard. He was wearing shorts and stout shoes. 'Right,' he snapped. 'What are you lot playing at?'

I strode towards him and held out my hand. 'Hello,' I said earnestly, 'I'm Che.'

He instinctively grabbed the hand I offered him. 'Keith,' he said.

'Keith, I hear there's some problem with the passes.'

'You could say that.' He held up the two passes for me to see. 'Look.' He held up the forgery beside a genuine pass. 'See that? The colours don't even match.'

'I don't believe it,' I said, drawing out the words slowly, like I was clutching for an explanation

'Well, nor do I. I can't believe someone would be so stupid as to try this on. Never mind the Festival, I'm taking this personally. Do you realise how pissed off I am?'

'Of course,' I said with a deferential nod. 'But to tell you the truth, Keith, I haven't got a clue how this happened. We've been contracted to provide a skate ramp for the Blue Field and these are the passes we were sent.'

'Who contracted you?'

'Robert Rustcombe. Create Collective.'

'Where is he?'

'He's not getting here for a day or two. He called this morning to say he couldn't make it.'

'He sounds like a complete amateur,' snarled Keith. 'Stay here. If this checks out, this clown won't be coming on site. You can take my word for that.'

He was back within five minutes. 'OK, I've spoken to the Blue Field. Tricia's absolutely furious. She told me not to let you in at all.' My heart sank. 'But I told her I thought you should be allowed on site. That way you can clear up this bloody mess with her.' My heart lifted. 'Now how many vehicles have you really got? And don't bullshit me because I can find out like that.' He snapped his fingers like a pair of castanets.

Temporary passes sorted, we moved the vehicles fast, passing through the gates before Keith had a change of mind. We followed the dusty track, winding our way through the site towards the Blue Field. Around us, piece-by-piece, the festival framework was still being slotted together, the infrastructure of a citadel that by the weekend would be filled with a hundred thousand and more temporary citizens. Within the high steel walls lining the perimeter, the site sprawled over hilly slopes and the flat bottomed valley, carved up into different 'fields' where domed marquees and stages the size of churches rose out of the ground like vast medieval encampments. Today, the sun was shining and the festival site was lush with early summer vegetation and buzzing with insects. It was a wild, sprawling picture that conjured up images of everything that rural England meant to me.

There was something special about Glastonbury Festival. It

represented the annual shift from the grim winter into summer. The first gathering of the migrating tribes, drawn together for one big carnival of popular culture that stood for everything that wasn't screwed down and painted a conservative shade of grey. Admittedly, it was no longer the wild frontier town of yesteryear. The corporate sponsors had been knocking on the door for a while now and each year red tape, police concerns and brand sponsorship chipped away at the old free-for-all spirit of the festival. We'd heard rumours that things were going to be changing after this year's festival, that the porous perimeter fence was going to be pulled down and replaced by an impervious superstructure that would allow only ticket holders inside, but I didn't believe the talk…

Buoyed by the relief of making it on site in one piece we had, nonetheless, crawled in like dogs from the bush, our tails between our legs and guilt glinting in our eyes. It had been an inauspicious start to the festival, and I had the feeling our problems weren't over yet. Already, a siege mentality prevailed. We set up camp in the Blue Field crew area, placing our wagons in a loose circle, and putting up our tents within it. However, food, a few beers and a half-arsed game of football in the long grass helped to settle the atmosphere. We cheered when Glyn emerged from the caravan in a pair of cut-off denim shorts, and when Cas knocked the hippy over with a sliced shot on goal we cheered even louder.

I finally answered the phone to Nobit who'd been calling incessantly. I wanted to tell him what a prick he was for stiffing us on the passes, but in view of the gate incident a diplomatic approach was required. We'd got the cover story worked out, and invented a fall guy. He was the rogue who'd been contracted to bring the marquee. He'd doctored the passes while we'd been busy loading up and subsequently done a runner. As a result, I told Nobit, we didn't have a marquee and were raking through our contacts to find a replacement. You could see the night sky through the holes in the story but Nobit was too inexperienced to start looking. Besides, he'd been on the end of a severe phone lashing from the organisers, and was relieved just to get an explanation.

Blagging Nobit had been easy, but as the sun fell on our makeshift camp I was summoned for an audience with Tricia, the Blue Field head honcho, who had a ferocious reputation. She held court from a cluster of Portakabin offices housed within a security-fenced compound that was policed by her own praetorian guard. She was so important she even had her own Portaloo.

With the Pig along for technical support we were made to wait outside her office, listening to her bark through the thin walls. Eventually she called for us to enter. Stocky, with bloodhound eyes, Tricia had the collar of her Barbour jacket turned up and a pair of spectacles propped on top of her frown-furrowed forehead. It wasn't hard to picture her charging into battle in a sabre-wheeled chariot in a distant time gone by. She sat behind a desk stacked with paperwork and smoked aggressively.

Dispensing with any niceties, she launched her offensive. 'I'm a busy person with enough shit to sort out without having to deal with liars, cheats and undesirables. You're lucky I'm in a good mood. I was all for having you horse whipped and thrown off the site earlier. I've spoken to Keith, I've spoken to Robert Rustcombe – several times – and I can't be arsed to listen to any pathetic excuses. You've got three minutes of my valuable time to give me your version.'

I played the humble criminal before the judge. She listened while scribbling her signature on bits of paper, pausing every now and then to cast a disapproving eye over the two of us. I gave her the story and, second time round was even starting to believe it myself, throwing in a few examples of Nobit's incompetence for good measure. After all, if it hadn't been for that little prick messing us around, we wouldn't have had to try to sneak our way on site in the first place. All the while the Pig, by my side, looked like he was standing to attention. I finished my speech and stood for an uncomfortable few moments waiting for her response.

Laying down her pen, Tricia pulled out another cigarette, lit it, exhaled, flicked a bit of straw off her arm, looked for an ashtray, turned the volume down on one of the walkie talkies on her desk, then stared me in the eye. 'Very well. You've got a stay of execution. But I don't do second chances. Understood?'

I nodded.

'If this chap with the marquee turns up, I want to know about it.'

I nodded.

'Now then,' she said, flicking ash onto her desk. 'Will you tell me what that stack of speakers is doing sitting in the middle of my field? I've been around long enough to know that what you have there is bigger than 5K, which is the technical specification I gave Robert Rustcombe.' Another snippet of information he'd failed to pass on.

As if relieved from sentry duty, the Pig spoke. His answer was well spoken and totally out of character. 'It's 7K actually,' he said politely. 'I always like to have some spare speakers on hand. Obviously we'll be running at five.'

'You'd better be.' She shot him a withering look. 'And as for setting up, Mr Rustcombe should have told you that you weren't expected until later in the week. You'll have to liase with a chap called Fredo. He lives in a little office a way down there.' She pointed through a wall.

We got back to the camp to find it buzzing with activity, the troops cheerily digging in as if they were preparing for the big push over the top. Cas and the Grubby had knocked up some benches out of scrap wood and there was a campfire blazing. We ate a dinner of beans and smoked and drank like cowboys, the tensions of the day almost forgotten.

I went to bed early but was woken in the middle of the night by the sound of raindrops drum rolling on the top of my tent. I felt sick. When it rained at Glastonbury, there was only one inevitability: mud. With a hundred thousand pairs of feet trudging around the site, the ground would quickly turn to a sludge that swallowed shoes, and caused tents to slide down the slopes with their occupants still inside. The wellington boot would become a prized commodity, and locals would make a killing knocking them out for silly prices to desperate townies in city shoes. There was nothing you could do about the mud. The festival would go on, people would make the most of it, as they always did, but it wouldn't be pleasant. It was one thing to tie bin liners round your shoes, but that wouldn't really work with a skate ramp. I wasn't religious, but I offered a prayer all the same. Please let it be a passing shower, please let it be a passing shower…

On Site: Day Two

Fortunately the rain had been fleeting and the new day brought sunshine that quickly hardened the earth again. We'd had breakfast (more beans) and were surveying the plot we'd been allocated, and searching out the flattest ground available to lay the ramp. We weren't getting far and the phrase 'too many chiefs' came to mind. With my engineering skills limited to the role of holding wood, I wasn't qualified to give an opinion so I stood to one side listening to the crew bickering. The arguments had been going on for a while, and were beginning to get silly when I caught sight of a new camper van circling the space behind us and coming to a rest not far away.

'Boys,' I said. 'Check out who just arrived.'

The squabbles stopped and all heads turned to stare at the figure waddling towards us. He was wearing a pair of baggy trousers that were in constant need of hitching, and a pork pie hat that sat on his head at a crooked angle. He wore a Create Collective T-shirt and looked about 12 years old.

'I'm Robert Rustcombe,' he announced rather too grandly. 'I'm looking for Travis or Che.'

I could see my Sewerside site dogs baring their teeth as they snickered.

'I'm Che,' I said, walking over to shake his hand. His grip was limp. 'I thought you were coming tomorrow.'

'I was. I thought I'd better… you know, after the…'

'It's all sorted,' I said.

'That's a relief. Have you met Tricia?'

I nodded.

'She can be pretty scary.'

He introduced me to his crew. It comprised of his mother, his sister and a couple of mates who stood around with their hands in their pockets looking awkward. Nobit stood around talking about himself mostly. 'I've got loads more people coming. It's going to be a great laugh. Listen, we've got to assemble a sculpture. You haven't got any nails do you?'

How the hell had this kid managed to land the gig?

The festival didn't officially open for another couple of days but the site was already bustling with ticket holders laden down with bags and tents, and just as many swarming over the fences as security fought a losing battle to keep them out. The main strip that ran through the site had opened for business, with stalls selling everything from sleeping bags to novelty knapsacks and overpriced food. As afternoon turned to early evening, the marquee crew turned up with an army field-mass tent that had seen action in the Korean War. True to Sewerside form, once pitched it brought a shanty essence to our corner of the Blue Field.

With the marquee in place, the Pig was keen to set up sound, and for some reason I ended up being the only pair of hands he could pressgang into service (his own crew had disappeared). I spent much of the night helping him to rig up the sound system. Before we started, I made it clear that I couldn't be trusted with live electricity and that he'd have to tell me exactly what he wanted me to do. So, for the next five hours, I lugged speakers, uncoiled wires, fetched stuff from the van, changed over plugs, cable tied loose cables and stood with my head by speaker cabinets yelling 'Yes' every time the cone popped, for a reason that I soon forgot. The Pig had opted for four stacks of speakers, one in each corner of the marquee, pointing in towards the dance floor, so as to contain the sound.

Of course, we wouldn't be running the system at 5K. 'Do you

think I brought 14 kilowatts of sound up here for fucking decoration?' the Pig grunted.

Each stack comprised of three bass bins, two mid-range and one top speaker, arranged in a pyramid. The leads ran into a bank of amplifiers and compressors stacked in the van he'd parked at the back of the tent. He'd stopped referring to the van as a van. It was now his 'office'. The decks were set up on a spare bass bin pitched on its side, about four feet away from the back of it. 'This way,' said the Pig, with the wry smile of a master planner, 'I can control everything from here and won't have to leave my office at all.'

While we worked, I could hear the sounds of Nobit Rustcombe and his team merry-making around their camper van. His mother was tipsy and talking too loudly. As I wrestled with tightening guy ropes that had gone slack, I heard her exclaim, 'And Trish said to me, 'Who is this brilliant young promoter? I remember him when he was running round the garden with no clothes on.''

I heard Nobit counter with a cry of 'Mum!'

'Sorry, darling. But that's what she said.'

'You're so embarrassing.'

It was then that the penny dropped. Our little friend hadn't got here on merit at all. The little bastard had snuck in through the back door with a ticket that had nepotism stamped all over it. We had put the whole thing together and here he was taking all the props.

It was the same old, fucking same old.

I told the Pig. 'Doesn't surprise you, does it?' he snorted, as if he'd known all along. 'Don't you worry about him. Put it this way, it's better to be working for someone like him than someone who knows what they're doing, do-you-know-what-I-mean?'

The Pig was absolutely right, of course.

On Site: Day Three

I climbed out of my tent mid-morning, and had beans for breakfast again. I spent the afternoon busying myself with things to do. The ramp build was progressing slowly as we were still waiting for electricity to power the tools and a ton of sand to steady the foundations. I saw Travis briefly. He'd been flitting in and out of camp, off on a mission to tag the site with our name. Meanwhile, the pass situation was causing me headaches. We'd had ten wristbands allotted to us, and those had been used up getting the advance party on site. They were made of plastic and fitted with once-on, stay-on locking systems. We'd made them loose enough to slip on and off so they could be used again, but security on the gates was tight. Any wristband that looked as if it had been tampered with was being confiscated. The Grubby informed me we'd already lost two wristbands trying to get people in. 'Security are well on top,' he told me gravely. Meanwhile, our unofficial guest list was extensive and my phone was filled with messages from those due to arrive. I wanted to check the situation for myself and so as night fell I went to meet Natty at a rendezvous point outside the nearest gate. He'd turned up with a party of ten. Yes, ten.

The festival was a day away from its official opening, and the site was literally heaving. Rain had returned, turning dusty roads to slush under the feet of thousands, but this time I was too busy to worry about it. I fought against the tide of bodies arriving on site, until I reached the gate. On the other side it resembled a border crossing in a Third World country, and teemed with sketchy bastards touting everything from tickets to tins of beer and stick-up merchants scanning crowds for fresh-faced prey. This was the first sight of Glastonbury for many, and it was an intimidating one in the darkness. It must have seemed like they had arrived at the gates of Hades.

I found Natty and his entourage sitting on their bags in the rain, looking glum and slightly bewildered. 'Easy, man,' said Natty. He was happy to see me but subdued. 'Thank fuck you're here, there's some well-dodgy cunts hanging around. We've just seen one kid get robbed with a knife.'

'Don't worry,' I told him. 'A few minutes more and you'll be in.'

Two at a time, I got six in, no problem, but wasn't so lucky on the next run. One got through, the other got pulled, her wristband coming off in a steward's hand. She was turned back and the wristband confiscated. That left five still waiting to get in.

'I can't risk another band,' I told Natty. 'They're going to have to jump the fence.'

'Mate, they ain't country boys like you. They won't be able to do it on their own.'

A fence-jumping exercise was the last thing I wanted to be doing right then but I couldn't just leave them there. Besides, Natty was right, I knew the score and had always jumped the fence. Every year the talk was the same – higher fences, more security, snipers in the watch towers… and every year that fence was as easy to jump as the last. It wasn't out of disrespect for Michael Eavis, who owned the site (because he was the man and that was undisputed), but jumping the fence was one of those rites of passage you went through if you grew up in the West Country. It was all part of the buzz. Natty's crew weren't local though. They didn't know the lie of the land and they weren't equipped for the mission, so I gave Natty directions to our camp and ducked through the gate to round up the stragglers.

They chatted away nervously as I led them away from the gate. It was dark, but I knew my way. We travelled parallel to the fence, through a small apple orchard, and into the cover of a copse that ran beside a river. As usual, the perimeter was swarming with various rude boy outfits who'd staked their territorial claims to sections of the fence. They called to us in Bristolian and Scouse accents, offering to get us in for 20 quid a piece, through holes they'd bashed in the steel panelling or ladders over the top. To outward appearances they were sinister and intimidating but I knew that they were just preying on first-time jumpers and their fears of the unknown. Sometimes things got nasty though. I had to stop my charges breaking for cover when a disagreement over prices resulted in some kid being chased through the woods by three snarling Yardies threatening to kill him. Had it been on a council estate in the heart of the inner city things would have been different, but it wasn't, it was the countryside, and an environment I knew well. It wasn't long before I found a tree butting onto the fence, which provided a natural ladder to clamber up. I checked there were no security patrols passing, before helping the others up. Once on the other side we moved quickly for the cover provided by the sea of tents that now covered the grassy carpet.

Back at base camp, I called in to the Pig's office. He was smoking a joint surrounded by faces I didn't know. People were drifting in and out of our marquee, nodding their heads to the dub he was playing with the levels turned down. 'We can't turn it up,' he was berating a scrawny little raver, 'because the festival doesn't start until tomorrow. Now fuck off and leave me alone.'

'Everything OK?' I asked.

'Fine, chap, just fine,' he replied.

I didn't have time to chat. My phone was ringing again. Haze was at the gate and needed to be busted in…

On Site: Day Four

'How's it going?' I asked Cas. The festival had officially opened, but the ramp was only just being finished.

'Should be done in an hour or so. Health and safety are on our case though.' He turned to shout at the Grubby who was poised to hammer a six-inch nail into a thin sheet of ply.

I stepped back and onto Nobit, who'd ambled up behind me. 'Listen,' he said, 'have you got some spare hands to help with putting up our sculptures. Keeps falling down.' He pointed over his shoulder to where three of his mates were wrestling with a pathetic 3-D figure, 12 feet tall with a tiny head and hands on slender hips. 'It's our own take on the Burning Man,' he told me proudly.

'Looks more like AIDS Man to me,' sniped the Grubby.

Begrudgingly I agreed to help. I half-heartedly threw my weight behind the erection of the sculpture while Nobit and his mates squabbled and scrambled. Once set up, they stood back and admired their handiwork. 'Good job,' said Nobit with a sniff. 'What do you reckon?'

I shrugged. I wasn't in the most accommodating of moods. I was still seething over the revelation that this gig had been bequeathed to him rather than earned.

'Oh, Che, I almost forgot. Who should I give the play list to?' he asked, pulling out a piece of paper.

'The what?'

'The play list,' he warbled like a small bird. 'I've given people two-hour sets starting from midday and running until two in the morning, which is when the music has to shut down.'

I took the list from him. He'd been busy with those coloured pens again. 'What about our DJs?' I growled, scanning the unfamiliar names.

'I've marked you down for a few sets tomorrow.' He sneezed. 'Got terrible hay fever.'

Before I could take issue my phone started ringing. 'I'll have to sort this out with the Pig,' I told him.

'Oh,' he replied, with a look of concern. The Pig scared the hell out of him.

I had been hoping to set up the stall, but the stock was in the back of the green army truck and Glyn had gone AWOL with the keys. It was one of those fucked-up festival occurrences. With so many things to sort out, one of our financial cornerstones had become just another 'to do' on the list. Compounding the issue, Psychedelic Steve had appropriated our stall tarpaulin in order to construct a yurt for him and his crazy girlfriend to live in. It was very homely inside, I had to give him that, but I told him to take the thing down all the same.

I spent the rest of the day doing gate runs that I couldn't find anyone else to do. I was becoming a regular face, hanging outside the gate, talking business with pykie crews running their own little scams. Evening fell on the first day of the festival, which was already messy with caned casualties. Elsewhere, hundreds of artistic performances were taking place at any given time, but I had seen little of the festival apart from the immediate area round our ramp. Finally finished, it had brought out the skaters. There was Team

Sewerside, of course, but many more besides (build a ramp and skaters will always come). As the day wore on and the skaters got more inebriated, rampside manoeuvres had become more extreme and ever more dangerous.

I needn't have worried about staking a claim for our DJs that night. They were in no fit state to play. Natty had started popping pills soon after breakfast. Haze had turned up to the site fully charged the night before and had since been busy quaffing whatever nefarious substances he could get his hands on. The cumulative effects had rendered him incapable of stringing a sentence together, let alone playing a DJ set. He was so fucked he'd practically started speaking in tongues.

I returned from my latest gate-busting exercise to find the crew had vanished from the marquee. The Pig (who only ever left his rig to piss) told me they'd gone off to check out a band so I decided it was time I entered into the party spirit myself. He gave me a line in his office and I dropped a pill on top of it (not literally) before going off to find them. I bumped into Ginger Gaz along the way and ended up on an impromptu wander round the festival.

Every field had its own sound, its own vibe, and each one was as different as the next. The site grew larger every year, needing to accommodate more stuff and more people. The iconic image of the festival was the Pyramid stage that played host to the headline performers, but once on site it always seemed smaller than I remembered it, dwarfed as it was by the magnitude of everything else that was going on around it; The Green Field was populated by purveyors of alternative society, pioneering ways to live that proved you really didn't have to go along with the consumer crowd if you didn't want to. With their bio toilets, wind-powered generators, permaculture projects and traditional arts and crafts, on the outside they may have been dismissed as being eccentric fringe elements, but within the Glastonbury environment their visions of the future were given a rightful prominence. Once at the festival the stock of these 'hippies' went through the roof as, for three days, the tourists from conventional society kind of wished they were all a bit more like that themselves.

The Green Field was just one extreme on a festival site of extremes. Its embodiment of everything that was natural and organic sat juxtaposed by the chemical excesses of the Dance Field, which spent the festival rushing and gurning and pulsating to the synthesised sounds of the technology age. It was this place that epitomised the excesses of the festival environment, a kaleidoscope of uppers and downers, where the air either fizzed with the rush of endorphins or hung heavy with the crush of comedowns. In the early hours it could be a scary place, inhabited by sketchy characters and lost souls mutated by the toxic poison of too many chemicals, giving off a vibe that reeked of a place called Purgatory.

The main strip, a contemporary medieval bazaar of stalls where people bought and sold things they needed or which just shined particularly brightly in the light of their inebriated states, was a constant march of human traffic, shuffling along the dusty roads and bottlenecking at bridges and entrances to the many different fields that spider-webbed off them. The main strip was known as Babylon by old festival hands, and I for one avoided it when I could.

It was the first time that Ginger Gaz had been to the festival and I found myself showing him around like a tour guide, peppering my conversations with anecdotes from festivals gone by that probably sounded, to him, like the musings of an old hippy. Still, he indulged my lyrical waxings, and as we rambled over the few hours, we witnessed the spectrum of sights and sounds that made this festival the mammoth event that it was. We circled the site and wound our way back towards the Blue Field, climbing the hill that overlooked the Pyramid stage from where we looked down on dancing lights and the orange glow of the thousand campfires burning in the valley below.

On our return to the marquee, we found most of the tribe had regrouped by the ramp. Nobit wasn't around. I didn't think he would be. We'd got him to bump the last two DJs on the day's play list, in favour of a couple of DJs Natty had brought down, and he'd gone to ground in a sulk. The tent was busy, the Pig's system had been turned up a good few notches, the music now punching its way from the four speaker stacks making the ground quake.

'You know we've got to shut off at two, don't you?' Pig said to me.

'I think we can push it a little bit, can't we?'

His face was stern. He was leaning on the back sill of the van, his arms crossed and resting on the portly hump of his belly. He was talking to me but his eyes were wandering over the dance floor, and the speaker stacks at the back of the tent. I knew from experience that those piggy pointers were listening for any change in the quality of the sound, and when they detected it he would adjust a knob or fiddle with a dial until he was satisfied.

'Well, chap,' he said, 'you'd better sort that one out with Nobit.'

Nobit wasn't around. Two o'clock came and went, and the tent kept getting busier. After a full day of caning it, people weren't ready to stop their partying yet.

It was about 2.30 in the morning. Travis and I were sitting on the skate ramp, smoking a spliff, when we heard the bad news. Glyn and an accomplice had been busted. The harbinger of doom was the flower-powered grim reaper himself, Psychedelic Steve.

'Yuh, brother, they were just minding their own business when they got jumped by five plain clothes cops near the Dance Tent.'

I found it hard to believe they were 'minding their own business'. I'd seen them earlier that evening, shouting off about some shit hot pills they'd got from the Travellers' Field.

'Jesus!' said Travis, looking shocked.

Suddenly the realisation hit me. If they'd been caught and the police decided to follow a line of inquiry, they'd beat a path that led right back to our marquee.

'Oh my God,' I yelped, jumping to my feet. 'Were they selling?'

'Uh, uh,' said Steve, shaking his head. 'The last place they sold a pill was in our tent. Who knows, maybe they were followed from here.' He shrugged, as if it was a trifle detail.

'Christ oh fucking Jesus!' I whined. I looked at Travis, who was looking at me, and I could tell he was thinking the same. 'And if they run Glyn's name…'

'…And come up with his brother's.' Travis finished the sentence for me.

'And see he's got a conviction for selling ecstasy,' added Steve.

'We're fucked,' said Travis.

'Yuh,' said the hippy, hands on hips, and shaking his mange.

'Does the Pig know?'

'I've just told him, man.'

'What's he say?'

'Glyn's a big boy. He can look after himself.'

'Not about Glyn getting nicked.' My voice was getting louder. 'About the God knows how many pills he's punting out in this fucking tent.'

'Oh that,' nodded the hippy like it hadn't really crossed his mind. 'Yuh, I suppose it could make things a bit tricky.'

Inside the walls of the temporary citadel it was sometimes easy to forget that the laws of the outside world still applied, and this was reality giving us a kick in the nuts. I went to talk to the Pig. He didn't want to talk about it and the more questions I asked the more intensely he pretended to be working. Around me happy people were having fun, but my party had suddenly turned very sour. Travis and I passed the word on, but it had already spread.

We pulled the plug on the music at three. I was relieved to have the silence to think, though it didn't really help. As others headed off back to the camp, Travis and I spent two hours running through likely scenarios while defending the ramp from Ketamine cases trying to roll down it.

Back at the tent I tried to sleep but it was a fitful snatch of half-dozed moments in a world where the conscious and subconscious clashed in a series of dark dreams where everything that could go wrong did go wrong. We were a camp under siege again.

On Site: Day Five

I woke four hours later feeling like I hadn't been to bed. My head ached from thinking too much. I felt like shit and my mood was black. The day reflected it, grey with a chilly wind that moved black clouds across the sky and permanently threatened rain.

There was no news on Glyn and no news just fuelled the paranoia. There were other problems too. Health and safety were on our backs, concerned about the well-being of spectators. They'd turned up at the wrong time, just as a board left the ramp at high speed and hit a biker on the head. The biker had shrugged off the blood streaming down his face and showed us scars of 'real' injuries but H&S weren't so forgiving. They threatened to shut us down if there was another incident. We'd also had an official warning, on headed notepaper, for running the music late the night before. Queen Tricia had told Nobit that any more of the same tonight would land us in water so hot his balls would melt (her choice of words). 'I'm shitting my pants,' said Nobit after he'd told me, revelling in his minor drama. Maybe I should have told him what else was going on and see him do it for real. To compound matters, he had a whole new play list of DJs that were on site and lining up like planes on the runway ready to have their turn at the decks.

Right now, I'd had enough. I just wanted to crawl away and hide somewhere until it was all over. From the start, it seemed, this mission had been fucked, fucked, fucked... I was sitting in the back of the army truck, the only sanctuary I could find, looking at stock boxes that still hadn't been unpacked and turned into a clothes stall, when Natty popped his head in. 'You look like you want to go home, mate,' he chirruped.

'I feel like it,' I replied glumly.

He climbed inside the truck. 'There you go,' he said, dropping a pill into the palm of my hand. 'Get that little tinker down your neck and you'll soon forget about it all.'

I gave a sarcastic smile, but he was right. There was nothing I could do about anything until it actually happened. I took the pill and popped it into my mouth.

After the intensity of the first day's/night's partying it was as if there'd been a collective realization that there were still two days to go. The pace had slowed, and people were winding down before winding themselves back up again. Even Haze had finally gone to sleep. My spirits improved as the day wore on, chemical enhancement allowing me to sit back for the first time and let the festival wash over me. I had escaped into a cotton wool reality where rational thought had been pleasantly anaesthetised, and as darkness descended I was looking forward to tonight's session in the marquee. I'd even started to forget about Glyn and any impending police sting. It had begun to feel like yesterday's bad dream. Maybe it hadn't even happened at all...

I was in the Pig's office, running an eye over Nobit's 'Saturday' night play list when Haze suddenly sat up, dazed, like an infant roused from sleep. Unlike an infant, he looked like death, his face pale and eyes ringed with dark circles. He had grass in his hair and his clothes were ripped and stained.

'Jeeesus!' he screeched. 'What day is it?'

'Saturday.'

He shook his head, still grasping for consciousness. 'What day did I go to bed?'

'Saturday.'

He lay back down again. 'Fuck me. I was in a proper state. I can't even remember playing last night.'

'That's because you didn't, you munter,' cracked the Pig. 'You lunched it out with everybody else.'

'I feel terrible. Fink I need a bit of food down me. I ain't eaten for a few days,' said Haze softly.

Dr Jekyll had turned back into Mr Hyde.

I took him back to the camp and cooked him beans and a few pieces of toast, charred over the campfire. He gulped it down in lupine bites with a plastic cup full of brandy to set him on the level. While he sipped he tried to piece together the gaps in his memory. They involved some 'savage pills', some rocks scored off a Jamaican chick, and the coach journey to the festival that had culminated in him taking his clothes off and running up and down the aisles shouting 'I am the lizard king'. It wasn't long before Travis and Cas showed up at the caravan, along with a couple of the skaters, Natty and Turnist, a reggae DJ who also worked for a magazine called Upshot which was edgy and different and run by a dynamic German called G-Force. Turnist was here to cover the festival for the magazine, but right now he looked like he'd have trouble writing his own name.

I made a round of coffees with brandy chasers and we crowded round the table, shooting the breeze and slagging off Nobit and his Saturday night play list. We were all growing increasingly disgruntled at having to accommodate the Create Collective.

'So which DJs are we going to bounce from his list?' I thought out loud.

'Fuck it. Kick 'em all off,' Cas suddenly raged.

There was a murmur of general agreement.

'He's right,' said Travis. 'Enough of Nobit and his teddy bears' picnic.'

There were whoops of agreement all around me.

Haze snatched the list from my hands. 'The Hazelator's goin' to make an executive decision.' He stuck it in his mouth, chewed, and swallowed it. 'If Nobit gets in the way we'll just spike 'im with acid.'

The fighting talk had roused the troops, but I had concerns about the hot water we were already bathing in. 'What about the Glyn situation?' I asked.

'What the fuck?' spat Travis. 'What else can they do to us? We've been fucked around long enough. We didn't come all this way to end up as a side show in some kid's degree project.'

His words rang true, and as they did, I realised that since the festival had begun we'd all been so busy running around on our own little missions that we'd kind of forgotten why we were here. For the first time, the players, with the exception of the Pig (who point blank refused to leave his office) were sitting round the same table. Candlelight gave the conversation a conspiratorial feel. The tribal council was sitting, and there was no doubt that the word of the council was war. We'd been fucked about for long enough. It was time to storm the hill and fly our colours.

Buzzing with rejuvenated faith, I went off to brief the Pig. We'd let Nobit's DJs spin on until midnight and then close the book. No more politely slipping our DJs into Nobit's play list. From now on it was going to be a running session with Sewerside at the controls. This was our back yard, and we were going to put on a party that Glastonbury would remember...

The night had brought a thin mist that descended over the site. Friday night's session had gone down well and word had spread that we'd finished late. I had a feeling it was going to get busy and I wasn't wrong. By 12.30 there were between a thousand and fifteen hundred people either dancing inside the tent or milling around in the area outside.

I was with Travis and we'd just battened down the ramp for the night. Inside the marquee, Natty and another MC were working the crowd to a soundtrack of hip hop beats.

'Awright,' said a voice.

The face was hidden in the shadows of a deep hood and my vision wasn't too sharp on account of the drugs I'd been nibbling. I stared hard and the face stared back at me until the penny finally dropped. 'Glyn.' I embraced him (that was the ecstasy...). Despite the fact that he'd been such a liability, I was pleased to see him. 'Where did you come from?'

'Just got back,' he said. 'They bailed me at 6 o'clock this evening and I've just walked from Shepton Mallet.'

He wasn't his old self. He seemed shell shocked. Hands in pockets, drawing circles in the ground with the toe of his hobnailed boot, his conversation was animated. He explained the events of the night before. 'We'd left here last night with a couple of girls. Just going for a walk, like. Sat down on the grass by the Dance Tent to roll a spliff and then out of nowhere we were jumped by two blokes. We thought we were being fucking turned over or something. Well anyway, I smacked one of them and then a load more pile in, and suddenly we've been nicked. We thought they were having a laugh.' His voice grew quieter. 'Thing is, I can normally sniff an undercover a mile off, but this lot you'd never have guessed it. They were off their fucking faces.'

'What do you mean?' probed Travis.

'Their pupils were bigger than mine. I swear to God, they were all fucked.'

'You're kidding?' I said, a shiver running down my spine.

'Do I look like I'm fucking kidding?' said Glyn angrily. 'I swear to you. They were pilled out of their fucking heads. They didn't look like coppers, they didn't act like coppers, they looked just like anybody else.'

I looked at Travis, and the look on his face could have been the mirror image of my own. Despite the sound of the dirty bass line coming from the tent the world had gone very quiet and our conversation suddenly seemed very loud. My eyes panned over the faces around us, gradually, like the slow motion sweep of a movie camera.

'I'm telling you,' Glyn continued, his words plopping like small stones in a pond, 'everyone here needs to watch their back. You'd never know who they were and they're fucking everywhere…'

I was still trapped in a bubble, not moving, not saying anything, just looking at Glyn.

A face seemed to loom out of the mist. 'Oi, dread,' it hissed close to Travis' ear. 'Got any weed for sale?'

The bubble burst.

'No,' Travis shot back with a vehemence that made the figure step back suddenly.

'OK, mate, only asking.'

I needed more information. 'Did you have anything linking you with this place? A crew laminate?' I pressed Glyn.

He shook his head.

'Did they question you?'

'Course.'

'And?'

'And I told them that we had a sound system and were knocking out pills to underage kids,' he said sarcastically. 'What do you think I told them?'

'Sorry, mate. I didn't mean it like that.'

'I told them I was just a punter.'

I felt better with that knowledge. Nevertheless, we'd still have to watch our backs and hope there was nobody watching ours…

'Have you seen your brother?'

He shook his head. 'I don't think he's too pleased with me at the moment. I'll be on the mobile if he wants to talk to me. I'm going to get out of here and go up to the Travellers' Field. It's safer than this fucking Babylon.'

I went to inform the Pig, ducking under an open back door of the van and into his office, blinking in the harsh light of the halogen lamp he had taped to the inside. He was arguing with one of Nobit's DJs who, backed up by members of his posse, had invaded his office and was demanding to be allowed on the decks. His crew were doing their best to look sinister while their mate was giving it the gob and demanding to see the play list. Nobit, as usual, was absent.

'What's going on?' I asked.

'Mate. Where have you been? I'm having serious hassle off this lot.'

'Why?'

'They won't fucking leave me alone.'

'Then why don't you tell them to fuck off?'

'I don't want to be rude. I thought these boys were with you.'

'Do you recognise them?'

'No.'

'Then they're not part of our crew, are they?' I said simply.

'Oi, geezer,' said the DJ to me. 'Tell your mate here he'd better put me on the decks.' He was short, with a goatee beard and an attitude.

'Sorry, mate,' I said trying to be reasonable, 'but there's been a change in plans. You'll have to wait until tomorrow.'

'Uh, uh,' he replied. 'I'm goin' back to London tomorrow. I want to play now.'

'Can't help you, got DJs lined up ,' I shrugged.

'Well, you'd better get them off, then.'

'Why's that?' I said.

'Because if you don't, things might get a bit nasty.'

My mood changed. I stepped towards him. Unmoving, he tilted his head back, and held my gaze with mocking eyes. He was smug, and thought he was in control. I was high on ecstasy and anxiety, and his words had got me growling like an animal ready to bite. 'OK, enough. Get the fuck out now,' I spat.

'You gonna get fucked up,' sneered the DJ, leaning closer.

I was aware of the Pig beside me, but I wasn't looking at him. I never saw him turn into the wild boar that pushed me out of the way, thrusting his muzzle close to the DJ's face. 'If you don't fuck off in five seconds flat, I'm going to shut the system down and tell the people out there why I'm doing it.' He jabbed a trotter at the dance floor. 'You understand me?'

The DJ thought about a response, verbal or otherwise, his cronies squaring up behind him, but already more of our bodies had begun to gather. A tattooed punter with matted dreads and psychopathic body language stopped his dancing and leaned over the DJ decks. 'You got trouble, Pig?' he growled.

'No,' said the Pig. 'We haven't got trouble. Do we?'

The antagonist sucked in his cheeks and stood down.

'Now get the fuck out of my office,' growled the Pig.

They left with loping B-boy swaggers that tried to conceal the loss of face, tossing yokel insults behind them as they left. We watched them go.

'Do you think they'll be back?' I asked the Pig.

'Will they fuck. Probably on the way back to London right now.'

'Don't matter if they do come back,' added the psychopath. 'We'll just make 'em disappear.' His eyes grew wide in a way that spooked me and he undulated his hands in the air, like a magician conjuring over a top hat.

There was no need to make anyone disappear. They didn't return, and the only magic at work was the spell the hip hop boys were casting over the dance floor. Natty had his audience strapped in and was taking them for a lyrical ride, bumping along on a bass line so fat you could surf it. The crowd responded with cheers and whistles and shouts for more of the same. 'Turn it up,' they yelled, cheering when the Pig relented and clicked the sound up another notch. The walls of the marquee dripped with sweaty condensation, and the rising volume levels fed the atmosphere that bubbled towards boiling point. Just when it seemed like it couldn't get any better, the inevitable happened.

The music went off.

The rig fizzled, then spluttered, then died, replaced by an empty void that was soon filled with cheers and jeers of disappointment. The party tumbled into a state of confusion. The crowd began baying for more, clapping their hands and stamping their feet as if it would be enough to set their world turning again. It was 2.30.

'What's going on?' asked Turnist. 'Haze was just about to start his set.'

'Curfew,' replied Travis.

'I thought we were going on all night?'

'Cas,' I said. 'Go and see if the Pig's had the power turned off, or if it's voluntary.' He disappeared into the crowd.

Natty's microphone may have been disconnected but he continued to rhyme to his audience. 'Technical hitch... Broken down like the snitch... On a litre of Vodka... It's just an itch... That we can scratch (– Oi what's happened to the fuckin' sound?!)... Resurrect it like that... With a surgical patch... Sewerside gonna come back...' He kept it up for a while then walked away in mock disgust, as the crowd applauded and stepped up their calls for more.

I couldn't see the decks through the crowds on the dance floor, but I recognised the voice that came from the direction. It was timid, and shaking and had all the presence of a quick fart on a windy day. 'Sorry... Sorry...We've got to turn it off... Thanks a lot. You've all been great... If you come back tomorrow we've got some more great music,' squeaked Nobit, his voice but a ripple on the rising tide of discontent.

Cas came pushing back through the crowd. 'The power's still on, but Nobit told the Pig to kill the sound. Says if we don't shut down now we won't be able to run tomorrow.'

'What are we going to do?' I asked Travis.

'Fuck it. Who remembers Sunday night at Glastonbury? Half this lot won't be here tomorrow.'

'We made the decision,' said Cas.

Travis nodded. 'He's right.'

'OK, OK, OK...' I said, trying to buy myself time to think, but it was pointless. I knew what had to be done. 'OK, OK... Let's go.' I was still saying the words, trying to convince myself, as I began to push through the crowd. I didn't know what I was going to do but the drugs inside me were sparking neurons left, right and centre and suddenly a picture emerged. In my head, I saw it so clearly, it was almost as if it had already happened. This was going to be my Braveheart moment. My heart was racing and my body was fuzzy with the surge of adrenaline.

'Right!' I roared out loud, to everybody in the marquee and nobody in particular. 'We're the Sewerside and we're here to party. Are you ready to party?' It sounded clear as crystal in my mind but the words that tumbled out of my mouth were so shrill and dis-jointed they sounded like the mews of a cat being castrated.

In my thoughts I'd been expecting cheers of support but instead an embarrassed silence was all that greeted me, as a tent full of heads turned to look at me as if I was a crazy hobo who'd just crawled out of a pile of newspapers in the corner.

But there was no time to acknowledge my embarrassment as I forged on towards the front. Nobit stood transfixed, the proverbial rabbit in the headlights as I charged up to the decks. I saw Haze, waiting in the wings, looking pensive and confused. 'Haze, put a fucking tune on.'

With a look of confusion, he jumped to his feet and grabbed a record. By the time I'd got behind the decks, Travis had caught up with me. 'Right,' I said, gathering a modicum of composure. I didn't need to shout because my previous rant had served to silence the confused dance floor. 'We're playing on,' I told Nobit.

'But we can't!' he blubbed, his face twitching, 'I promised Tricia I'd...'

Travis turned to him. 'It's Saturday night. People want to party.'

Before he could answer a girl in the crowd yelled out, 'Let's tie the little fucker up to a tree and beat the fuck out of him!'

'Turn the fucking music back on,' barked another to general shouts of encouragement.

'But I promised Tricia,' Nobit began. 'She said if I didn't do it I wouldn't be allowed back next year...' His statement trailed off as he realised he'd just put his foot into a pile of shit so big it was going to swallow him whole. He snapped his mouth shut as if it would be enough to retract his confession.

'Sorry, Robert,' I said, turning to him. I felt sorry for the kid, I really did. At that moment he was the object of universal hatred, and he knew it. I was sorry but I was also defiant. 'We're not part of a package you put together like a piece of furniture. You've had your 15 minutes of festival fame and now it's time to stop. This is no Create Collective, this is Sewerside, and we haven't worked our arses off so you can turn it in a university project. We're doing this because this is what we do.'

Nobit shrugged a hopeless shrug and stepped aside.

'Mr Pig,' I said loudly, and for the crowd's benefit. 'Would you please take us to warp speed five.'

The Pig looked at me blankly. Not again, I thought. As a performer, I was dying a death here. Fortunately Travis's prompt spared me any more embarrassment.

'Haze, you ready?' I asked.

Haze nodded, dropped the needle to the record, and the rig exploded into life again, the thunder of drum and bass splitting the ground like the strike of an atom bomb...

On Site: Day Six

We'd been shut down at six. There hadn't been any discussion. The Blue Field organisers just cut the power at the main supply. But it hadn't mattered. We'd achieved what we'd come to do. We'd rocked our little corner of Glastonbury with a running session from Haze and Natty, our two secret weapons, who'd rinsed the place dry.

'What a fuckin larf,' said Natty cackling to himself in an easy chair out the back of the green army truck. Haze was now asleep, snoring away in the sun, his hand down the front of his trousers. He looked like Rumpelstiltskin after a hard night's work. Cas and another of our Liddleton crew, Big Dan, were sprawling over two more chairs. Still buzzing off the back of a Saturday night that had finally come good, I hadn't been to sleep yet. I found a half-crate of beers that someone had either stashed or forgotten about in the back of the truck, and passed them round. Even Haze stirred long enough to crack one.

The stall was finally up, two days later than scheduled, three days too late. I had four rails of stock that looked like washing on the line no matter how I arranged them. Halfway through the morning, still having not sold anything, I took off my rose-tinted spectacles and looked at the stall objectively. With the boys sprawled all over the stall like a litter of site dogs nobody was likely to buy any clothes from us. I coaxed or physically dragged them to less prominent positions in the hope that people would mistake them for ravers chilling out, but that didn't really work either. I went to bed at around two in the afternoon, leaving Big Dan and Natty in charge. I didn't want to leave the stall but my body was demanding sleep.

I woke four hours later, my body feeling like a well-used bongo, my mind operating on a two second delay. I guzzled a bottle of foul-tasting water to cure my dehydration, and emerged into the sunlight.

I wasn't hungry but I knew I should eat. The camp was empty except for Psychedelic Steve's crazy Italian girlfriend who was doing yoga in a pair of stained tie-dye leggings. The sight was enough to banish all thoughts of food so I cleaned my teeth, lit a cigarette and headed back to the stall. The skate ramp had emptied of skaters and was now littered with bodies lying in various comatose states. The site dogs were still sitting in exactly the same position I'd left them. Having finished off the beers and procured some more, they'd spent the day drinking in the sun, and were now in various states of debilitation and dangerously leery.

'Afternoon, boys.'

'Look who it isn't,' cackled Natty. 'About fucking time you got your arse out of bed, we've been rushed off our fucking feet.'

'You're joking?' I said excitedly.

'Course I am,' he laughed.

'Not so fast, Natty,' said Haze, with a theatrical lick of the lips. He reached into his back pocket. He passed me a grimy tenner wrapped round a handful of shrapnel. 'Sold a T-shirt, mate,' he said.

'I sold another one,' murmured Big Dan who was still sprawled over the same easy chair, a can of lager in one hand. Despite the sunshine, he was wearing a heavy jacket. 'I'll have to owe you the money though. Bought some beers with it.'

'Thirty quid. Not bad for a day's work,' I said sarcastically.

'Che,' said Haze before I had time to dwell on it. 'Got a question for you, son. Who'd win in a fight between Taxi Driver and Scarface?'

'Taxi Driver,' I said after a pause.

'I fuckin' told ya!' roared Haze, thumping Turnist so hard he toppled back off his chair.

'Che, you wouldn't believe the hassle we've been having,' said Natty, removing his sunglasses to reveal eyes that rotated independently of each other. 'They won't turn the sound back on.'

'How come?'

He shrugged. 'Cause that organiser's a bitch?'

'Natty,' I said, trying to coax the information out of him like a parent trying to get a phone message out of a toddler. 'What's been going on?'

'Nothing. She just started giving us grief about the music and I just said...' His voice trailed off as he tried to remember.

'Something about her being dead,' said Big Dan, slumping lower into his chair.

'What?' I yelped.

'Oh yeah,' Natty drawled, trawling the shallows of his memory. 'I remember now...' Then he went silent again.

'Turnist?'

'Yeah. She came over and gave us grief then Natty said something like, "Don't worry about it, she's old, she'll be dead soon anyway," and then she went off on one.'

'She was a right stroppy cow,' chipped in Haze, dropping one of the cans he was attempting to juggle with on top of Stig, who was stretched out and sleeping. 'Don't worry though, I gave her an earful.'

'You did what?'

'She said we were crap. I told her she was a fat cow.'

'Then what happened?'

'She left.'

'I remember now...' said Natty, before collapsing into a cackling heap again.

In truth, they were probably no worse than half the walking wounded stumbling round the site after nearly three days and nights of festival spirits. The difference was though, in my absence these boys had been our ambassadorial representatives. It was one thing to square up to DJs with attitude, squaring up to Queen Tricia, however, was an entirely different matter.

'Oh yeah,' added Turnist, as an afterthought. 'She said she wanted to see you.'

I went to visit the organiser's office and announced myself and was told to wait. I smoked a cigarette sitting on the step, listening to the sounds coming from her inner chamber. Her tone was boisterous and she was swearing heavily. 'Show him in,' I heard her say. 'Actually, don't bother, I need to piss anyway.'

I heard the door slam open, and jumped up from my seat to see Tricia stumble against a wall and come to the door. Her clothes were crumpled and showed signs of having been slept in and her eyes were bloodshot and watery. Her breath smelt of booze.

'You,' she said with a slur.

'Tricia,' I replied politely.

'You were supposed to shut the music off at two.'

'I didn't know that,' I lied.

'I told Robert.'

'He didn't tell me,' I lied.

'He's in charge of your area,' she huffed.

I shrugged.

'I suppose you've heard about what happened to me?'

'No.'

'I was threatened by those animals. I assume you know who I'm talking about? They threatened to kill me.'

No more lies. Time to come clean. 'I heard there was an altercation and I apologise. They've been drinking. Perhaps their words were taken out of context, though.'

'Out of context? Those little bastards threatened me with violence. You ask anyone round here, I was extremely…' She stabbed a finger in the air for emphasis,' …upset by the whole thing.'

'I'm very sorry.'

'Your area has been the bane of this festival.'

'We haven't been that bad,' I replied with a half-smile.

'Robert was supposed to provide an art installation. What you do isn't art. It's…' She paused, grasping for the right word. 'It's fart!' she yelled triumphantly.

'Hang on a minute,' I said, suddenly indignant. 'Who are you to say that? Do you know how much work we've put in to this? How much money we've spent to get here, how many favours we've had to pull? And all the time we've been doing it blindfolded because you decided to ignore us in the first place and deal with some kid who hasn't got a clue what he's doing.'

She bristled. 'Robert Rustcombe came to us with a very attractive proposal.'

'Robert Rustcombe would struggle to propose marriage. What the hell's he doing running this gig anyway? He admits himself that he's never done anything like this before.'

'It's too late,' she said, with a brush of her hand. She fixed me in her sights. 'It's trash like you that gives this festival a bad name.' She spat the words at me.

She was wrong. It was trash like us that made Glastonbury. It was trash like us that brought the spontaneity and the diversity and the party spirit that had marked this festival's history as something different. Glastonbury wasn't about feudal fiefdoms or festival politics or who was headlining on the main stage. It was about the colourful mishmash that celebrated everything that was organic, vibrant and raw about the culture of our times. It was people like us who sowed the seeds of creativity in the next generation, just as those generations before had sown the seeds in us. Take away that and you were left with a stadium rock concert with rules and regulations where corporate branding was as important as the performers who were headlining the stages. And if that made us trash, then…

'I want you out of my field and off site by sundown!' barked Tricia before I had a chance to articulate my case. 'If you're not off by then, I'm going to call in the police.'

Chapter Eleven

The comedown from Glastonbury had been a heavy one and for three days all I'd been fit for was sleeping. Reality had finally bitten with a visit to the Job Centre. It had been busy, filled with people who'd missed their signing-on-days because of the festival.

'I couldn't sign on. I was at Glastonbury,' I'd heard three people before me in the queue say.

'Were you looking for work?' they were asked.

The answer had been no.

'I'm sorry, that's not a valid excuse. You'll have to fill in a form. Next...'

When it was my turn I tried a different tact. 'I've been at Glastonbury.'

'Were you looking for work?'

'Yes.'

'What kind of work were you looking for?'

'I'm quite a good juggler and I was trying to get work with a circus troupe there.'

The girl behind the desk nodded. 'OK, fill in this form. Your payment may be a day late.'

I'd caught up with the Pig, who'd been in a good mood. He'd done his accounts and was happy to report that the trip had paid for itself, even if he was still waiting for most of the money to come in. The rest of the crew had made it home in various states of disrepair but the hot gossip was that Psychedelic Steve and his girlfriend had run off with the Hare Krishnas. We hadn't heard from Nobit since the festival and I had the feeling we never would.

The ignominy of being kicked out of Glastonbury had been re-interpreted as a badge of kudos by the Sewerside crew, who saw our ejection as evidence that we had the balls 'to keep it real'. However, for me the festival had illustrated the reality, and that reality was this: that the system, whether it was the economic battleground we'd been fighting on since the business' inception or the feudal fiefdom of the Blue Field, was both omnipresent and omni-powerful, and it wasn't going to be changed by a ragtag band of creative upstarts keeping it real.

Deep down, I also knew that the festival had been a catalyst. We'd founded Sewerside on a set of ideals, to be our own masters and live life on our own terms and spent the past few years chasing our dream with a blind passion. If the essence of keeping it real was a refusal to sell out, then the practical reality was that the only thing in life that was free was the air you breathed, and everything else cost money. Those were the rules of the world we were living in and they were non-negotiable. The dream had foundered because you need money to make money and we didn't have any money. Nevertheless, our Glastonbury victory, however hollow, had been achieved by playing to our strengths and fighting guerrilla-style – hitting hard and then running back to the hills when the odds grew too great. Perhaps if we could do the same thing with the business…

We'd skirted round the subject before, but the stark reality of our financial situation was such that we could ignore it no longer. We had reached the point where we no longer had the reserves to function as a going business concern. The bank was on our case, as were the credit card companies and a list of creditors as long as a happy tapeworm. We didn't have enough money to buy more stock, and it would only be a matter of time before we sold out of what stock we had. Once that was gone, we'd be at the mercy of them all.

So it was, against this background, that I found myself sitting in the yard having a conversation with Travis that had been entirely unintended but had been on the cards for a while. Neither of us had woken up that morning thinking 'Today we'll discuss the possibility of bankruptcy.' It was just the way it unfolded. I guess it goes back to that small businessman's handbook they never gave us at the beginning. There comes a time when you have to step back and take a look at what you've got and make a realistic decision about the future, even if it's a decision that breaks your heart.

'Tell me truthfully,' said Travis, twirling a cigarette between his fingers. 'What are our chances of making it through the winter?'

I shrugged. 'Best case scenario or my honest opinion?'

'The truth,' he said. 'You know me. I haven't got a fucking clue when it comes to the figures.'

'It's not looking good.'

'I knew that much.'

'The loan's gone. Our orders are down, and even if they were up we wouldn't have the money to manufacture anyway. We owe money all over the place and the loan repayments are bleeding us dry. But you know, things happen.'

'Like miracles?'

'Yeah. Like miracles.'

He laughed. 'Always waiting for a fucking miracle.'

'Why do you ask?' I said.

'Glastonbury kind of brought it all home.'

I resisted the urge to say 'snap!' It's funny, but after so long working together there was often a certain synergy to our thoughts. I raised my eyebrows instead and let him continue.

He carried on talking. 'I can't help feeling that we're caught in the rip tide. We spend our time paddling, but we never get anywhere. Sometimes it looks like we're just about to get out of it, then...'

'We get dumped right back in the middle again.'

He nodded. 'I don't know if I can carry on paddling.'

I didn't answer. Not because I didn't have an answer. It's just that Travis had let the jack out of the box and I was just taken aback by it. 'Don't get me wrong,' he added, 'it's not that I want out, it's just that it isn't working the way it is. We've got talent. It's just that the business, it's starting to feel like a millstone around our necks.

All the time we're struggling just to survive and to be honest I've stopped believing we can make it anymore. And that belief was what kept me going this long. Without it…' His sentence trailed off. 'Does that make sense?'

I nodded.

'Maybe it's just time to regroup. You know, get rid of the shit and concentrate on the bits that work. Just make some fucking money really. I don't know. What do you think?'

I shrugged. 'I'm hearing you.'

'At the end of the day, what've we got to lose?'

'If the business goes tits up?'

He nodded. 'It's not like we've got assets. We don't have anything to lose.'

'Except for a whole lot of debt.'

'Exactly. Maybe we should just strip things down. Shed a skin.'

'You know you'd take the knock, don't you?' I said. And he would. In our unorthodox business manner, we never formalised our business partnership on paper. What we had was what I guess you would term as an old-fashioned gentleman's agreement, forged over a handshake, a cup of tea and a spliff. We had no need for legal formalities between us, and with me signing on that option had become a practical impossibility.

'To be honest, I don't really give a fuck at this moment.'

We sat in silence for a few moments.

'Well, we can sit tight and wait for them to come for us, or we can engineer our retreat.'

'A tactical withdrawal?'

I smiled. 'Get as much out as we can before the system sucks us up, and then mutate.'

'Mutate,' Travis nodded. 'Mutate, survive, move on.'

The conversation, far from depressing our spirits seemed to galvanise them. As funny as it sounds, for the first time in longer than I could remember, I felt positive. We had been struggling for so long with the dead weight of dread crushing our shoulders that acknowledging it made the load lighter to carry. We spent the rest of the day discussing our options and sketching out a loose timetable for the tactical withdrawal. It was now July, and we both agreed that Christmas would be a good deadline. This would give us the opportunity to take advantage of summer sales and the retail frenzy of Christmas. It was agreed that the plan should remain a secret between us. To outward appearances, it would be business as usual until we figured out just how the hell we were going to bring things to a close.

Our first decisive move would be to abandon wholesaling to most of the shops we dealt with, and sell the clothes ourselves. This way, we could get prime bang for our buck by cutting out the middleman. With this in mind, we decided to organise a yard sale to raise some cash. Nothing fancy, just a few flyers advertising a Friday night session with a small sound system and some direct sales from our clothes rails. There was just one problem. Our relationship with the landlord had been frosty for some time now.

Nigel Lesnik was the director of a charity organisation with a non-specific mandate to promote community relations. Financed by government grants, he'd taken over the lease of the building a year ago and turned the two floors below us into office space. At first he'd turned up at the yard door with smiles and reassurances that we were safe where we were and trumpeted his right-on credentials. His ambitions were grand. 'I want to wake Liddleton up to the modern world,' he'd claimed triumphantly. It was obvious he hadn't been living in Devon long. If he had, he'd have known that people didn't like to be told to wake up. They liked Liddleton the way it was. He'd seemed harmless enough to begin with, just another pony-tailed idealist trying to do his own thing. But he changed.

Once installed behind a large desk, Lesnik had begun to develop an unhealthy sense of his own importance. He started turning up at our door with niggling little gripes about the volume of our music or us slamming the doors. It wasn't long, however, before his niggling started to become obsessive. Within three months, we were blamed for everything from missing mail to the migraines of his volunteer workforce. It was clear that Lesnik had developed a hidden agenda. We were the wart on the portrait of his ambition and his new ambition was to have the whole building to himself, and for that he wanted us out. However, he couldn't get rid of us just like that as we'd refused to sign the lease he'd forced on us. We'd also been in the building long enough to have sitting tenant rights. So long as we kept paying the rent he couldn't evict us without good cause and to date he hadn't found one good enough. It was inevitable, then, that the yard sale could cause some friction. Not that we gave a fuck about what Lesnik thought, it just meant that we'd have to go about things quietly. After all, a ranting landlord turning up on the doorstep wouldn't be good for business. Midway through our discussion, the phone went.

'Hiya, Che, it's Michelle.'

She was calling from the council. They were desperate to raise their profile following recent criticism that they weren't doing enough for the kids and had contracted us to organise a skate competition. A no travel operation that was good for us, good for the kids, and good for the bank account. Michelle was in her late twenties, had the kind of body that looked good in a summer dress and a flirtatious way about her that probably set male pulses racing in council building corridors. I'd taken the Grubby along for our first meeting, seeing as he was the authority on all things skate. As we'd been busy in the run up to the festival, I'd given him the job of coming up with a flyer.

'Did you have a good time at Glastonbury?' Michelle asked.

'Yeah, it was fun, thanks.'

'I saw it on the TV. It looked excellent. Go on, make me jealous, what bands did you see?'

I told her I hadn't seen any.

'Oh,' she said. 'What were you doing the whole time?'

If I told her even a fraction of what I'd been doing, she would have pulled the deal there and then so I told her I'd been working too hard.

'What a drag,' she mewed. 'Listen, I'm just calling because I've just had a meeting about the competition.'

'OK.'

'We've just got the flyers back.'

'Great. How do they look?'

'OK,' she said, uncertainly. 'The spelling's not very good though.'

I'd forgotten about the Grubby's dyslexia.

'How bad is it?' I asked through gritted teeth.

'It's pretty bad,' she said. 'The 'T' and 'E' are missing out of 'competition'.'

'Oh,' I said, relieved. 'I thought it was something serious.'

'Well, it is really. It's the strap line and it's in quite big type.'

'Don't worry, the kids will know what it means.'

'Maybe,' she said, 'but the date's missing too.'

'Oh no. How many have you had made up?'

'Two thousand.'

I called the Grubby to see what he had to say. He blamed the mistakes on the computer spell checker

'You didn't put in the date either,' I told him.

'Yeah I did. The printers must have cocked it up.'

'You know we're going to have to write it on two thousand flyers by hand.'

'That's OK then, isn't it?' he said as if it was par for the course.

'Yes,' I replied. 'Because you're doing it.'

Chapter Twelve

July: Council Tax

I had a box of prizes in the car to be given away at the skate competition. The Pig had sorted out a job lot of trophies that were either rusty or made of plastic and bore the engraved names of past golf tournament winners. I'd peeled them off and replaced them with gold 'Skate Comp Winner' stickers that looked quite impressive, but only from a distance. We'd put the skate ramp up the day before and conscripted Stig and his mates to sleep under it and protect it from Saturday night beer boys.

It was warm when I arrived at Liddleton park, but a large bank of black cloud was looming off the coast, bringing a breeze that threatened rain. I was late. Michelle was already there, nervously setting out her organiser's table and fretting with risk assessments and health and safety concerns about skateboarders not wearing pads and helmets. 'Where is everyone?' she asked breathlessly. 'The competition's supposed to start in ten minutes.'

She was used to organising swimming galas and gymnastics events and tended to assume that this was going to be no different. I'd tried to tell her beforehand that a 9am kick off was ambitious, skaters not being known for their early starts. They began to trickle in over the next hour or two to register for the competition, but we had to roll the start time forward. The Pig arrived late too, bringing a couple of bass bins, mid-range and tops and a small marquee with him. 'Oh,' said Michelle, 'the speakers are warm.' I didn't tell her that the sound system had come straight from a rave.

By lunchtime the event was looking livelier, the street course and the ramp fizzing with some hardcore skate action. With '20 years' experience in the business', the Grubby was playing master of ceremonies and his commentary was littered with profanities and double entendres that had Michelle nervously biting her bottom lip. She looked out of her depth. As the day wore on the crowd had begun to swell with Liddleton low life who'd been attracted by the prospect of sinking a few brews and smoking some fatties in the great outdoors, watching the free show and listening to the tunes belting out from the Pig's rig. You could differentiate the parents who'd come to watch their kids compete, as they weren't the ones skinning up on the grass or offering Michelle cans of extra-strong lager. Neither did they endorse the event with comments like, 'Fair shout love' and 'About fuckin' time the council put something on that's worth going to...'

'D-you-know-what-I-mean?' said the Pig enthusiastically. 'This is what summer's all about. I bet that bird from the council's dead chuffed with the turnout today.'

I wasn't so sure.

'Are you OK?' I asked Michelle. She hadn't moved from her desk for the past three hours.

'Fine,' she said, flashing me a smile that was as false as her eye-lashes. 'Bit different to what I'd expected.'

'The kids are enjoying it. Great turnout too.'

She nodded. 'Some of them are quite scary,' she whispered.

'They're not so bad,' I said. 'A different kind of crowd to swimming galas I'd imagine.'

'You can say that again. You know some of the kids are drinking, don't you?' She nodded in the direction of some teenage skaters slaloming around empty cider cans.

'Perhaps you'd better say something.'

'I think it's probably best if I leave it for now,' she frowned.

The big event was the final in the 16+ class of the competition. From the start it was clear that it was going to be a showdown between our own Ginger Gaz and a flashy grockel from out of town. The grockel had a sponsorship deal with one of the bigger skate labels and was good in a technical way but he wasn't as smooth as our boy, who flipped some sick tricks with a fluidity that flowed. There was no mistaking who the partisan crowd was rooting for either. With the competition over, the judges retired to the Pig's van to compare score sheets. Grubby, Travis and a couple of old boy skaters were the judges. I was there to collate scores. While I totted up the totals from the rest of the day, I had half an ear on the debate regarding the final showdown.

'It's got to be Ginger Gaz really,' commented one of the judges.

'I don't know about that, mate,' replied the Grubby spitting sausage roll crumbs. 'He was good and that – don't get me wrong – but did he try hard enough? We know what Gaz is capable of.' He had a habit of placing illogical obstacles for no reason. It had something to do with the dog in his nature.

'That doesn't come into it. We're not judging on what skaters can do,' said Travis.

'Is it good for business though? Might be seen as favouritism.'

'It doesn't have anything to do with business, mate,' said another judge with some exasperation. 'It's about who was the best skater in today's competition.'

'True,' said the Grubby with a nod of deference. 'I'm just playing the Devil's Graduate.'

'Advocate,' I added.

Michelle presided over the prize-giving ceremony, and made an elaborate show of placing the trophies on her table. Already I'd had to put my boot up the arse of one little bastard who'd tried to make off with one while her back was turned. She'd prepared what was supposed to be a thank-you speech but seemed, in fact, to be a council manifesto trumpeting their achievements. It rambled for far too long and sections of the crowd were growing restless after a day of drinking in the sun. They didn't want to hear the speech, they just wanted to hear the winners and it wasn't long before the heckling started.

'Get on with it,' came the first shout.

'Get your kit off,' came the second.

The more 'respectable' spectators tutted and hushed them out of sympathy for Michelle's obvious embarrassment. If I'd been her I would have cut my losses there and then, given my thanks and announced the winner. Michelle, however, had a speech to deliver and she stuck to her guns '…The council is committed to spending more on public services and giving the people of Liddleton the standard of service that they deserve. Like the competitors today we are, as a community, all true winners thanks to the Millennium Initiative…'

'Did you hear that?' yelled one of the cider grommets. 'We're all winners. That means we've all won a trophy.'

Moments later, I found myself dragging Michelle to safety as a grubby horde rushed the organiser's table in a scramble to loot the trophies that had been standing on it. Before our eyes the award ceremony deteriorated into a free-for-all.

'I've never seen anything like it,' said Michelle. She was still crying, large teardrops turning her mascara to a black slush that ringed her eyes and made her look like a panda.

We were sitting in the Pig's van. 'They're just excitable,' I said. 'All the adrenalin.' I offered her a bit of bog roll.

'I never want to see another skateboarder again. Those kids were like animals.'

I didn't know what to say. They were just skaters.

'Oh well,' I said, 'there wasn't any real damage done. We did get most of the trophies back.'

'They ruined the whole day.'

'I don't think so,' I said. 'Put it this way, you probably won a lot of sympathy for the Millennium Initiative.'

She blew her nose and I saw that her blotchy eyes no longer leaked tears. She brushed away the hair that had become stuck to her cheek. A faint crack of a smile appeared on her lips. 'Do you really think so?' she asked.

Chapter Thirteen

The skate competition had been a debacle, but for once we hadn't been to blame. In fact, the council had commended us for our part in rescuing Michelle. Two days after the event we had a cheque through the post. In the spirit of Glastonbury and the tactical withdrawal, I'd had it made out in the name of The Castro Trading Company. I took the cheque and used it to open a new bank account.

The skate event over, we'd turned our attentions to the yard sale. As the retail revolution had pretty much sidelined Liddleton, the prospect of a sale at the yard had stirred some excitement amongst anyone in town that didn't think wearing your jumper tucked into your trousers was trendy. I took the lack of a memo from downstairs as a sign that Lesnik was still oblivious to the fact that it was taking place, and that was encouraging news. The yard was in its usual state of gross untidiness, so we borrowed a vacuum cleaner and blitzed the place until we got bored of tidying and shifted the remaining crap into a pile that could be camouflaged. With a set of decks and a couple of the Pig's speakers (moved in under the cover of darkness the night before), the yard now resembled a trendy metropolitan loft space.

We racked stock up on rails and packed the yard out with boxes marked 'Bargain Buys'. These boxes were filled with the freak and unique by-products of the manufacturing process; prototypes, samples and garments with defects. It was a marketing ploy, of course. There were no bargains, just cheap rejects we couldn't get rid of any other way.

The same skate grubbies that had rioted at the skate competition were banging on the office doors long before the sale was about to begin. When I opened up they surged past me like a wave of soldier ants.

The youths had seen the flyers saying 'Sales Party' and once they'd spent their savings they hung around on the sidelines, swigging from contraband bottles of grog, waiting for the 'party' to start.

Then came the second wave of customers. This crowd was older and predominantly male, blokes who spent their lives living in the same set of clothes because they didn't like shopping. They picked through the rails with an embarrassed tentativeness and bought items without trying them on.

'Sure you don't want to try that one on?' I asked repeatedly.

'No, looks like it's the right size,' they'd reply, holding the garment against the relevant body zone. 'What do you reckon?' they'd add with the same hint of not-that-I'm-a-homo-or-anything aggression males tend to adopt when performing the act of eating a banana.

'I'd try it on if I were you,' I told them.

'Nah. It'll be all right. I'll take it.'

Some of the blokes had girlfriends in tow and it was always a pleasure doing business with members of the opposite sex. If they liked it, they bought it and they generally didn't care what the price was. They also wielded the power to cajole or publicly embarrass their partners into parting with their money.

Business was swift. In two hours we took over six hundred. It was cold, hard cash, and the easiest money we'd made in a long time.

As time wore on, the teenagers were beginning to annoy me. One kid in particular wouldn't leave me alone. Pissed on alcopops, he kept asking if I'd sell him a T-shirt for the change he had in his pocket, which wouldn't even buy a chocolate bar. 'Go on, mate,' he'd slur, 'all I want is one T-shirt. I won't tell anyone if you give it to me cheap.' Eventually my patience snapped. I took a line out of the Pig's PR book and told him to fuck off.

There hadn't been any trade through the door for a while. Travis had already left, having had an earful from his missus about a forgotten family dinner, so it was just Cas, Big Dan and me hanging around behind the decks, drinking beers. The teenagers had started drunkenly play-fighting amongst themselves and I knew it wouldn't be long before it got serious. I was getting ready to call time and close the doors when we had an unexpected visitor. My heart sank when I caught sight of the figure come walking through the door.

I knew who it was just by clocking the dodgy gait and spider's web tattooed around his eye. His name was Sid-the-Dog and he was something of a low life legend in town. He was renowned for being Liddleton's biggest smack dealer and myth had it that he kept an ounce of heroin shoved up the arse of his pitbull (although I never could work out how that worked). Hence his nickname. Sid didn't need to rob to pay for his own habit like many of his customers, but his penchant for burglary was well known. A compulsive thief, he burgled as a hobby, much the same way that law-abiding citizens went fishing. It was said that he was addicted to the buzz of nearly getting caught. He frequently had been, of course, and was in and out of jail. Anyway, Sid-the-Dog was now in our yard and had a perfect opportunity to scope out the place. Half of me thought that we were probably safe anyway, as our network of contacts ran deep into the local underworld, but with a character like Sid-the-Dog you couldn't be sure. He flicked through the clothes rails, picking out garments and dumping them on the table in front of me.

'How much do I owe you?' He asked once he was done.

'A hundred and fifty,' I said. 'Tell you what, though, you're the last sale of the night, so we'll call it a hundred.' The clothes were worth more, but I took an executive decision to defer to his reputation and give the man a bit of respect. I hoped my gesture would appeal to his thief's sense of honour and insure us against being broken and entered.

'Cheers, mate,' Sid-the-Dog said with a smile that was so genuine it was almost touching. 'I appreciate that.' He peeled off some notes and handed them over.

It was all going to plan until the young grubby who'd been hassling me earlier croaked up from behind his bottle of cider. 'That's not fair!' he yelled. 'How come he gets his stuff cheap and you won't even sell me a cheap T-shirt?'

I ignored him and continued bagging up the clothes.

'You only done it because it's Sid-the-Dog.'

I turned to Sid-the-Dog and raised an eyebrow, but his face was blank.

Fortunately, Cas interceded. 'I think it's time you lot fucked off,' he said, standing to his feet.

'Yeah, right, you fucking twat,' sneered the kid, buoyed by booze. He made a dash for the door with Cas lumbering after him like a riled park keeper. The kid's cronies de-flocked from their perches like vultures following the kill.

Sid-the-Dog watched them go. He tapped his long fingernails (I wondered if they were intentional – you know, for extracting the smack out the dog's arse…) on the tabletop. 'Nice place you've got here,' he said, looking around.

Oh no, here we go. 'Yeah,' I said, 'It's OK.'

'I never knew you had so much stuff.'

'We don't normally.'

He looked up and gave a little smile, like he knew I was lying.

'Well, thanks for that anyway,' he nodded, motioning to his bags. 'I owe you one.'

'No worries,' I said.

'See you around, maybe.'

'Yeah,' I replied, wondering what he'd meant by the word maybe…

While I locked up, Cas and Big Dan left to bring round the car. I was on my way downstairs when I bumped into the landlord.

'I suppose you think that was funny?' he said curtly, pointing to a computer printed sign on his office door. 'Quiet please. Meeting in progress. Can't you read?'

I shrugged. 'Not really.'

'Well, I'm glad you can afford to be so flippant,' he said, in a nasal monotone. 'I don't think the police and the council will see it the same way once I notify them that you've been holding a rave in the building.'

'What are you talking about?' I said, screwing my face up in annoyance.

'I think you know what I mean,' he said smugly. 'You've been having a party up there.'

'Believe me,' I scoffed, 'if we'd been running a rave up there you'd know about it.'

'And you believe me,' he said with a self importance that made his double chin wobble, 'I had to cancel a very important meeting and send people home because of the noise.'

'Not another paperclip audit?' I sniped.

'You're in big trouble, mate,' he countered, pulling an addressed envelope out of his back pocket. 'You see this? It's going to the council first thing in the morning. Let's see what they have to say about the matter. Some of us are trying to run a business, you know.'

'Really,' I said sarcastically, pushing past him down the stairs, before I did something I'd regret 'and all this time I just thought you were being a fucking jobsworth.'

'I'll remember that,' he said, invoking school day memories of zealous teachers.

'Why don't you just get a life and let us get on with ours?' I made a note to find some dog shit and post it through his letterbox.

Chapter Fourteen

<u>August: The Dog Dance</u>

The good times had been rolling since Glastonbury and the start of the summer season. Maybe it had something to do with our decision to seek a tactical withdrawal or maybe it was just the sunshine that had brought a little bit of the feel good factor we'd been lacking. The inflow of cash from summer sales and a few weed runnings on the side had allowed me to keep the creditors quiet with cash bungs, and so long as there was enough in the bank to keep up the monthly loan repayments we had time to consolidate our resources and prepare for the endgame.

Travis had been in London for the best part of the week. He was part of a crew of graf artists spraying up boards at an event called 'The Street Olympics'. I'd been tempted to go up myself, but I didn't really fancy hanging around handing him spray cans for three days and had enough to do anyway. I changed my mind though when Turnist called to say that Upshot had been given a stand at the event to promote the magazine. He was running it and suggested I come up with some clothes.

'It'll be easy, man,' he'd told me on the phone. 'Just bring up a couple of boxes and hang out a rail. If anyone says anything, I'll tell

them it's our clothes we're selling. Come on, it'll be a laugh. Haze is going to give me a hand.'

He was right, it probably would be a laugh and I hadn't been up to town for a while so I loaded up the Shove-it with a couple of boxes and some rails and left Devon early on Friday morning. The day was overcast, hot and humid, and passers-by stared as I eased the orange jalopy through posh London streets on my way to the Street Olympics.

It was being sponsored by one of the major soft drinks corporations, desperate to brand its product at street level. The whole extreme sports scene was now being seen as a 'cool' way for the corporates to brand their products for the youth market. They were dying to get their grubby mitts on a slice of 'street' culture as it would give their brands the kind of kudos that 'the kids' would buy into. From my days in New York, I knew that this strategy had probably been decided in a boardroom by men in suits who wouldn't know the back end of a skateboard from the front and thought riding 'goofy' had something to do with looking like the Disney character.

What these people failed to realise was that skaters were without doubt the biggest bunch of anti-corporate animals running around those streets the big brands were so desperate to paint in their corporate colours. Sponsoring an event like the Street Olympics got them little respect at all. Besides, after an afternoon of sweaty skating, the last thing the 'kids' wanted to be necking was a gacky soft drink with zero calories and packed full of artificial sweeteners. At the very least they wanted the full caffeine, sugar energy hit, and more often than not skaters wanted to be knocking back a can of something alcoholic. Nevertheless, the suits had decided this was how they were going to raise the profile of their consumable goods, and were content to throw as much money at it as was needed to stick. Sadly, I knew from experience that if they banged the drum hard enough and for long enough, people would begin to forget the phoniness of their intentions and it wouldn't be too long before the scene would become corporatised. It was just a question of keeping the propaganda pumping.

The event was taking place on a five-acre site within a park, south of the river. Ringed by security fencing and licensed for eight thousand people, the site was circular in shape and patrolled by a team of security guards who'd been re-branded with the more user-friendly 'stewards' label. Inside, there was a collection of ramps, from a huge vert construction that was playing host to some of the biggest stars on the worldwide skate scene, to midi and mini ramps and a pur-pose-built street course inside a large marquee. As well as stuff to watch, there was a heap of stalls selling product as well as food and drinks at the kind of exorbitant prices that none of the real skaters there would be able to afford.

Regardless of the sponsors' ulterior motives, the Street Olympics was indeed an impressive sight, and there was genuine excitement at the prospect of three days of hardcore skate competition. As faces on the circuit, we knew a lot of those competing, and would have brought our own skate team up for the occasion were it not for the fact that we missed the entry date on account of all our Glastonbury running around. In addition to the skate features and the usual extreme sports tack-ons, such as bungee jumps and climbing walls, there was a live stage and a couple of music tents.

Here again, the sponsors had looked to the street for inspira-tion and the bill was packed with punk, hip hop and dance music performers and DJs that were bubbling on the underground music scene. Generally, they too were unimpressed by the corporate over-tures of such an event but – as with everybody on the underground scene – faced that same old prisoner's dilemma. Do you 'sell out' and get paid for being on the bill, or 'keep it real', not perform and not get paid. Of course, the answer came down to economics in the end, as most people operating from the 'underground' were skint and few would actually turn down the opportunity to make a few quid.

And so the Street Olympics arena had been cast, heralded as the premier extreme sports event of the year by a slick PR campaign that appealed to the mainstream, ensuring interest from broadsheet newspapers whose readers were the first ones to call the police at the sight of a gang of skaters grinding rails in their local parks.

'Che', yelled Haze, who'd come to meet me with a wristband. 'How're ya doin', bruv?'

'Good. You?'

'All right, mate. Bit of a mad one last night though. I've only 'ad a couple o' hours' kip.'

'What happened to your face?' I asked. He had a large black bruise over one eye and scratches on his cheeks.

'Had a fight with me brother down the fishing lakes.' Haze had taken up fishing to keep him away from the chemicals after his Glastonbury excursion, and it had become his latest addiction.

'Pretty nasty one as it goes. Lost both me rods and ended up chucking the little bastard in the lake.'

The Street Olympics was quiet. It was Friday and most of the people milling around were either media or people working there. The Upshot stand was no more than a table on the grass, a couple of easy chairs and a stack of magazines. Turnist was pleased to see me.

'What happened to the stall?' I asked.

'Thought we'd go al fresco', he laughed.

'Where's Travis?'

'Painting. Just follow the smell of weed.'

"'Ere', said Haze, passing me a drink, 'get that down your neck. Rum and coke. They're givin' out free samples. Been drinkin' the fuckin' stuff all day. Come on, I'll show you where Travis is.'

As predicted, I could smell Travis before I could see him. A half-smoked spliff hung from the corner of his mouth and he was squinting at the rough outlines he'd started putting on a four-by-eight feet whitewashed board.

'Hey,' he said, as we shook hands.

'How's things?'

'Same as usual, mate,' he replied, nodding at the etched lines. 'Slowly.'

'You should 'ave a lick of this charlie I've got,' said Haze. 'You'd be finished in a couple of hours.'

'Nah,' said Travis screwing up his nose. 'That's the last thing I need.'

'What about you, Che?'

I dawdled but finally followed him into the kind of plastic toilet cubicle that tended to get very messy at festivals and snorted one of the lines he chopped out on the top of the seat. 'Got some savage little tinkers as well,' said Haze grinning like a hobgoblin and pulling out a wrap of cellophane. It was filled with fractions of pills and a lot of powder. 'Geezer the charlie came from gave it to me. Sells fousands of pills. This is just what 'e 'ad left at the bottom of a bin liner.'

I emerged from the cubicle blinking in the sunlight, no longer able to feel my teeth. With only a couple of hours left, there wasn't much point in setting the clothes out so I smoked spliffs, horsed around, caught up with a few old faces, and downed the free drinks that Haze passed me.

The day's proceedings were winding down and I was helping Turnist to stash the stall away, my thoughts on where I was going to stay for the night. Travis was staying with a country man we knew from Devon who now lived in London and was making his name as a hip hop producer, and there was no room at the inn. Turnist was between places at the moment and sleeping on someone's floor himself. Haze didn't have anywhere to stay either, although he didn't tend to worry about things like that... The sun was beginning to set and the site lights had been turned on, casting a halogen glow over the site that made the blackness of the clouds above even more pronounced. As I cast my gaze over the site I was suddenly aware that the faces of people around me appeared to be glowing orange.

'Haze,' I said presently.

'Yes, bruv.'

'I'm feeling a little bit strange.'

Haze laughed. 'Course you are, mate. You've been knockin' back tinker brews for the past hour. Been spikin' ya since you got 'ere.'

'Haze, you bastard,' I groaned. It was clear Haze's fishing habit hadn't quite replaced his old ones.

'Don't worry, mate, it's not just you. I did a round for us all.'

'How much was in there?'

He shrugged. 'There's still loads left in the bag. Can't 'ave been that much.'

'Great, spiked with fucking ecstasy,' I muttered, though as it was now taking effect my grumble was half-arsed.

'Tell me about it,' chipped in Turnist. I noticed his jaw was starting to tremble.

'I've got nowhere to stay.'

'Don't worry about it,' Haze assured me, 'I'll find ya somewhere.'

'You sure?'

'You're in my town,' said Haze, his arms out stretched, though it wasn't strictly true as Haze was living with his parents in Colchester at the moment.

'I hope so, Haze. I can't be dealing with doing an all-nighter and then working this place tomorrow.'

'Trust me.'

I stopped off to see Travis before we left. He was talking to one of the security guys when I found him.

'Trouble?' I said when security had gone.

He shook his head. 'Buying weed,' he said with a laugh. 'Think I must have sorted half the security crew since I've been here.' He looked up, clocking my eyes, which probably looked like they were on stalks. 'What the fuck have you been up to?'

I was now putty in Haze's hands, spiked and homeless in the city. I had a small backpack with a sleeping bag, toothbrush and a pair of clean pants inside – basic kit that prepared me for most eventualities. I gave Travis the keys to the Shove-it and, with a 'when in Rome' attitude, accompanied Haze on another visit to the toilet cubicle before we left. It was a move I regretted as soon as we descended down the stairs to the tube platform. There weren't any seats on the train and I was forced to spend the next half-hour leaning against the window and praying for the journey to end, like a kid strapped onto the Waltzers, as Haze rattled off ecstasy-fuelled fisherman's tales.

'Now a lot of people are unfamiliar with the Zander,' roared Haze over the noise of the train, his head cocked to one side, 'but I know it quite well, because the lakes where I fish are full of 'em. Now a Zander is a cross between a pike and a perch, and 'e's a nasty little bastard too…'

I was aware that people were giving us wary looks, and it wasn't just my drug paranoia.

After a few drinks, Haze took us to a club in the East End where a friend of his called Elsa was playing. We'd be able to kip at her place for the night he'd assured the two of us (Turnist having now decided that he was too out of it to go back to where he was staying). Unfortunately, the bouncers wouldn't let us in. They told Haze he was too inebriated.

'Inebriated! All I've 'ad to drink today is a couple of rum and cokes, yoo cunts!' spat Haze, his face contorting. He would probably have had a kicking were it not for the fact that he was frothing at the mouth from another dip into his bag of crushed pills.

'Ay curumba,' I said, as we sat on a step, reviewing our options. I hadn't eaten all day and the nefarious cocktail I'd been sipping on since I'd arrived in London was catching up with me.

'Fancy a salmon (salmon and trout – snout)?' Haze asked.

I shook my head and then puked up on the pavement. When I had stopped puking, I forced myself into a newsagent and bought a melted chocolate bar that was hard work to swallow. Meanwhile, Haze made some phone calls. Unfortunately, his own Street Olympics cocktail had done little for his phone manner and I could picture the people at the end of the line inventing excuses to deter him from turning up on their doorstep. Eventually he hit lucky, finding a friend of a friend who was living in a squat in Dalston. We caught a bus then walked the rest of the way to the flat, arriving there at about three in the morning. It was on a run-down housing estate filled with faceless buildings that loomed large around a broken concrete courtyard. The only vegetation was a single tree that had long since been killed off by vandals. The lifts didn't work and the stairwell crunched with broken glass.

'Not a bad little place, really,' wheezed Haze, surveying the estate over the side of the balcony. I couldn't say I shared his opinion.

Our host for the night was a skater called Hank, and I could tell straight away that he had his reservations. His eyebrows raised when he clocked Haze with his baseball cap pulled to one side exposing the scratches on his face, the powdery evidence of what he'd been up to caked round the corners of his mouth.

The squat showed signs of grubby habitation. Skate mags lay around the place, creased and stained like old pornos, and the sink overflowed with used take away cartons. Stinking rubbish had burst through black bags, spewing out over the uncarpeted floor, and chunks had been gouged out of the plasterwork where someone had made a lean-to skate ramp against one of the walls. The furniture consisted of a kitchen table, a few broken chairs and some pallets on the floor covered with dirty mattresses. Hank told us the squat had formerly been office space, but the building had been condemned and was about to be demolished. He was expecting the bailiffs any day now and kept his belongings in a bag by the door so that when it got kicked down he'd be ready to go. I could tell that Hank thought it was pretty cool living in a squat. It reinforced his image as being slightly screw-loose and hardcore. I could also tell that Hank was doing a lot of pretending. Every now and again he dropped his dropped vowels, his speech giving away the hint of a cosy middle class upbringing. I could tell Haze unnerved him. Haze did have a screw loose and was most definitely hardcore without having to live in a squat.

It was late and I wanted to sleep. There was nothing to drink in the flat except for half a bottle of opened wine that tasted like vinegar and off-colour water from the tap that could have easily come from the canal outside. Hank had the wine, I braved the water, Turnist rolled a spliff, and Haze had another line. It wasn't long before he was on a wild one again and talking about knocking up an acquaintance to get some more white powder. I'd been in this position too many times to know where this early morning conversation was going – nowhere – and rather than put myself through an hour of chasing that conclusion I took the nearest soiled mattress, rolled out my sleeping bag and did my best to sleep.

I'd slept for about three hours. Hardly enough to prepare me for a day on the stand (let alone sorting out the stand under the noses of the organisers) but it was better than the no hours Haze had had. He was smoking a cigarette and reading a magazine when I woke. Beside him, the Turnist was sleeping, his large frame wound round a small chair. It was a hot day, breaks in the morning cloud hinting the sun was on its way. Once at the Street Olympics I borrowed a wristband and a wheelbarrow and went off site to fetch the stock boxes out of the car. The secret of a good blag is to act like you know what you're doing and as I wheeled my stock back through the gates security nodded and smiled.

I'd brought up the small tent we used for events like this, a customised garden gazebo (available from all good garden centres) that had come in a box with a picture on the front showing a happy family and sausages sizzling on a barbecue. The gazebo took about five minutes to slot together and we set it up at the end of a row of retail stalls and as far away from the organiser's office as we could get it. We aroused no undue suspicion as we put the clothes out on the two rails I'd brought. Just as we were finishing around came the first sample tray of rum for the day. I kicked back in one of the easy chairs, the grass beneath my bare feet, the sun on my face, and settled down to my breakfast brew, nodding my head to the laid-back beats rolling out of the music tent opposite.

It was Saturday and the good weather had brought out the people. In addition to the extreme sport crowds there were families, weekend warriors, skate trendy wannabes, and a multitude of sun seekers making the best of a summer's day out. Extreme Sports was the latest fashion look and everyone, it seemed, was clamouring to pull on a pair of baggy pants and a baseball cap and pass themselves off as being part of the scene. Naturally this translated as being good for sales. I wasn't really in the mood to play shopkeeper but to my surprise I didn't even need to. GP, it seemed, was coming straight to me.

GP was a Grubbyism – it was the name he gave to punters at events like this – and was short for 'General Public'. There's a lot of psychology behind getting people to part with their money, and it had taken me time to learn. The Grubby had been my finest teacher too. It's all about the vibe you give off. Try too hard, or make them feel too pressured and a curious punter scuttles away, even if they're interested in purchasing. By the same token, people avoid an empty stand like the pox, reasoning there's nobody in there because there's nothing in there worth looking at. A crowd always attracts a crowd, and the key to selling is to exude a state of relaxed indifference. That said, there's a difference between relaxed indifference and totally ignoring your customers, which was precisely what we were doing at the Street Olympics. However, far from being perturbed by our ramshackle appearance and a sales team ensconced in easy chairs, punters were drawn to the stall like flies round a fresh turd, and business was brisk and effortless.

Later in the afternoon, I took a stroll round the Street Olympics site. Around the perimeter, there was some pretty good graffiti going up and I noticed one piece in particular. It featured a well-known politician on hands and knees and being fucked up the arse by a demonic looking Mickey Mouse. I didn't need to read the tag to know that it was the Menace's work. I went to check out the skating on the street course where the big competition of the day was taking place. There I bumped into Hank, who was competing and had won through to the final.

'Your mate who was foaming at the mouth, what was he on last night?' he asked.

I told him it looked worse than it actually was, but he didn't believe me and I wasn't surprised when he gave a half-arsed excuse as to why we couldn't stay at the squat again that night.

Travis had negotiated with his security guard contacts and they'd let us leave the car inside the Street Olympics perimeter, and we'd left the site after a very respectable day's business. I was now squashed in the backseat of Carlos' small car, between Turnist and Haze with a record box on my lap, zipping through Saturday night streets. Travis was up front. We'd hooked up with him earlier in the evening. Because he ran a record label, Saturday night was a work night for Carlos that involved club hopping across the capital to check out crowds, dance floors and the tunes that were making them move. We were en-route to a monthly drum and bass night in a large converted church and from there back to his flat in north London to grab a patch of floor space.

We got to the club shortly after midnight and by-passed the queue that snaked round the block. The urgency of the music literally shook the walls inside and the dance floor was jumping. It had been a long time since I'd done much dancing (I'd been on the other side of the promotional fence for too long) but the cocktail coursing through my veins was looking for an escape and it wasn't long before I found myself swept along with the heaving mass of fucked-up party people. The place kind of rekindled nostalgic memories of the big raves of years gone by I used to go to, only the faces were younger – or rather mine was older. I soon lost sight of the others but it didn't bother me. I was having an enjoyable time watching the night unfold without the worry of being responsible for it, and talking crap to complete strangers for no good reason other than the fact I was off my head.

I finally caught up with Haze in the chill out room. He had a fag hanging out of his mouth and was talking to three foreign girls who were heavily pierced and tattooed.

"Ere's a man who can help,' Haze said to one of the girls. 'You got a light, me old sunshine?'

I fumbled through four pockets before I found it.

'In my country, we say a man without fire is like a man without cock,' said one of the girls, with a sultry gaze. She stuck out her tongue.

'Fruit bats, this lot,' grinned Haze. 'I'm havin' the blonde one. You take your pick.'

I smiled and asked if he'd seen Travis. 'You missed 'im, mate. Him and Carlos was lookin' for ya.' Haze had eyes like saucers. 'I offered him a tinker to stay on, but 'e wasn't havin' any of it.'

'Shit. That was my bed for the night.'

'Don't worry about it, Che. 'Ere, 'ave another pill.'

It was against my character, but totally in character with the weekend I'd been having, so I shrugged, swallowed the pill he gave me, and gave myself up to the dance floor again.

We left the club at five. It was already light, and the streets were deserted except for a couple of early-morning commuters off to work the Sunday shift. I laughed at their misfortune until I remembered that I was working the Sunday shift too. I'd had four hours' sleep in the past 48 and had spent much of my waking time ingesting substances. At this stage of the night, morning, weekend, I was incapable of assessing any options that required looking beyond the end of my nose, so when Haze suggested we go back to the Street Olympics and kip in the gazebo I didn't think twice. We took a gypsy cab, with loud Reggae blasting, that drove so fast we could have been doing a hospital run.

The Street Olympics site may have had all-night security patrols but there was scant evidence of them as we climbed under a section of the fence and belly-crawled our way to the gazebo. Haze, the terminal pykie, left on a mission to scour the site for items to loot and it wasn't long before he returned with a case of rum from the sampling tent. I took a medicinal tot, despite the furriness of my mouth and the banging headache of dehydration. Stretching out on the grass floor of the stall, my ears ringing, I closed my eyes and tried to sleep. Behind the lidded veils my mind raced with images of the previous couple of days that my brain had yet to file in the memory bank. Eventually, however, I dozed off.

'Che,' said Haze, with a sudden dig to my ribs, 'check it out.'

'What?' I said, groggy and annoyed at having been woken.

'Listen to the dogs.'

'What?'

'Listen to the dogs. They're barkin' one of the tunes we 'eard in the club.'

I opened one eye and listened. I could hear the dogs barking. It was an early morning mutt chorus that was rolling across the neighbourhood beyond the park, and on a normal morning it would have sounded exactly that.

'Shit, I wish I had a microphone,' said Haze.

'That's unbelievable,' mused Turnist, listening intently.

'It's just dogs barking,' I yawned.

'I disagree, you cynical ole bastard!' snapped Haze. 'I would say that what we're listenin' to is a bunch of very musical – and intelligent – dogs.'

'Believe me, the tune's all in your head,' I told him.

'He's probably right,' said Turnist, disappointed.

'Believe me. I know I'm right.'

'I don't fink you are, Che. Listen to it. They're doin' the dog dance. Fuckin' ell, it's bringin' me back up...'

I fell back to sleep, listening to a discussion on dog dancing, and before long had entered a world of twisted dreams: I was in the orange Shove-it and on my way to a club for the dog dancing championships. I was wearing all the clothes that we had on the rails and had a bottle of rum balanced on my head, which was making it difficult to drive. The car was stalled in the queue of people waiting to enter the venue and I was sweating under the many layers of clothes I was wearing. I was aware that I was soiling fresh stock and then had the horrible realisation that I'd forgotten about the rabid dog I'd stashed in the trunk. But it was too late now, I was at the front of the queue and the bouncers were already demanding to know where the barking was coming from. They opened my door and three of them grabbed me...

I woke with a start, Turnist looming large over me, his hand shaking my shoulder. For a few moments I was caught in an altered state somewhere between my dream and the reality, where nothing really made sense. 'What time is it?' I grunted.

'About 9.30,' he said without looking at his watch. 'Security have just been over.'

I sat bolt upright. 'Are we being kicked out?'

'No. They want to open the gates for the day but they can't because your orange car's parked in the middle of the site.'

'You're joking?'

As if on cue there came an announcement over the site speaker system. I didn't have the keys, Travis did. I asked if he was here.

'No.'

'Oh fuck.' I jumped up, and promptly lost balance. I found my phone. Travis was running late.

'Leave it to me,' he told me, not seeming to grasp the seriousness of the situation, 'I'll give Ainsley a call.'

'Who the fuck's Ainsley?'

'Head of security. I've sorted them all out since I've been up there so I reckon I can buy some time.'

He was right too. I was there to meet him when he eventually turned up, the orange car having already delayed the opening of the Street Olympics by half an hour. As we didn't officially exist on the organiser's books they hadn't been able to trace the car.

'You're a lucky bastard,' growled Ainsley, a hulk of a man with a skinhead and thick cockney accent.

'Sorry about that,' said Travis. 'Taxi had a puncture coming over the bridge. Would you fuckin' believe it?'

'No,' leered Ainsley. 'I fink you woz in bed.' He had a sinister laugh. 'You know the organisers fought it was a fuckin' IRA bomb, don't ya?'

'Shit.' Travis scratched his head guiltily.

'Don' you worry about it, dread,' said the security man, slapping Travis on the shoulders. 'I enjoyed seeing the lickle fuckers squirm to be honest wiv ya.'

'I'll sort you out, mate.'

'Yeah. I know ya fuckin' will.'

The car got moved. Ainsley got sorted, and the organisers were still oblivious to our speakeasy retail outfit. On any other day the car would have been blown up by the bomb squad but this weekend, it seemed, luck was running with us. By mid-morning, the incident had been forgotten and back at the stall we'd picked up the sales where we'd left off the day before. Turnist, Haze and myself were fizzling with a delirious kind of electricity in a post-club, no-sleep, comedown sort of way. As the day progressed we became that drunken rabble in the park that mothers steered their toddlers away from, and yet garments were flying off the rails with a regularity that was alarming. I was even starting to run out of pocket space to put all the money that was being thrown at me. I could only think that everyone else's stall was so crap that punters were passing them by, following the trail of the weed smoke that wafted from our gazebo. Or perhaps, I thought, with a logic that could only be born from three days of substance abuse, this was the very future of sales...

Halfway through the day, one of the other stallholders wandered over and introduced himself. His name was Jerry. He had a pot belly, bad breath and his face glowed red with sunburn. He was wearing some of the clothes that he was selling on the stall but he wore them uncomfortably, like a Dad trying to impress his teenage son. 'I was going to say it's a bit quiet today but I can see it's not the same for you,' was his opening line.

I tried to rein in my large grin and gave a shrug. 'Don't know why. Sometimes you just have a good run.'

'I should bloody say so,' said Jerry with some bitterness. 'I haven't broken even yet.'

'It'll be OK,' I said. 'Usually is.'

'I wish I shared your confidence,' he said, taking his shades off to reveal a pair of white circles around his eyes. Behind me, Turnist and Haze had broken into yet another rendition of the dog dance.

'Those guys are completely out of it, aren't they?'

'They've been on the free rum,' I said.

'And smoking a bit of the old funny stuff,' Jerry added with a wink. 'Are they with you?'

'Kind of. Turnist works for Upshot, and Haze is just… Haze.'

'He works for Upshot, does he? Love the magazine, maybe I'll have a word.'

'Shall I introduce you?'

He took another look at the Turnist who was now rolling on the floor, barking. 'I think I'll probably leave it for now,' he replied.

I watched him waddle back over to his stall, and caught the gaze of another couple of stallholders wearing long faces, who were staring disapprovingly in our direction. 'Afternoon,' I chirped in my best camper-go-lucky voice.

They looked away.

There's something to the old adage that money makes money, because by mid-afternoon, on top of all the sales we were chalking up we had another little scam on the go. Haze had taken a couple of our exhibitor's wristbands and gone to the gate to bring in the foreign girls he'd met at the club. While waiting, he'd been approached by a couple of blokes who'd asked if he could get them in. He'd charged them half-price, walked them in with loosely fitted wristbands and then taken the bands back once inside. We had five wristbands between us. Entry into the Olympics was a tenner. One person out, with four wristbands at a fiver a piece translated as…

'Twenty quid for ten minutes fuckin' work,' exclaimed Haze on his return from another run.

'What about security?' I asked as he handed me the wristbands for my turn.

He shrugged. 'Che,' he said melodramatically. 'From what you've seen of the security boys this weekend, do you really think they give a fuck?'

He had a point.

I left the sanctuary of the stall and made the very short walk to the main gate, passing through it and strolling by the long line of people who were waiting to pay. Even though there was only an afternoon of the event left there were still a lot of people arriving. Following Haze's advice, I walked away from the site to a spot underneath the cover of bushy trees. I lay in wait. There was no shortage of passers by, it was just a case of picking the right ones. I asked a middle-aged couple if they were going to the Olympics and knew straight away they had been a bad choice. They practically ran away from me, prompting a thought to flash into my head. It was one of those life-flashing-before-you moments. What the fuck was I doing? How had I gone from being a career professional with a high salary and a trendy New York pad to being a sketchy drugged-up bastard so desperate for cash that I was prepared to lurk in park bushes touting dodgy wristbands to innocent passers-by? I didn't have the answer, but the dark thought vanished as soon as I spotted a group of four teenagers in their late teens carrying skateboards.

'Boys,' I said, affecting the kind of corner of the mouth delivery

I'd observed the ticket touts using on Glastonbury's Hades Gate. 'Anyone looking to get into the Olympics for half-price?'

We agreed the price and I gave them the instructions like Haze had told me. 'Keep it short an' sweet,' he'd said, 'an' act like a pykie. That way they won't try and do a runner.' I directed them to follow me and we strolled through the back gate with nothing but a friendly nod of recognition from the two security guards on the door.

'What did I tell you, Che?' said Haze, as I took the money and the wristbands from the teenagers. Before I could answer, he had his arm round one of the boys. 'Now you look like you could do with some new clothes, mate. Come an' 'ave a look at what we've got 'ere...'

We ran the wristband scam in shifts until there were no longer any people waiting outside to gain entry. Meanwhile at the stall, our clothing rails had been picked bare. By the time the PA announcement came saying that the Street Olympics was over, the only stock we had to our name were three ubiquitous yellow T-shirt hanging on the rail (we always got left with yellow. Yellow never sold but was good for breaking up the colours). Everyone had made money. The weekend had been profitable beyond our wildest expectations. We counted the cash in the garden gazebo and whooped up our good fortune. Sewerside had cleared nearly fifteen hundred over the two days, and that didn't include weed sales and wristband runs. Not bad for an event where we didn't officially exist.

Chapter Fifteen

August: Smoke 'n' Bacon

It was the height of the tourist season and Liddleton was its usual patchwork of pale, tanned and lobster-red flesh. Working days were slotted around the sunshine. I'd speak to people in London who complained about being stuck in a hot, airless office unable to enjoy the sun, and wind up the conversation by slipping in the fact I was nipping off early to go to the beach.

As well as selling our clothes direct to the punter we were also shifting a fair amount of weed. Travis had a new Cornish connection – the supply was plentiful, the price was cheap and, because I was acting as the bagman, our credit was good. It was tempting to think that we could keep it going and hustle our way out of trouble, but I knew it was just temporary. The feel-good factor would disappear with the first dead leaves of autumn, and as profitable as it was, running drugs wasn't a long-term business solution. With the tactical withdrawal never far from the back of my mind, I was stashing as much cash as I could while we were still able to make financial hay. In the meantime, we were trying to sort out a party. The Sewerside summer bash had become something of an annual ritual since we'd begun, as it was an opportunity to gather the tribes from around the country for a weekend in Devon.

I went to see the Pig to find out if he had any ideas for a venue. He was working, or rather slaving, on a building project for Micky Vendell. While the sun blazed, he was spending his days labouring inside an old grain warehouse Vendell was converting into flats. Not that the Pig minded missing out on the sunshine. It was his lunch break and we were sitting in the gloom of a room without windows.

'Suits me fine, chap,' he said, when I mentioned the lack of sun. 'I hate this bastard weather.' He wiped a trotter across his brow. 'So let's go through this again. You want to do a party next weekend. Where?'

'I was hoping you'd have some ideas?' I told him.

He thought for a minute, smoking a cigarette between mouthfuls of a Scotch egg. 'Give this bloke a call. A farmer. Has been known to have parties on his land. Might want a bit of cash for it though.' The Pig scribbled a number on a scrap of three be' two timber.

'I'll ask my 'ubby,' said the farmer's wife (the farmer was off in the fields). She was friendly but proper local and I had trouble understanding her. 'But I don' thank 'e'll wanna do it, an' I'll tell 'e faw why. T'is ower busiest time o' yeare, 'an I don' know if it all wouln' be too much on top o' the 'arvestin'. T'other thing is us's got a funny lot o' naybours, an' the last time we let a field faw a pardy they kicked up 'elluva stink. 'Tis a shame really, 'cause I loike a bit of a pardy meself.'

No sooner had I put the phone down, when I got a call from Stig. 'Don't know if you're interested,' he said. 'There's a kid from college called Scott, who lives on a farm. His parents are on holiday for a couple of weeks and he wants us to do a party for his 18th birthday.'

Bingo!

The farm was set within a maze of winding country lanes flanked by high hedges. It was deep in the tractor belt, about 20 miles inland. Travis, Cas, the Pig and myself were in the car and on our way to do a site inspection.

'No one's going to be able to find this place,' whistled Travis.

'If there's a party, they'll find it,' replied the Pig stoically.

Scott was waiting for us, his face beaming from beneath a woollen beanie. He was young, impressionable, desperate for a party and exactly the kind of person we could do business with. The farm was set in the side of a hill and surrounded on all sides by rolling fields and bushy hedgerows. In the distance loomed the peaks of Dartmoor. The air was filled with the sound of birds, the smell of warm grass, wild flowers and cow manure that wafted from the dairy farm across the valley. There were two barns, one of which was a corrugated iron structure, walled on three sides. It had a dirt floor, covered in straw, which posed a health and safety risk but one that wasn't insurmountable. The other was more of a stable with a couple of mangers, a low ceiling and a concrete floor. It was used as a storeroom, but it wouldn't take much to clear the stuff away. There were electricity feeds for both barns, which was a bonus as it meant we wouldn't have to use generators. The two barns were set at a right angle to each other. The farmhouse was out of the way and could be easily secured. Fortunately, there were no animals either which was a blessing as livestock always complicated matters when it came to a rural rumble.

'What are the neighbours like?' I asked Scott, as we stood in the stable, running through logistics.

'There aren't many. Just the farm over there, and another one up the lane, but there's a hill between us.'

The Pig was more thorough. 'Do you know them?' he asked bluntly.

'No.'

'Well, you're going to have to meet them before the weekend and tell them it might be a bit noisy. Say it's your 18th birthday and they'll probably be all right about it.'

'But it is my birthday.'

'There you go then.'

'What about your parents?' I asked.

'Don't worry about them. They've gone to Greece for two weeks.'

'And they won't come back early?'

'I don't think so.'

'And if they did?'

'That's something I'd have to deal with.'

I nodded. 'As long as we're clear on that.' The kid had a sense of responsibility, and I liked that.

'Office,' barked the Pig. 'I'm going to need one. VIP and crew access only. Got anything?'

'Not really. There's a room that links the two barns, but it's more of a cupboard really.'

'The one with the fuse boxes in it?'

'That's the one.'

'That'll do me, chap,' said the Pig, flashing a thumbs up sign.

'What about car parking?' I asked.

'We've got a field at the bottom of the track.'

The field was large and on a slope, meaning that it was unlikely to become waterlogged, but the track leading up to it was about 50 metres long and farm vehicles had churned up the mud so that unless you were driving a tractor it was impassable. We tentatively ran a car down it to assess the situation, but became stuck before we'd gone ten metres.

'This is a fucking mess,' said Cas shaking his head. 'We're going to have to dig it out.'

'We've got some shovels,' offered Scott.

'It'll take more than shovels.'

'It would be easier if we fuck it off altogether, and just mow down this field instead,' said the Pig pointing to another meadow.

'Um, not really. It's an orchard my Dad's just planted.'

'Fair point. If you don't ask you don't know. Plan A it is then.'

The Pig's solution to the track problem was labour intensive. He recommended we dig it out as best we could and then lay a new road using rubble from the building job he was working on as hardcore. We'd all laughed his suggestion off until we realised it was the only option we had...

After all the jokes, the arguments and allegations of security breaches, it was inevitable that at some time or another my sister would bring her new boyfriend to meet the family, and tonight was the night. My mother had invited him over for dinner.

I had hoped that Maddy's romance with the copper would be a flash in the pan, but things had gone quite the opposite and after two months of seeing each other, she was claiming to be in love.

'I can't believe it, Che,' said Haze when I told him. 'Your house'll never be the same. Imagine, you're goin' t' be sitting round the table after Christmas dinner, slap the papers together to roll a spliff, and… bang… you won't be able to because you've got fuckin' Bacon sittin' next to ya.'

To get things into perspective you had to see it in context. Since I'd moved back from America I'd been living at home, a terrace house overlooking the sea, that I shared with my mother, two brothers, Cas and Toad, and my sister Maddy. The atmosphere of the house was very laid back and liberal. The reason for this was my mother. After a difficult few years she'd got an unexpected inheritance from an old lady she used to care for, and now she was able to live life a little easier. As such, she had embraced middle age by re-kindling the youthful flame snuffed out by becoming a mother so young. The shackles of the habitual conservatism that ruled the first part of her life had been thrown off and she had replaced them with a pragmatic and very tolerant view of the world. This tolerance extended to her children and she was of the opinion that it was better to let us all get up to what we got up to under her roof than be doing it somewhere else. Although this sometimes made our house feel a little like a drop-in centre, her attitude made for no secrets, few tensions and a tight family unit.

Toad (a nickname that had stuck from the time he was in a cot) had just entered his teenage years. With a couple of older brothers who knew most of the curves and bends along the rocky road to adulthood my only fear for him was that he might rebel the other way and decide to become an accountant. Maddy was 19 and worked in a medical centre, and it was here that she'd first clapped eyes on Bacon. Not only was Bacon a copper, he was also CID, and in the circle of Liddleton acquaintances I moved in, that was tantamount to being one of the Devil's own. I had gone to great lengths to keep my sister's romance a secret. After all, letting it be known that my sister was going out with a copper wouldn't have been good for business.

Even though it was Bacon meeting the family for the first time, it was me who was feeling the nerves. Before his visit I tried to list the points not to be discussed at the dinner table, but the whole exercise was rather like trying to fit Pandora's Box with a plastic lid that was made for an ice cream tub. Eventually a heavy knock at the front door announced his arrival, and my mum invited him in (as I watched him step over the threshold, I was reminded of every bad vampire movie) and Maddy did the introductions. Bacon's real name was Terry, and I was aware that my palms were clammy when he shook my hand. He fixed me with a stare that was firm and probably meant to be friendly, but I couldn't help feeling he was trying to use it to read my mind. I let the hand drop and shifted around uncomfortably while my mother played the hostess, filling the silent gaps with small talk that wasn't going anywhere.

Bacon was about the same age as me, but not as big as I'd expected, his black hair cropped squaddy style, a thick coppers' moustache furring his top lip. He was wearing a white shirt tucked into jeans that were too narrow in the leg to be anything other than a cheap generic brand, and black shoes that looked like they'd been shined for the parade ground. He left a smell of aftershave wherever he stood. To calm my nerves I tried to imagine him doing another job – insurance salesman, shopkeeper, a farmer even – but it was no use, everything about him yelled copper, and very loudly. All through the small talk I did my best to guard my body language. Meanwhile, Cas had adopted the cocksure persona he adopted when he was working on the roofs. It was obvious by the way Maddy kept looking over, that neither of us were being ourselves. Toad on the other hand was oblivious to 'us' and 'them' divisions and was busy showing off. I was glad he was. It was a welcome distraction.

'He seems really nice,' whispered my mother to me, as I prepared drinks in the kitchen. 'Don't you think?'

'He's OK,' I replied, biting my tongue to prevent from adding 'for a copper'.

'You don't like him, then?' she asked, interpreting my reply like only a mother could. She was whispering, but loudly, and I flashed her a look that implored her to stop.

I took the drinks back through, dismayed to discover that the others had vanished, leaving the room with only the copper in it. I had no choice. Now I would have to engage the enemy.

'Are you local?' I asked.

He told me he was originally from Reading, but had been down here five years. He lived in a village nearby. 'And you?' he quizzed.

'Here,' I said. Surely he already knew that.

'Looking for your own place?'

'Not at the moment.'

'Right.' He wrapped a hand round the glass of wine in a way that told me tell he wasn't comfortable drinking from a glass with a stem. 'Cheers,' he added, giving me a strange look as I downed half my glass. 'Maddy tells me you've got your own business.'

'That's right.' I forced a smile.

'You make clothes or something, don't you?' How much more had she let slip from the pillow? 'Got an office down near the sea. Number 37. Red door isn't it?'

How did he know that? 'Yeah. That's right,' I said after a pause I could count in seconds.

'Business good?'

'Now's not too bad.'

'It must be tough working for yourself.'

'There are two of us, actually.'

'Yeah. Who's your partner?'

Oh no, I'd drawn Travis in too. 'An old mate.'

'What's his name?'

'Travis,' I said. Why did he want to know?

'Is that his first name or his last name?'

'Last.' It wasn't at all, it was his nickname.

'Right,' he said, obviously finding the conversation as hard going as I was. 'Where do you sell your stuff?'

'All over, really.' I reeled off the list of big cities that sounded more impressive than the little shops we dealt to within them.

'Do you sell anywhere in Liddleton?'

'Sometimes we sell from our…' I was going to say office, but decided against it. '…house. This house,' I reiterated pointing a finger, 'you know, when we've got stock we need to get rid of. Sales parties, that kind of thing.'

'Oh. Maddy said you sold stuff out of your office.'

'No,' I shook my head too hard. 'Not really.'

'That's a shame. I was just saying to her the other day that I needed to get some new clothes. Could have put a bit of business your way.'

And scared enough of it off. 'I don't know if we'd have anything your size, to be honest,' I said rubbing my nose in a way that he would have been right to interpret as a sign of guilt.

Fortunately, Toad's arrival saved me from further interrogation. He burst into the room with a grubby white garment in his hand. 'Don't move, you're under a-vest!' he yelled. It was the kind of corny teenage humour that I'd have normally dismissed with a scowl. Tonight, however, I laughed at his joke so hard the poor kid believed he had a glittering career in comedy ahead of him.

Dinner was a Q and A affair, with my mother doing most of the questioning. I concentrated on eating my food in a state of natural indifference, but the more I tried to act indifferently the more conscious I was of trying. I had hoped that alcohol would help me to relax but I was drinking so quickly it only seemed to make things worse. I kept my eyes on my plate when he expressed a preference for pork over lamb, and did my best to react to his story of a stolen work site generator and the ensuing car chase as if I didn't know the people involved. Nevertheless, it was looking like the evening might pass without further incident when my mother dropped a bomb into the gravy boat. Wine had loosened her tongue and the words that came next fell like scorching lumps of lava.

'…So every quote I got on the car was so ridiculously expensive that Che suggested I talk to a friend of his…'

She was talking about the Pig. I knew where this was going and I prayed for a comic diversion from Toad but he had his nose in the feedbag and couldn't be prompted.

One of the Pig's sidelines was dabbling with motors. It was the most legal of his various activities, but that wasn't saying a lot.

My mother continued. 'He took one look at my car and said he'd do the work for half of what everyone else was quoting.'

'Sounds like a handy bloke to know,' said Bacon, with a polite smile.

'He's lovely,' said my mother.

'Maybe I should give him a call. My car needs a bit of work doing before its MOT. What's his name?'

'Gosh, that's a point,' said my mother, turning to me. 'What is his name? I only know him as the Pig.'

'Oh no. It's not who I'm thinking of, is it?' said Bacon looking at me. As I've said before, the Pig had a big reputation in our small town and it didn't take much for Bacon to register the name on his radar, on- or off-duty. In unison, Cas and I gave nods that had cat-out-of-the-bag written all over them.

'I think I'll stay quiet on this one,' said Bacon, raising his eyebrows.

'Why, do you know him?' Why didn't my mother just hand us over right now?

'Our paths have crossed before,' he said tactfully, pushing peas around his plate. 'Let's just say that I've been round to his house a couple of times, but they weren't social calls.'

I wondered if he was the good cop or the bad cop.

'You didn't let him do the work on your car, did you, mum?' implored Maddy, showing a concern born out of a desire to impress her new boyfriend.

'Not yet. He's due to come over this week. Why, he's not dodgy, is he?'

'Well, if you asked me for my professional advice,' responded Bacon diplomatically, 'I'd suggest you get someone else to have a look at it.' He paused. 'But having said that, he's probably no more of a crook than the majority of garage owners out there.'

'Exactly,' clapped my mother, misinterpreting his professional tact for a full endorsement. 'I'm so glad it was you who said that.'

Bacon smiled uncomfortably. 'Know him well, do you?' He asked me.

Here we go. 'Friend of a friend,' I said, addressing a piece of potato snagged in his moustache.

'Good friend?'

I shrugged. 'You know what it's like. Liddleton's a small town.'

'Isn't it just,' he said, holding my gaze until I turned away. I aimed a kick at Toad under the table in the hope that he'd think it was Cas. I was looking to promote a diversionary dinner table argument.

'What?' said Toad, fixing his stare on me and me alone.

'What?' I feigned surprise.

'You kicked me under the table.'

'Sorry, mate, I thought it was the dog.'

But Toad didn't buy it, and from the expression on Bacon's face, I knew he wasn't buying it either...

Chapter Sixteen

August: Rural Rumble

Since our inspection of the farm Devon had been on the end of a five-day deluge of monsoon proportions, and the forecast for the party weekend was scattered showers, frequently heavy. We'd been fielding calls from our upcountry guests, concerned about the weather, and Travis and I had been reading from a well-worn script which went a little like this; 'Nah, man, it's hardly been raining at all. You people in the city forget, the climate's different down here. Besides, we've got a couple of barns. It'll all be fine…'

I'd told Carlos the truth, however. We'd colluded on many of our previous parties, and I was looking for some wise words of guidance.

'I'll be honest with you. The sites looking like the Somme. We've got four days to lay a new frigging road, or else we'll have to bring people in by tractor.'

'Is that an option?' he'd asked, deadpan.

'No. I was joking about that bit.'

'It sounds like you're up against the one thing you can't conquer.'

'What's that?'

'Nature.' Oh how easy to troubleshoot from behind a desk in a London. 'I'm sure it'll all work out,' he'd added. 'It always does.'

'I'm not so

sure this time.' I'd said through gritted teeth.

'That's what you always say,' he'd laughed.

I'd painstakingly typed out directions to the farm in a language that even the village idiot would be able to understand and sent them out with maps to contacts as far afield as Liverpool, Bristol, Birmingham and London. Like I said before, our parties had a bit of a reputation and, for many city slickers, our summer parties in Devon had become the poor man's Ibiza. We'd left spreading the word locally until the last minute to prevent arousing the suspicion of the local law enforcement. I had purposely avoided telling Maddy about the party, which I didn't like doing. I felt bad, but it wasn't really an option. Bacon may have won temporary membership to the family, but he was still a copper. Besides, what if he wanted to come along to the party as a civilian? That didn't even bear thinking about. Fortunately, they'd decided to go camping for the weekend.

'I don't know why you're so cloak and dagger,' my mother had clucked. 'He probably wouldn't care anyway.'

'Probably isn't good enough,' I'd replied.

'You don't understand, mum,' Cas had chided.

'I think he's a nice bloke.'

'So do I,' I replied. 'But he's a copper, and unfortunately we mix in different circles.'

'It's only a job, for God's sake. I think you two should just bloody well chill out!' she'd snapped impatiently.

It had taken a chain gang of unwilling conscripts and four days of heavy graft to lay the new road to the car park field. Despite our efforts the track was only just passable and none of us knew if it would be able to take the kind of traffic we were expecting. Expenses were mounting. Putting on a decent party didn't come cheap. We'd decided to run two sound systems – a drum and bass rig in the larger barn, and a hip hop sound in the stable. That meant money for the Pig's rig, DJ and MC travel costs and a whole bundle of miscellaneous expenses on top. I'd discussed things with the Pig, and we'd decided to run a gate. The farm lay at the end of a paved track, meaning we could charge people as they came in. Five quid a car was deemed a fair price. I'd managed to source some cheap bar stock by hooking up with a continental booze runner who was expecting a knock from Customs and Excise. We'd also sell teas and coffees. Cas had found a musty bag of powdered magic mushrooms he'd picked the year before that he was intending to brew, although I didn't think they were a good idea. There was nothing worse than a party full of twanged-out trippers.

The Pig was already setting up when Travis, Cas, and I turned up to the farm on the Saturday morning with a van full of booze, decks, mixers, and assorted crap. Soon after, the Grubby arrived with a couple of the skaters, and was soon wielding hammer and nails with the ferocity of Thor. We weren't trying to make the place look like a club as that would be missing the point – the rustic vibe was all part of the magic and the countryside surroundings were aesthetic enough – but it still took a few hours to get the place ready. There were still concerns regarding the state of the road, but fortunately the predicted showers hadn't materialised. Better than that, the sun was actually shining.

We finished up our work and lazed in the sun, smoking spliffs and drinking warm beers, as we ran through last minute logistics. The atmosphere was chilled and I should have been enjoying the summer's day, but I found it difficult to chill with so many things to be sorted at the last minute no matter how well prepared I was. There was an unpredictability that came with putting on an event in a deregulated environment. A club night was easy. You turned up to a purpose-built venue, whacked a few backdrops up, plugged in and were ready to roll. You didn't have to worry about security, or people finding the place, or a visit from the local rozzers halfway through the night. With a party, however, you had all these things to worry about, and it was usually me who did all the worrying. I hated the run up to a do. It was always filled with anxiety and doubt. Would people come? Would it get busted? Would it rain? Only time would tell.

My mum was away for the weekend and had left Toad in my care. I couldn't leave him behind so had brought him along with the proviso that he bring a tent to sleep in. He asked if he could bring his new girlfriend and I eventually relented. I'd made a trip back to Liddleton to pick up him and another load of sundries from the yard, and by the time I got back to the farm it was evening and the light was beginning to fade. The wind had dropped, the air was still, and as I drew close to the barn I could hear the gentle thud of a bass line. The Pig was running the system low, giving it a warm-up before the night kicked in. Natty had already arrived with four carloads from Kent, and was complaining they'd had to drive 15 miles to find the 'local' fish and chip shop. Carlos and Turnist had also turned up after a long drive from London.

'I've forgotten what clean air tastes like,' Carlos laughed. 'You boys have done it again.' He motioned to the glorious countryside that surrounded us.

'Tell me that tomorrow morning,' I grimaced.

Haze was lost somewhere, chasing around country lanes and periodically calling me up on the mobile to tell me the map was wrong.

'Haze. It's not wrong. It's taken from a road atlas.'

'I'm tellin' ya, Che, it's fuckin' wrong. All the roads look the same.' The signal was bad and his voice was cracking up.

'OK. Tell me what you see. At least give me a landmark.'

'Che, all I can see are fuckin' hedges or fields full of animals.'

'Keep an eye out for balloons,' I said. I'd marked the route with party balloons.

'Baboons?' screamed Haze before the signal went dead.

I was preparing to man the gate. I knew from experience that it was a job that few people either wanted or could be trusted to do. Punters didn't like paying in our neck of the woods and the Pig, knowing far too many people for his own good, was susceptible to the blag. But he was also blunt to the point of being intimidating, so I reasoned that so long as I kept a leash on him we could pull off a fairly effective good cop, bad cop routine. At 11 we made our way to the end of the track.

I'd left the Sewerside crew primed and in position. Cas was keeping an eye on the bar. He was also overseeing the security with a praetorian guard that included Big Dan, his deaf mate Danny D, and a couple of pill-popping roofing acquaintances you wouldn't want to get on the wrong side of. Travis was keeping an eye on the DJs, and the Pig had left his brother monitoring the sound systems. The Grubby was on standby with hammer and nails to deal with any maintenance issues. Carlos and Turnist had volunteered to organise the car parking. Experienced hands were at the helm and I knew I could rely on them all. The Sewerside guerrillas had secured the farm and were ready to rumble. However, in all my rushing around, I'd totally forgotten about the birthday boy. I saw Stig, on the way to the gate. He told me Scott was already fucked and had shut himself away in his farmhouse with a stash of drugs and a gang of hammerhead mates. It was all good...

The Pig and I took up our positions. We had acquired walkie talkies for the night, had a couple of heavy flashlights, and a flower pot to stash the cash in. There was no moon, and the sky above had the pitch of newly laid road tar and we talked the turkey and smoked cigarettes while we waited. By 11.30 I was starting to wonder if my worst fears were being realised. So far we'd only had five cars through the gate, and two of those had been filled with DJs and associates. We stared into the black searching out headlights and straining to hear the noise of approaching cars, but the only noise we heard was Toad. I heard him coming down the track, long before I could see either him or his girlfriend, or the large bottle of cider with only a couple of inches of backwash left inside.

'Awright, mate... my bruver... my best bruver,' he slurred, hugging me from the darkness.

I shrugged him off. 'What's it like down there?' I asked curtly.

'Pretty shit,' he said with a drunken honesty that stung. 'There's no one dancing except for some mad old woman who's trying to snog everyone.'

'Great,' I muttered.

'Do you want some cider?'

I got rid of him before he became the proverbial cat I kicked in frustration, and went back to scanning the horizon. At 11.45, our wait finally came to an end. We saw the headlights pretty early but it was only when they came over the brow of the hill that we were able to see another set behind, and another one behind that, until we counted 12 cars snaking down the country lane towards us.

'Here we go,' said the Pig, straightening the collar of his jacket like an usher preparing to greet the wedding guests. We had our routine all worked out. The Pig would flag the cars down with a torch and direct them into the mouth of the track at which point I would turn on my beam, block their way, and demand their cash. It was textbook highwayman stuff. Vehicles kept coming, the majority packed with more than the manufacturer's recommended passenger allowance; skaters in beaten-up bangers, free party ravers in the back of vans plastered with the names of local building contractors, rich club kids in parents' new cars and dusty Land Rovers filled with farmers' kids from the sticks. One pillock even turned up in a sports car. I counted 45 vehicles before the traffic got too heavy to count any more. Every so often the walkie talkie would crackle with urgent messages calls to halt the traffic coming down the lane as people were getting stuck in the mud of our new road. However, we had to keep things moving fast at our end so as to prevent traffic jams in the country lane. We'd heard from some that there was police activity on the main roads, and they'd obviously sussed there was a party going on but couldn't find it. It fuelled the fear, but I was sure it didn't matter anymore. There were far too many people on site for the party to be stopped now.

It was 2 o'clock when the Pig and I called it a day. The flower pot was filled with coins, and I had a wad of notes stuffed in my back pocket. We walked back up to the party and stumbled upon a scene that bore no resemblance to the one we had left behind hours earlier. Scott's farm was now teeming with people. The sound systems were firing close to full capacity and the bass was no longer a gentle rumble but a thunderous boom. We stopped by the big barn. Strobes and the strafe of coloured lights morphed the faces of those on the dance floor into one big swirl of movement as DJ Haze, the sorcerer's apprentice, threw down rhythm after rhythm.

I went to check out the stable. I stepped through the door into a wall of heat. Natty and his boys had unleashed the hip hop and the place was going wild. Natty clocked me pushing through the crowd and threw me a shout from the microphone. I nodded in reciprocation, and he mouthed back that he wanted a beer. At his side was Toad, a mic in hand, and before I knew what was happening, Natty had introduced him and the kid had begun dropping the rhymes he spent dinner times trying out on the family. I couldn't believe it when the crowd erupted in rapturous applause.

That night Toad got a new name. From now on, he'd be known as…

'Make some noise for Mr Kishi,' yelled Natty from the stage, his arm round Toad's shoulder. 'Next generation! Thirteen years old and you heard him here first…'

It took me a while to get to the besieged bar. I wriggled between the legs of those waiting for drinks, and pushed my way under the makeshift bar top. Cas flashed a look of irritation as I emerged beneath him. Realising who it was, he wrapped an arm round me.

'Did you see the boy on stage?' he laughed.

'Our little bro! What's all that Mr Kishi business though?' I shouted over the noise of the music.

Happy and smiling, he shrugged.

'Any problems?' I yelled cracking open a beer.

He shook his head.

'What about the car parking?'

'It's a fucking mess. But we'll worry about that in the morning.'

'I've just got some shit to sort out and then I'll be back to take over,' I told him.

It was that time of night when things were starting to take a turn for the weird as drugs and booze started to kick in. I called in behind the decks to say hello to Haze. He'd been melancholic since arriving and was extremely unhappy now. Some dickhead had sprayed the decks with one of the fire extinguishers. They were still covered in foam. There was always one. I looked at the guilty party who was sitting against the wall behind the decks, eyes rolling, conducting an imaginary orchestra with his hands. I went over and booted him. He flashed me a loony's grin and carried on conducting.

'Out,' I said.

'Wha'?' he stammered.

'Get the fuck out from behind here.'

I kicked him again. He got to his feet, lurched in my direction, and I pushed him hard against the wall. A couple of his mates came over and began to remonstrate with me until I told them what he'd done. Apologising, they dragged him away.

I was trying my best to sit back and observe the party but it was difficult. It's not that I wanted to be working, I just couldn't stop, and secretly I didn't want to. Despite the frown marks etched onto my forehead and a look on my face that made people get out of the way, I was actually enjoying myself. For me, the act of pulling it all off was the biggest buzz of all. I didn't stay in one place too long. I flitted between barns, did stints on the bar with Cas and Big Dan, serving up teas, coffees and the occasional Farmhouse Special, an evil brew consisting of coffee, brandy and two heaped teaspoons' of powdered magic mushrooms.

'What's it like?' I asked Big Dan.

'Fuckin''orrible, mate,' he said. 'Just the smell makes me gag. Natty seems to like it though. He's been drinking them all night.'

Against my better judgement, I went to take a look at the car park. The road that we had so diligently laid a few days before had practically disappeared under the weight of so many vehicles passing over the top of it. People had given up trying to get down there, and had abandoned cars wherever they could. The red sports car that had wheel spinned down the track earlier in the night was stuck in a rut of its own making. The driver of the car was losing it. His sporty number may have ruled the roads, but in the middle of the field it had been reduced to a heap of metal with an engine in it.

The party was still rattling away at full tilt. It was around four, and to the east the sky was beginning to pale. The temperature had dropped, the cooling ground giving rise to a mist that was so thick it blanked out the landscape around us. I went to seek the Pig in his office. He was sitting in a deck chair, his hands crossed over the hump of his belly, legs outstretched. I looked up to see Haze shuffle in behind me.

'Gents,' he nodded. He was subdued, and the colour of his face matched the white puffer jacket he was wearing. He didn't look well.

'That's a brave move,' I said.

'What's that?'

'Wearing white to a party on a farm.'

'I s'pose,' he shrugged, digging his hands deeper into his pockets and yawning.

'You all right?' I asked.

'Not really. Just can't seem to get into it.' He pushed his baseball cap to the back and started scratching his head. 'I'm a bit darked out to be honest. Ain't slept for a couple of days. 'Ad a heavy session Friday night and done all the drugs I was supposed to be bringing down 'ere. Hit the old rocks a bit 'ard.'

Haze had been smoking crack for the past couple of months and I wasn't the only one who was concerned. It had started off as odd toot here and there but recently had turned into a habit. He'd called me a few times in the early hours of the morning, coming down from sessions that had lasted a couple of days, crying down the phone that he couldn't breathe and was about to die.

'You should knock that shit off,' I told him.

'Yeah. I should do. Listen, I'm thinkin' of headin' off.'

'You're joking?'

'Nah. Old Bovva wants to get back to Colchester. And I've got work tomorra.'

'You want some expenses?'

He nodded.

I needed to sort out a few bits of money, so I went to the van with the Pig as there would be fewer interruptions. It was cold in there and the Pig's feet were wet after treading through the dewy grass (I'd been wearing wellington boots all night – Hey, I was putting on the party, I could wear what the fuck I liked), so I turned on the engine and whacked up the heat.

'Do you want a line?' he asked.

'I don't know.' I was feeling quite pleased with having made it this far without any chemical enhancement. I was exhausted though, starting to feel it in my legs, and there was still a while left to go so I took him up on his offer. The coke was enough to pick me up by the scruff of the neck and breathe some energy into me – the best lines were always the ones that came when you were exhausted. I counted the money. We had almost six hundred quid, a hundred in shrapnel. I gave the Pig three and took the rest to pay off the DJ's travel expenses.

'What about the kid?' asked the Pig, referring to Scott.

'I think he's had a pretty good birthday party,' I replied.

'Yeah,' The Pig yawned.

'Not a bad old night,' I added. 'No sign of the rozzers, either.'

'No. There were a couple of undercover here though.'

'How do you know?'

He shrugged. 'That's what I heard. Could just be party rumours though.'

'Let's fucking hope so.' I said, Terry's face looming large in my imagination.

When we emerged from the van, the sky was split in two by an east–west divide, light at one end and pitch black at the other. I looked in on the dance floor in the big barn. The driving rhythm and bass that had bundled the crowd through the night was starting to sound tedious with the coming of dawn, and the only souls still dancing were the speed freaks and the hardcore. I went into the stable where Natty and the boys had finally hung up their microphones. Carlos had taken over the helm, flicking classic soul 45s that brought out the smiles, and plenty of people were still grooving. Big Dan, wearing shades, was slouched over the bar top. I passed beneath him but he didn't stir.

'Dan?' I said.

'Yes, mate,' he replied, without moving.

'I thought you were asleep.'

'No, mate, just fucked.'

'How's business?'

'Teas and coffees mostly.'

Behind the bar, Cas's deaf mate Danny D was sitting on an upturned crate, a cup of tea in his hands. The beers had pretty much gone and the floor behind the bar was wet and littered with ripped packaging, empty cans and crumpled plastic cups.

'Good party?' I mouthed.

He grinned and gave the thumbs up sign. I wondered if he had any concept of the sounds that were going on around him. Cas told me that he got off on the vibrations, which I suppose made sense.

'Where's Cas?'

He shrugged and held up a hand for me to wait. He rooted around under the debris and fished out six plastic cups, three of them packed tight with bundles of notes, the others filled with more shrapnel. I found a corner and sat down to count it. We'd made four hundred profit on the bar. It meant Travis and I would be in for a little cash bonus.

Outside it was light. Dawn had taken hold of the new day, and the sun was beginning its journey across the sky, which had turned a mixture of pink and blue. The curtain of mist was beginning to dissipate and the majority of partygoers had abandoned the dance floor and taken to fields filled with hay bales, or leant over fences, nodding their heads to the music, eyes on the sunrise. It was my favourite time at a party, the birth of a new day. As I sipped on my coffee and watched the sun rising I felt strangely elated. Someone caught my eye and nodded. It was the munter who had let the fire extinguisher off somewhere in the madness of the early hours. I wondered if he remembered what he'd done. It didn't matter, bygones were bygones, and I nodded back.

I found Travis round the back of the barns, sitting in a corner that was already trapping what heat the sun had to offer. He was leaning against the wall, his eyes closed. Natty and a couple of his hip hop crew sat beside him rolling spliffs. They nodded as I came over.

'Travis.' I tapped his leg gently with my foot, and he opened his eyes. 'How's it going?'

'Shattered,' he replied.

I nodded, and eased myself down beside him. 'Good night, though.'

'Wicked night,' he smiled. 'How long are we going on for?'

'Until nine, maybe ten.'

'What's the time now?'

'Just gone seven.'

He nodded. 'I'm going to have to make a move soon. Do the Sunday family thing. If I can keep my eyes open, that is.'

I nodded. 'Listen. I'm going to go and see how things are in the car park. I bet it's not a pretty picture this morning.'

He nodded. 'Got some cash for you,' he said.

I stood up too fast and had a rush of blood to the head that made me feel as if I were about to faint. I dropped to my knees and waited for it to pass. 'Keep hold of it for now. I've got too much money to deal with at the moment.'

'I fucking hope some of it's for me?' piped Natty, cackling to nobody in particular.

'Didn't Travis tell you?'

'What's that?'

'You got paid in Farmhouse Specials.'

'Don't!' he howled. 'I ain't never going to be the same again. I do not have a single clue what I was rapping about last night.'

I left them in the sunshine and I headed off on my way to the car park field. As I walked, I clocked a couple of girls walking towards me. They were wrapped up in jackets against the early morning chill, holding hands and laughing. One of them, a pretty girl with short blonde hair, the bottom of her jeans wet from walking through the long grass, looked up at me. I nodded and she returned the smile I threw her way. Neither of us said anything in that moment and neither of us had to. I knew what she was thinking. It was as if we were sharing the same secret. The smile between us had 'glad to be alive' written all over it. I carried on walking, the sun now burning orange above the tops of a copse of trees on the brow of the hill. I breathed in a lungful of morning air and even though I was plodding through the farmyard in my wellies, I felt like I was ten feet tall...

Chapter Seventeen

<u>September: Pork Roast</u>

We hadn't seen Haze since the party but I'd heard he'd been losing it in London. Eventually, I'd had a call from him.

'Che,' he'd wheezed down the phone.

'Haze. How are you?'

'Not good, mate, I've just come out of 'ospital. Went a bit over-board at the weekend.'

'In what way?'

'Took too many tinkers after a day on the rocks. Ended up collapsing in a club and bein' taken to 'ospital. Doctors pumped me stomach an' that. Proper told me I almost died.'

'Haze, you've got to slow down,' I implored.

'That's what they said. Was quite funny in a dark kind of way. Apparently, I was walkin' round casualty taking drinks orders. Fought the reception was a bar.' It wasn't funny but I couldn't help laughing at the image. 'It got worse than that. Turned round and saw a geezer walk past me with a 25-pound carp that wasn't even there. I fink it done 'im in as much as it done me.'

'Haze,' I'd told him, 'you've got to get a grip. You can't keep caning like this. You've got to learn moderation.'

'You're right,' he said with muted resignation.

'I know I'm right, mate. Look, I've been around the block enough times. I've had mates lose it on drugs and I've had mates lose their lives on drugs. You understand?'

'Yeah, I see what you're sayin' and it's all true, bruv. It's the rocks though, Che. Those fuckin' rocks send me crazy.'

Two days later, I'd got a call from the Turnist to tell me Haze had been in a car accident. He'd been coming back from a party when the driver ran a red light, collided with a truck and flipped over. Haze and the driver had been trapped inside the wreckage for three hours while firemen tried to cut them free. The driver died on the way to hospital and Haze had almost gone the same way. One of his legs had been broken and the other had been completely shattered. They'd just sewn him up, pieced him together with pins and sent him home after a couple of days because they needed his hospital bed.

In a strange way, though, the accident was probably the best thing that could have happened to him. He'd been hurtling through the summer towards a crash of a different kind and at least now he couldn't do any more drugs, even if he wanted to.

On other fronts, there had been little time to rest on the laurels of a successful party, and we'd soon been on the march again, hitting and running in the name of operation cash flow. It was tempting to think that we could carry on going but I had to remind myself that the last three months were as good as it got. So it was that halfway through September our summer offensive ground to a halt.

We'd been sailing very close to the wind of our overdraft limit. I'd been putting just enough in to ensure that the loan repayments and a cluster of direct debits got covered each month, but that was about it. I covered my tracks with optimistic conversations with the bank manager, the promise of big things coming down the line. He was too busy worrying about surviving the corporate downsizing that was taking place and fortunately craved reassurance more than hard evidence. He even offered us another loan. I felt kind of bad stringing him along, but if he wanted to believe the let's pretend stories I was feeding him, then so be it. At least it gave us more time.

We'd stopped selling to shops altogether now. We had stock reserves left but they were dwindling and what we really needed was one big cash hit to clear the lot. The weed money was keeping us in petty cash for now, but I didn't like it. Liddleton was too small a town to keep your head down and avoid attention for long and with Bacon now popping up with an alarming regularity at home, it only added to my anxiety. Thoughts of the end game had never been far from our minds but it was like having a toothache that came and went. When you were in pain you'd think about making an appointment with the dentist, but you forgot about it once the tooth stopped hurting.

On top of everything else I was under pressure from the dole. I'd been in for another three-month review and been told that getting the long-term unemployed back to work had become a key objective in the district. As such, I'd been told, I had to attend Job Club.

'There's some great bonuses,' bubbled Tina, my personal adviser. 'I think it will be a great help to you. You have full use of the computers and photocopier and you can use as many free stamps and envelopes as you like.' I'd asked her what the alternative was. She'd frowned and told me there wasn't one if I wanted to continue to be eligible for benefits.

I hopped out of the car, and ran the rest of the way to Job Club. It was my first meeting and I was late. The office had a new paint and disinfectant smell that was synonymous with doctors' waiting rooms and village halls. It took place on the top floor of a building, and was arranged around three working rooms, partitioned by paper-thin walls. The woman behind the desk gave me a glance that said 'lazy-arsed slacker', and pointed to a door. I knocked and entered before getting a reply. The room was small, cramped with a couple of desks and three computers and a circle of uncomfortable plastic chairs. Bored faces sat around the bespectacled woman addressing them. Everyone looked up when I walked in.

'And you are?' beamed the woman, peering over the top of her spectacles.

'Late,' I said. 'Sorry.'

'No, your name?'

'Che.'

'Of course you are. Grab a seat.' She mouthed the words slowly in a way that was patronising without being intentional. 'My name's Joan Fielgud,' she added. 'Just call me Joan though. We don't stand on ceremony here. You've missed a bit of the presentation, but I'll go over it quickly again for your benefit. Sorry folks,' she apologised to nobody in particular. Nobody in particular gave a silent groan and narrowed their eyes.

My other Job Club peers included a roly-poly man with pens sticking out of his shirt pocket, a blind man with a serene smile and a guide dog called Bouncer, a woman in her 40s whose permanent scowl hinted at a history of mental illness and two bored teenagers who looked like they'd just left school.

'Obviously, the reason you're all here,' said Joan, 'is that you've been unemployed for a long time. I'm sure you're all a bit rusty so we'll take things nice and easy. And please, if you don't understand anything just ask. Now if you look into your folders, you'll find a copy of the Job Club agreement. It's not as scary as it looks, but represents your commitment to attend at least three times a week until you find work.'

Three times a week?

Joan rambled on. 'We're informal here so if you want to go to the toilet, just go. It's not like you have to have my permission or anything.' She paused waiting for polite laughter, but it didn't come. 'I can see we're not very lively today,' she laughed softly herself. 'The same goes for tea and coffee. Help yourself, but please, please, please, wash up after you. One more thing, please can you make sure your mobile phones are switched off. There's nothing more distracting when you're trying to concentrate.'

We left the 'briefing room', and were taken next door to the 'resources room'. Newspapers covered a table in the middle and the shelves were stacked with manuals, supposedly stuffed with handy tips to get us back into work. Our induction tour lasted the best part of an hour. Joan moved round the room explaining everything from changing the size of the paper on the photocopier to how to turn off the computer. She went through it all, to the tiniest detail, and my head ached with the tedium of it all. I was grateful when she finally declared it was lunch break. I went downstairs for a cigarette. I caught up with the two teenagers who were already smoking.

'What do you think of it so far?' I asked.

'Shite,' said one. The other just shrugged.

After lunch, we were ushered back into the briefing room for a health and safety talk. This covered everything from fire drill procedures to how to pick up heavy boxes without straining your back. I asked her if we were likely to be picking up any heavy boxes in the Job Club.

'No,' she laughed. 'Still, better to be safe than sorry. There's no such thing as too much health and safety.'

Then it was back to the resources room, where Joan held up a copy of a sample CV. 'Now I'm sure all of you are familiar with what a CV is, even if you haven't written one before. CV is short for 'Curriculum Vitae' which comes from Latin – not Italian as someone in another group thought.' She paused again, still waiting for that polite ripple of laughter, but the only sound was Bouncer panting. 'It's your chance to sell yourself. I like to think of it as a shop window, a place where people can browse. Like an item in a shop window, you want to stand out so you can grab the employer's attention.'

For the best part of an hour, we went through the CV writing process until eventually we were deemed fit to be let loose on the computers. 'Don't worry if you don't get it finished today. There's no rush. I'd rather you took your time and gave it some real thought. I always say if a job's worth doing it's worth doing well.'

It didn't take long for me to type up mine (fictionalised, of course) and I asked if I could go. 'What's your name?' she asked, 'Speedy Gonzales?'

I forced a meek smile.

'I can't let you go until four. It's in your agreement,' she added, tapping my file. 'Why don't you take a comfy chair and look through some job sections in the papers.'

Seething, I grabbed a paper off the table. I didn't bother looking at the job section because I wasn't looking for a job, so I read the sports section instead and eavesdropped on Joan as she typed out the blind man's CV.

'Have you got any disabilities?' she asked.

'Yeah. I can't see,' said the blind man.

'Course you can't. Gosh, aren't I silly? Ignore that. You'll have to excuse me, you're the first visually impaired person I've had up here.'

'I'm not visually impaired,' he chirped, 'I'm totally blind.'

'I'm not sure we're allowed to use that term,' said Joan, looking worried.

'Why not?'

'Some people might find it offensive.'

'But I am.'

'Right,' she said, like she wasn't really sure. 'Well, let's put down visual impairment for now, and we can sort it out later.' She tapped away for a minute or so, before the computer screen froze. 'Hmmm,' she frowned, 'looks like this is a good time to call it a day. OK folks, I'll see you all back here on Wednesday. You've survived your first day. Now tell me, it wasn't that bad, was it?'

If she'd been expecting a reaction she didn't get one.

Released from Job Club, I made my way down to the yard, carrying that dumb folder with me like it was a ball and chain. Unwittingly, the Job Centre had given me an incentive to get off the dole, even if it wasn't the incentive they'd intended. The thought of spending three days a week at Job Club was something I couldn't even start to comprehend.

Lesnik was on the stairs when I came into the building, talking with a man wearing a suit and a hard hat. 'I'm going to need to get into your office,' he sniffed. 'This gentleman is a structural engineer and he's surveying the building.'

'OK,' I said, letting them in. Travis wasn't around and fortunately the yard smelt of nothing more innocuous than gone-off milk. It looked a bit of a state, but it was rare that it didn't. I hadn't got around to setting the place straight after the summer campaign, and it was filled with piles that hadn't been moved since being dumped there after one event or another. Stock boxes were untidily stacked, the contents spilling over the top of them, and lights, tarpaulins, speaker leads, backdrops and accumulated crap covered the floor. I left them to it and turned my computer on.

As I waited for it to boot up, I caught snatches of conversation. Lesnik was talking about the various crack lines in the brickwork. They'd been there long before we had, but I knew he was desperate to pin them on us. He spoke in hushed tones, which naturally stirred my curiosity and although they moved out of earshot, I noticed the man in the hard hat kept shaking his head, as if he was disagreeing with what Lesnik was saying.

They left and I made a couple of calls but it wasn't long before Lesnik knocked on the door again. He looked smugly contented. 'I just thought I'd inform you that I have proof that you've undermined the structure of the building,' he said sanctimoniously.

'I don't believe you.'

He looked taken aback, only confirming my suspicions. 'Are you calling me a liar? You saw the engineer yourself.'

'Yeah, I saw him shaking his head a lot.'

'What's that supposed to mean?'

'Nigel,' I said. He cringed. He was the kind of bloke who liked to be known as 'Nige'. 'You know as well as I do that this is an old building and I've told you before that the cracks were here when we moved in.'

'Can you prove that?'

'Of course I can't prove it.'

'Then I'm afraid you're going to have to contribute to the repairs. You're legally obliged to maintain your share of the building, you know.'

'Meaning?'

'You wait and see.' His beady eyes sparkled with spite.

God, I wanted to take that lank ponytail and use it to throttle the fucker with, but the ring of the telephone saved me from a lengthy jail sentence for his murder.

'Nigel. I'm very busy. Thank you for your time, but I really do have to get on,' I said with a feigned weariness that I knew would make his blood pressure rise. I closed the door on him and answered the phone. It was the Pig.

'Hello, chap. I'm in the neighbourhood. Just checking to see if you're in.'

'Come on over.'

The Pig looked pleased with himself. He slapped his mobile and a large bundle of keys on top of my desk and pulled out a packet of cigarettes.

'I've got a bit of news,' he said, hopping from one foot to another and blinking furiously. 'I've just had a meeting with Micky.'

'Vendell?' The Pig had been doing a fair bit of work for him recently.

'Who else?' spluttered the Pig, irritated that I'd interrupted his flow.

'Go on.'

'You know the Golden Shower.' I knew the holiday complex he was talking about. With a name like that who didn't? 'Well, Micky's just bought it. Signed the papers today and he gets the keys next week.'

'Don't tell me he's going into the tourist business?'

The Pig gave an incredulous snort. 'Is he fuck. Do you know how much social security spend out in housing benefits?'

I shrugged.

'Well, let's put it this way. There's 50 chalets at the Golden. In rent alone you're talking about five grand a month, never mind what can be screwed out of people for utilities. Not only that, he's got a grant to do them up, which is worth so much money it's ridiculous.'

'How come?'

'Because he's going to fill the place with the kind of punters that no one else wants to give housing to.'

'Like who?'

'Fuck knows. Alcoholics, drug addicts, asylum seekers, people from up north, you name them.'

'So why's it good news?'

'Have you seen the Golden?' I shook my head. 'As well as the chalets it comes with a main building which has got three decent sized rooms in it and a late-night bar license.'

'And?'

'And – if you'll let me finish, you munter – he wants to start doing club nights down there. You're looking at the new entertainments manager.' He proudly poked his chest. 'I get my own fucking office and everything.'

'You are joking?'

'Am I fuck. Start tomorrow, and I want to set up a meeting with you boys about putting a night on.'

'Well, talk to me about it now.'

'I'd prefer it if you came to see me in my office.'

'Don't be weird.'

'All right then,' he replied, somewhat disappointed to have to talk the turkey here and not in his new office. He reached into his back pocket for the crumpled piece of paper he called his diary. 'OK. I've sorted these dates for you. First one's in three weeks.'

'Don't give us too much notice, will you?' I said sarcastically.

'Travis'll do us a flyer, won't he?'

'Don't know, mate. You'd better ask him. What kind of budget are we talking about?'

'Whatever you need.'

'What, and Vendell's going to back it?'

'Doesn't matter,' shrugged the Pig. 'Things are going pretty well at the moment, and once the club's up and running they'll be a whole lot better. Money won't be a problem, chap.'

I didn't have to look very far behind the words to see where the

Pig was coming from. While we did a bit of wheeling and dealing to subsidise our business, wheeling and dealing was the Pig's business. His missus was expecting another kid and he'd stepped up his activities on the black market to pay for it.

In the whole scheme of things the Pig wasn't a Mr Big or even a Mr Nice. That was the thing about the drugs business. There may be barons sitting at the top, but it's a long ladder and the Pig was always going to be clawing around on the bottom rungs. While the Pig shifted a lot of consumables his operation was always going to be more cottage industry than cartel. His merchandise came to him on credit and because he was running his business in Liddleton his customers bought on credit too. Somewhere along the line he scraped a living off the margins but it was hard work and if a consignment got lunched, or busted, the Pig became liable for the merchandise that hadn't been paid for. It didn't take an economist to deduce the system was flawed.

'I'd be careful if I were you, Archie,' I warned.

'Course I'm fucking careful,' the Pig retorted.

This was a lie. To be a successful drug dealer you needed the guile of a fox, the stealth of a leopard and the anonymity of a pigeon, but the Pig at his blundering best had none of these qualities.

'Just watch your back.'

'At the end of the day I need the money, Che. Got the missus about to pop and I'm telling you, sprogs don't come cheap.'

'What about your new job?'

'I've told Micky wages are secondary until the club's up and running properly. I'm looking at this long-term.'

'Archie,' I groaned. It was bad enough making a pact with the Devil, let alone giving him your soul on a six-month free trial.

'Don't you worry about me, chap. Things are looking up and life's looking good. Anyway, if you've noticed, I've changed my identity.'

'How?' I asked incredulously.

'Had my hair cut, haven't I.' He took his cap off to show me.

'You're winding me up?'

Unfortunately he was being serious. 'I'm telling you. I've had three people walk past me on the street and not recognise me.'

'Just be careful,' I snapped, irritated at his Pig-headed logic.

There was a knock at the door that I ignored.

'Aren't you going to get that?' the Pig asked.

'No. It's probably the landlord.'

'Like that, is it?'

'You don't want to know.'

I hoped he would go away, but he kept banging on the door. 'Jesus Christ,' I fumed, 'I swear I'm going to kill him.'

But it wasn't Lesnik at the door, it was Bacon, and the sight of him there caught me by surprise.

'There you are,' he said, 'I was just about to leave.'

'Terry,' I said. My body language was defensive and I remained wedged between the door and the wall.

'Well, can I come in?'

'Sure,' I said, not moving.

'After you,' he added, looking slightly puzzled.

I backtracked through the door, and tried to signal a warning to the Pig. Predictably, he was oblivious to anything I was doing and had his tongue wrapped round a cigarette paper busily in the process of wrapping one up. I leaned against a stock shelf trying to look casual. 'So Terry, what can I do you for?' I asked.

'I've got a bag of Maddy's.' He gestured to the holdall in his hand as he swept an eye round the yard. He clocked the Pig, but only his back as fortunately he was hunched over the desk busy rolling his joint. 'She said to leave it here.'

'Sure. Let me take it off you.'

'Now that I'm up here, though, thought I might have a browse.'

'Fine, fine, that's totally fine,' I replied, aware that my tone was far too ingratiating. Fortunately there was a rail with some gear on it within easy reach. I pulled it over so that it better obscured the view of the Pig. 'Take a look through this rail. If you find anything you like, tell me, and I'll find you the size and colour.'

'How much are these?' he asked, picking up a couple of T-shirts.

'Fifteen a piece.'

I looked over to the Pig. He'd finished rolling his joint and now had it in his mouth, his phone clamped to his ear. He exhaled as the person on the other end picked up the call. 'Hello, chap. It's me... Greg around?... No? OK, can you give him a message from me... Just tell him it's green.' I didn't know if Bacon was listening or not, but from where I was standing I could hear the conversation clear as crystal.

'What was that, mate?... No, not until Thursday... Got some of the other though... ScoobEES... Yeah.' The Pig was now absent-mindedly walking in our direction as he talked, and obviously not receiving the telepathic message I was trying to send him. 'OK, chap. Do us a favour and tell Greg I need the paperwork too…' He took a big lug on the joint, blinked as the smoke hit his eyes, and carried on walking towards us. '…OK, mate, speak to you later. Cheers.'

Bacon didn't look up because he was looking in a mirror with a pair of trousers held up against him. The Pig didn't look up because as far as he was concerned Bacon was just another punter dropping in after work. But then it happened. Bacon and the Pig lifted their gaze at exactly the same moment, with nothing between them but the clothes rail and a sweet-smelling fug of smoke. From where I was standing, I saw them both double take.

'Jesus,' spluttered the Pig, spitting the joint on the floor and pretending to cough. Bacon looked at me and raised his eyebrows. I looked at Bacon and grinned sheepishly. The Pig looked first at Bacon and then at me.

'Evening,' said Bacon, breaking the embarrassed silence.

'Evening.'

'Have you two met?' I asked.

'Oh yes,' said Bacon, his eyes narrowed.

The Pig nodded. 'He's been round my house before, haven't you, mate?'

I tried to look surprised.

Bacon smiled. 'Once or twice. I almost didn't recognise you with your clothes on.'

'Is this business or...?' The Pig asked casually.

Bacon gave a short scoff. 'Don't worry yourself, mate, I'm not on duty.'

'I thought you boys were always on duty.'

'Well, that depends on whether there's a law being broken,' said Bacon, flashing a crocodile's smile.

'That's fine by me,' said the Pig, bowing his head in deference. 'I'm just up here for the same reason you are.'

'Just a couple of blokes looking at clothes, eh?'

'Yeah. That's right,' nodded the Pig, picking up the sleeve of a sweatshirt for inspection.

Bacon smiled again and turned back to me. 'How much for the trousers?'

'Forty,' I said.

'Do I get a family discount?'

The Pig looked confused.

'Thirty-five.'

'Sold.' He reached for his wallet.

'Don't you want to try them on?'

'No. They look like the right size. If not, I know where to find you,' he laughed.

I bagged up Bacon's purchase and handed it over. 'Right,' he said, 'that's my shopping done. Tell Maddy I'll pick her up around eight.' He nodded to the Pig. 'See you around,' he said. 'You shouldn't smoke, by the way. It's bad for your health.'

The Pig said nothing for a few moments as we listened to Bacon's footsteps retreating down the stairs. Once he was sure he'd left the building, he erupted. 'You know who that fucking is don't you?'

'Yes. I know.'

'What the fuck's he doing up here?'

'He's going out with my sister,' I said apologetically.

It took him a couple of seconds to take the information on board.

'Why didn't you tell me that before?' he roared.

'Sorry, mate, I didn't exactly want to shout about it.'

'Last time I saw that bastard he was kicking down my door and dragging me out of bed in nothing but a pair of socks.'

'You go to bed in your socks?' I asked, struck by the ridiculousness of his statement.

'Course,' snorted the Pig like it was the most obvious thing in the world. 'Not in the summer, obviously.'

'Obviously,' I echoed.

'Did he hear me on the phone?'

'I don't know.'

'Did you hear me?'

'Course I heard you.'

'Why the fuck didn't you stop me then?'

'Believe me, I tried, mate. Maybe I just heard you because he was here.'

The Pig shrugged. 'Oh well, there's fuck-all we can do about it now. Anyway, he probably wouldn't have known what I was talking about.'

'How do you figure that?'

'You heard me. I was talking in code.'

'Archie,' I said exasperated. 'A fucking police dog could break your code.'

Chapter Eighteen

The day we'd picked to see the accountant was somehow appropriate. The coming of autumn had brought a succession of Atlantic squalls that had stripped the trees of their leaves and recast our surroundings in drizzle-drenched bleakness. We sat drinking coffee, waiting for the accountant to finish with a client. Travis had looked bored. He didn't like being in this sort of environment and tended to switch off where figures were concerned. He wouldn't have been there at all if it wasn't for the fact that he had to be.

'Right then,' the accountant said when we sat down in his office. 'What can I do for you two?'

We'd spent the past three months carrying around the tactical withdrawal between us like a guilty secret. Nobody knew what we were planning to do, not even the rest of the crew. The accountant was the first person we'd told. Travis left me to do most of the talking and I gave him all the facts. He listened intently as I explained it was only a matter of time before the business ran aground, whether we had a say in it or not. The accountant turned to Travis. 'What have you got to lose?' he asked him.

'How do you mean?'

'Do you own your house?'

'No,' Travis laughed.

'Do you have any savings?'

'No.'

'Do you have any assets?'

Travis thought for a moment before answering. 'My record collection.'

He'd been serious, but the accountant brushed him away with a wave of his hand. 'The answer is simple. I assume you already know it. You have two choices. You either file for bankruptcy, or you wait until one of your creditors does it for you. The choice is yours. In the meantime, I suggest you get your accounts in order and start thinking about the liabilities you want to list. When you've made your decision let me know.'

It was true, the accountant hadn't told us anything that we hadn't already known, but the visit had been the first psychological hurdle. Nevertheless, the visit also confirmed that our whole adventure really was about to come to a close and precipitated my fall into a dark depression as black as the brooding autumnal skies outside. There was nothing to look forward to but uncertainty, and the taint of failure. As I started getting our books in order, poring over the last four years of figures that told the story of our business, a melancholic introspection began to stir within me. I felt nostalgic cramps for times gone by that would never be seen again. I didn't know what would come next, but I was sure of one thing, it would be the end of an era. And accompanying the nostalgia were the stabbing pains of self doubt, brought on by the knowledge that as a business we had failed.

So it was that I was walking into work one day when I found my gaze following the lines between the flagstones on the pavement. It made me think of a game I used to play when I was a kid. Don't step on the cracks because the bears would eat you if you did. That was the way I was feeling in my head. I'd slipped through the cracks and was running from the bears whose jaws were snapping at my heels. I was 30 and still living at home. I didn't have a pot to piss in. All my possessions could be packed into a rucksack. All my savings had gone, sunk into the business, and I had nothing to show for it except a few new clothes. Where did it all go wrong? I asked myself over and over and over.

When I'd first swaggered through the door, fresh from America,

I'd had dreams of a business empire and a belief that I was going to make Travis and myself the money to live out our dreams. It was me who was supposed to be the organiser. It was me who was supposed to be the businessman. It was me who was supposed to guide us to the pot of gold at the end of the rainbow. But it hadn't happened that way. We'd fallen through the cracks and become stuck in a world where hustling had become a way of life, a way to survive, the only way to survive.

I wasn't bothered about stitching up the bank. As far as I was concerned, the bank and the credit card companies were fair game – it was stitch or be stitched with them. It was the weak ones like us that kept them in spare change, paralysed and helpless and gasping for the air to breathe, while they sucked our lifeblood away with constant charges and crippling interest payments. I know what you're thinking. We were happy enough to take the money off them in the first place, and now things hadn't worked out it was easy for us to lay the blame at someone else's door. Yes we'd taken the money, but it had already been running back into the pockets of the system before it had hit our own. It was never really our money at all. Our business was just another fly caught up in the globalised web, and while we may have created a temporary buzz with the frenetic beating of our wings, we'd never really been anything more significant than the next meal for the spider at the core. As for the creditors, I'd made sure we'd paid off the small ones and the bigger fish wouldn't be left so high and dry. Except for the bank and the credit card companies we weren't taking anyone for a ride, and that was probably where I'd gone so wrong. You needed to be a bastard to be good at business. You needed to be a hard-nosed cunt willing to step on the face of anyone who got in your way, but I wasn't. We weren't. We were the quiet tribe from the hills who'd greet our enemies with smiles, and be wiped out because of it.

My thoughts brewed ever darker, ever more questioning. What had we achieved in the past four years? We'd put a few clothes on people's backs, brought some entertainment along the way and put a few smiles on people's faces, but so what? Nothing had changed. Life would go on without us. And then my thoughts turned selfish; why hadn't I just taken the easy option in the first place? Why hadn't I just got myself a safe, reliable career with a ladder I could work my way up? Spent my life worrying about pension schemes and mortgages, job security and dishwashers that blew up on a Tuesday afternoon?

I knew the answers, of course, but the cloud above my head was too black for the light to filter through. I hadn't fallen through the cracks at all. I'd jumped through them. We all had. And running with the bears?

Running with the bears was part of the fun, you dummy...

I'd spent the best part of two weeks at home, locked into the accounts and rifling through filing cabinets for receipts and scraps of paper. When I wasn't doing this, I was hanging out with my new pals down at the Job Club. I'd tried desperately to snap out of my malaise, to wake up the next morning and roar out of bed with the fury of the beast. But instead I woke each morning only to slump deeper into the depressed rut I'd dug for myself.

I was in the yard, looking for a receipt. It was cold inside, and raining out. Travis wasn't there. We were working swing shifts again. While I'd buried myself in the accounts and darkest thoughts, he'd thrown himself headlong into his artwork. I knew he'd worked right through the night because the kettle was still warm, and a half-finished canvas was stapled to one of the walls. The phone rang.

'Hello.'

'Is that Che?' said the voice on the other end of the phone. It was shrill and could belong to only one person.

'Felicity?' I hadn't spoken to her since the Party Porpoise fashion show.

'Yes, darling, it's Fliss,' she cooed as if she was talking to a baby. 'I want to talk to you about something.'

'What about?'

'Well, we've changed our mind.'

'About what?'

'About being a pressure group. We've decided that it's all very well throwing parties but we need to get a bit more radical.'

'Uh huh,' I said.

'So we've decided to organise an outing.'

'Where to?'

'No, darling. Silly Che. Not an outing, an outing.'

'Felicity, what are you talking about?' I said impatiently.

'We've decided to organise a dinner. With me so far?'

'Yeah.'

'What we're going to do is horribly naughty, but it's going to get oodles of publicity.'

'Go on.'

'We're going to send out invites to as many environmental criminals as we can; politicians, factory owners, corporate chairmen that go around polluting the planet. We're talking the real scum of the earth here.' There was something very pantomime about the way she said 'scum of the earth'.

'And?'

'And we're going to invite them to a special dinner to receive an award for their contribution to society.'

'Right.'

'Che,' she whimpered, 'I can tell you're not taking me seriously.'

'I am, Felicity,' I lied, wishing for the phone call to end.

'We're going to tell them the event's going to have loads of media coverage, so of course they'll all turn up because, apart from having little pricks, they've all got huge egos. And it's not a lie. The press will cover it because we're going to leak the real reason these people are going to be there.'

'And what's that?' I said, even more convinced that Felicity was absolutely barking mad.

'That's the best bit,' she giggled. 'We're going to line them up to receive their awards, and then we're going to spray them with gunk.'

'Gunk?'

'Yes, darling, gunk. You know, the sort of stuff they use on game shows, to dunk people in when they get the answers wrong.'

'Gunk. Of course. How silly of me.' She really had lost it.

'We're going to hose them down with gunk, and denounce them on stage for the criminals that they really are.'

'Wow,' I said, trying to sound enthusiastic. 'That's some plan.'

'Isn't it just? It's going to be bloody brilliant. I can't wait. It's just what the Party Porpoise needs.'

'So why are you calling me?'

'Che, my innocent little country mouse. I'm calling you because I want to know if you'd like to nominate anyone.'

'Like who?'

'I don't know, dumb brain. Think of someone.'

'I can't.'

'Don't worry, the dinner's not until the beginning of December. I'm sure you'll be able to come up with a name before then.'

'I'll think about it,' I assured her, while flicking a V sign at the handset.

'OK, sweetie, well I'll let you get back to the cows or whatever it is you tend to down there.'

I put the phone down only for it to ring again. This time it was John Pinfold, the bank manager.

'Is that Travis?' he sounded weary.

I'd been caught by surprise, answering the phone to the one person I most wanted to avoid. For the past month we'd been screening calls through the answer machine, and I cursed my absent mindedness.

'Yes,' I said. It was probably unwise, but it was important for me to start fading into the background in view of what was going to happen in the not too distant future. Pinfold didn't twig.

'I wonder if I could have a couple of minutes of your time.'

'Course.'

'I got a note today from head office. They're getting quite concerned. You're now two and a half thousand pounds over your overdraft limit, and the deposits in your account have dropped off dramatically in the past couple of months.'

'I know.'

'Is there any reason for that?'

'Tough summer.'

'Look, I don't want to worry you, but your bank account is in a fairly critical state.'

'I know,' I said. 'We've had a few problems, but we're in the process of sorting them out.'

'I see. Do you have any idea when you might be able to consolidate?'

'We're waiting for money for summer orders to come in, but I can't say when.'

'How much will that be?'

'Couple of grand, maybe more.'

'OK. That's not really going to be enough, is it?'

'I suppose not.'

'I spoke to Che about a further loan. Have you had any more thoughts on that?'

'Che isn't working for me anymore,' I said.

'Oh,' his tone was grave. 'Well, is it something you would consider?'

'Not at the moment.'

'What about borrowing the money off your parents?'

'No,' I bristled, annoyed at his nerve to ask. 'Out of the question.'

'I don't want to sound like the prophet of doom but I do have to reiterate that your account really is in a critical state. You've set the alarm bells ringing at head office and I shouldn't be saying this but some of the younger managers up there can get a bit trigger-happy at times. I have to warn you that unless you act soon, the bank will foreclose.'

'I'm trying my best to sort some finance,' I told him. 'I've got a meeting with a potential investor early next week. An old school friend who struck it lucky. Made a million in the internet game.' I made the lie up on the spot and didn't even bother wrapping it up in my usual sugar-coated enthusiasm.

'Well, he's certainly in the right sector to make money,' said Pinfold, but his tone was unenthusiastic too. 'Look, I'll put a note on your file to say I've talked to you, and if you could give me a ring after the meeting, we can discuss the situation further. But please do call me, because this thing won't go away.'

'Sure. Thanks for the call.'

Poor Pinfold. He was as much a victim of the system as we were. In the past four years we hadn't even seen him because he never had time to get away from the office. Still, I hoped he wouldn't cop a slap for letting us slip away. That was, of course, if we managed to do so…

I was still in the yard, stocktaking, when Travis arrived. He looked rough, but he was in good spirits, and I was glad to see him. He was the only one I could talk to about what was going on, the only one who could understand the twisted pain I was feeling, but not all of it. Because I also carried with me the guilt that he was the one who was going to take the financial knock for the bankruptcy. I could never quite find the words or the moment to articulate this, but today I had to try.

Travis was philosophical. It wasn't the end, he said. We still had the crew, still had the creative talent that had spawned the Sewerside adventure in the first place. We were fluid, he said with a shrug, like the guerrillas disappearing into the hills and biding their time until they were strong enough to return. He didn't care about the bank, or the creditors, or the bankruptcy any more, he told me. It was only money, and it wasn't even like it was a lot of money. That was the sad thing about this whole bankruptcy business. In the whole scheme of things our debts were small change.

'Put it this way, mate,' said Travis, drawing on a joint, 'at the end of the day we've been surviving at rock bottom for so long, our income can hardly sink any further. The only way is up.'

The truth made me laugh, and it had been a long time since I'd done that. There was also the feeling that Travis's words were an absolution of sorts. He was taking the knock but we were still in this together, and no matter what happened our friendship was stronger than the shit that was going on around us, and perhaps that had been the fear that had been lying at the heart of my decline.

With my guilt bared I felt a weight lift from me, and a sense of purpose fill the void it left behind. For the first time since the trip to the accountant I stopped drowning in the depths of my dark depression and felt the urge to kick for the surface and fill my lungs with clean air for the fight that was to come.

As Travis and I came down the stairs, Lesnik was outside his door locking up for the night. He scowled at us, and I couldn't help laughing. He narrowed his eyes and pursed his thin lips so that the frown marks on his forehead tightened. 'I'm expecting a cheque from you,' he shot, snidely, as we passed him by.

He was referring to the invoice that had arrived in our mailbox around about the same time we'd gone to see the accountant. The invoice was for four thousand pounds, half the costs of repairing the structural damage to the building. An accompanying letter informed us that we had 30 days to pay or else the matter would go to court. He'd refused to show us a copy of the engineer's report claiming that legally he didn't have to. This had obviously led us to doubt that such a report even existed. Lesnik was stepping up the ante though, trying to scare us into moving out. He knew we didn't have the money to pay and he knew that we didn't have the money to fight the case in court either.

'And I can tell you're smoking dope up there...' he called after us. '...You know I can have you closed down.'

I was aware that Travis had stopped. He spun on his heels so fast I clocked a mouthful of flailing dreadlocks. He dropped his bag and bolted back up the stairs, two at a time.

'You know what,' Travis yelled, pushing his face close to the landlord's. 'I've had enough of you. Ever since you moved into the place it's just been one thing after another. All you've ever fucking done is give us a hard time.'

Lesnik shrank his head so low into his shoulder that he resembled a tortoise withdrawing into its shell. He was shaken, but he didn't back down. 'The only reason for that is because there are rules and regulations.' The words rolled out like he'd memorised the script. 'By disobeying them you're jeopardising the charity work I do with the whole community.'

'That's bullshit!' snarled Travis. 'You do it because deep down you're just a fucking traffic warden without the hat.'

'As I've told you before, I'm not the one who makes the rules, I only enforce them. If you've got a problem, take it up with the committee.'

'"Take it up with the committee",' Travis mimicked in a tattle tale voice. 'You are the fucking committee, you twat.' He jabbed his finger up close to Lesnik's face.

'I'm warning you. Don't touch me or I'll...'

'I'm not going to touch you, dickhead. You're not worth it. Believe me, life's fucking hard enough for us without you slapping us with bullshit bills for damages we haven't even done. I'll tell you where the damage really is. It's up there. Up there in your stupid, small-minded little head.'

He stopped as abruptly as he'd started. He gave Lesnik one final glare then turned his back and casually walked back down the stairs. 'Jesus Christ,' I thought, 'Travis has flipped!' In all the time I'd known him I'd never once seen him lose his temper like that. But he hadn't flipped at all and was grinning when I caught up with him.

'Should have done that a long time ago,' he said. 'I'm telling you, I'm going to nail that bastard before we leave this place.'

'Don't worry,' I told him. The Grubby had a saying; 'Snakes never prosper'. I didn't say any more to Travis, but already the seeds of a plan were formulating in my head…

Chapter Nineteen

<u>November: Default</u>

The man who delivered the envelope was small, bald and apologetic. Travis had let him into the office thinking he was a courier. Inside the envelope was an eviction notice, citing non-payment of building repair costs. We had 28 days to leave the building.

'Sorry, mate I feel bad,' said the bald guy, 'what with Christmas coming up and that.'

'It's only November,' I said.

'In 28 days, Christmas will be just round the corner,' he corrected, pulling out a packet of cigarettes.

'Done this before?' Travis asked sarcastically..

'All the time, mate,' he chirped. 'Fucking hate the job. I get paid for bringing people misery, and there's not much job satisfaction in that. You know how it is, though – got to live somehow.' He paused long enough to light his cigarette. 'All the best with everything,' he added and left.

The eviction notice had been unexpected, but didn't come as a surprise. We could have contested it in court, but what was the point? We were going to be out of here soon enough under our own steam anyway. We'd let Lesnik win his little turf war and become king of not two, but three floors of the building, but we certainly wouldn't make it an easy victory.

The eviction notice had been the second unexpected envelope of the day. The first had been a default notice from the bank. 'Important: you should read this carefully,' it said at the top, in bold type. It detailed the fact that we had failed to supply sufficient funds to meet our monthly loan repayments. We had been given two weeks to come up with sufficient funds to clear our overdraft or face further action. The alarm bells had clearly stopped ringing at head office and a tactical strike was being primed. We'd spent a long time preparing ourselves for this day, and now it actually had come, I couldn't help feeling a sense of relief. No more uncertainties, it was time to get it on.

I called the accountant. He was frank and straight to the point. 'You'd better start listing your liabilities. Sounds like they're coming to get you, and once they've decided that, they don't hang around.'

However, as the Grubby also liked to say, every fag packet has a silver lining, and that day of bad news also brought a rather interesting phone call. I was sitting in Job Club when it came. My mobile rang and Joan flashed me a look of disapproval, so I excused myself and took the call in the toilet. It was Brian McTafferty from the Rustcombe Corporation and I was expecting him to try and sell me something. I was about to cut him short when he asked me about the availability of our skate ramp.

'Do you remember I spoke to you at the beginning of the year and told you that we were taking over the running of the OTP (Off The Peg) Show?' he asked.

I didn't remember the call, but I knew the show well. It was glitzy and commercial and made no bones about being anything other than a retail orgy. It took place every year, two weeks before Christmas, in a cavernous exhibition centre on the outskirts of London.

'I know it's short notice,' Brian continued, 'but we've just landed a sponsor for the sports fashion area on the condition that we provide an urban feature, and someone in the office mentioned you had a ramp and a sound system. We think it would be the perfect thing for the area – after all, sports fashion is about the lifestyle, and Off The Peg, like the Sixty Million Dollar Show is all about keeping it real.'

The words stung, coming from McTafferty's lips. What did he know about keeping it real?

I asked him how much money they were offering and he back-peddled and told me the budget wasn't actually that much. I wasn't interested in hearing him plead poverty though. The Rustcombe Corporation was a multinational, multimedia conglomerate and hardly lacking for cash. If they wanted something badly enough they'd pay out, especially if there was a corporate sponsor to appease, and so I started to spar with him over the price.

'What's the least you could do it for?' he finally said.

I was suddenly aware that there was someone outside the door waiting to use the toilet. I told Brian I'd have to think it through and fax over a quote. Feigning a stomach upset I left Job Club and hurried to the yard. I picked a figure that was overly ambitious and faxed it through to McTafferty. He rejected it and countered with a proposal of his own. I countered back and we settled for the difference. The deal involved cash and a free stand. I came off the phone feeling as if the Red Sea had suddenly parted before us and shown Sewerside the way through. The hire fee was good but the free stand gave us the perfect opportunity to shift the remainder of our stock before we initiated the bankruptcy.

Travis and I spent the rest of the afternoon locked in crisis talks. After months of sitting around waiting for things to move there was suddenly more than enough to be done, and we would be running against the clock. We had two weeks to comply with the default notice, OTP was in three, and in four we would be evicted. Looking at the timetable, I figured we'd be at our most vulnerable in the week between the expiry of the bank's default notice deadline and the beginning of the show. Of course, if the bank were on it they could wipe us out before we even got the stuff out the door, but I thought there was slim chance of that. They were under the impression that it was them who were calling the shots and would probably agree to give us more time in the hope we worked something out before they foreclosed. However, we couldn't be one hundred per cent sure. The solution, we concluded, was to clear everything of value out of the yard before the bank deadline was up. That way, if bailiffs did come crashing through the door, there'd be nothing for them to take. We needed somewhere to store the stuff though, and I wrote down 'Pig' on my list and added a question mark.

There was also the small matter of the landlord. I wanted to teach the power junky a lesson and I'd been kicking the plan around in my head for a while. I put in a discreet call to Felicity. I did have a name for her after all. The Community Umbrella Network Trust, I told her, was run by an environmental menace that was backing calls for a dam project that would flood the famous Devon Seven Valleys. Of course, there was no dam project and the Seven Valleys didn't exist, but what did she know sitting in her London office?

'He's a real slippery character,' I told her. 'Best to tread carefully.'

'He sounds perfect,' she simmered. 'Just the kind of scumbag who deserves to be outed.'

I couldn't agree more. I knew Lesnik would probably take the bait too. It was the kind of ego opportunity that would give him a hard-on.

The Pig was accommodating. I told him that we had to move out of the yard and he didn't ask any questions. An hour later he called back to say he'd cleared a room at the Golden Shower. There was only one condition. We had to commit to another club night. I had my reservations but I told him yes. We didn't really have a choice in the matter and besides I hadn't finished on the favour front. I needed his sound system for the show, and a wagon and driver to get us up there.

I returned home feeling exhausted, but revitalised. Buzzing off the adrenalin, but at the same time scared shitless about what the next month held in store for us. I'd stopped off on the way and bought a couple of cans of cheap alcohol in order to bring me down a bit. Everyone was out except for Cas. I told him about the Off The Peg Show and he was his usual box of itching powder, throwing up obstacles for the sake of it and querying the reason for doing it in the first place. I snapped at him and the snap became a lash that became a vicious sibling scrap on the kitchen floor.

'What's your fucking problem?' he yelled at me. His nostrils were flaring, eyes bulging wide, as I writhed in a headlock, his weight pressing down on me.

'My fucking problem is that the business is going tits up,' I gasped with the last of my breath.

'What did you say?' He eased his grip.

'We're going bust. Tits up. In two weeks the bank's going to foreclose.'

'Jesus!' he said, sitting back on his heels. 'Why didn't you tell me that?'

'Couldn't,' I said, rubbing my neck. 'Had to keep it a secret. You know what this fucking place is like for gossip. Can't afford to have that information out in the open.'

'Shit,' he said. 'I don't know what to say.'

'You don't have to say anything.'

We made up. That was the thing about family. You fought like wild dogs, insulted each other in ways you wouldn't even contemplate were possible, and then you made up. I handed over one of my beers and told him the facts. He was the first person I'd told. I told him everything, and once I began to spill it out it didn't stop.

Chapter Twenty

The past three weeks had been a bit of a blur. We'd been busy clearing four years of accumulated crap out of the yard, under the cover of darkness and right under Lesnik's nose. It would be to our advantage if he believed we were still there and intending to challenge our eviction.

Upholding our part of the bargain with the Pig we'd run a club night at the Golden Shower. It had been successful but I'd had far too much on my mind to enjoy it. Two memories stuck out. Haze playing a three-hour set on crutches, after which he collapsed in exhaustion, and the occasional sighting of black shapes scuttling along the roof beams. The club had a rodent problem, and despite the Pig's assurances that the bass would scare the rats away I'd had a farcical encounter with a wide-eyed punter who'd claimed she'd been bitten by a small cat.

The date set by the default notice had passed and we'd heard nothing from the bank, which was what we'd been hoping for. At the end of the day, it was the bank that stood to lose if it brought bankruptcy proceedings against us and Pinfold probably had the impression we were running around like headless chickens trying to arrange new financing.

I'd finished preparing the books and had filled in the bankruptcy forms, but we'd decided to do the show first before submitting them. The accountant had looked them over and run through the routine. 'You're going to have to present your forms to the court,' he told me. 'It sounds worse than it is. Travis might have to see a judge, it all depends on how busy they are. Afterwards, he'll be interviewed. It could just be to run through the motions, or they might decide to give him a grilling. It's a bit like a driving test, it all depends on who he gets on the day. If they do give him a hard time he'll just have to ride it out. He is bankrupt so that's that. He's also going to have to pay 350 pounds in cash for the privilege of doing so.' The irony of having to pay in cash for the privilege wasn't lost on me.

With the shit about to hit the fan I ditched Job Club and signed off the dole. 'Smashing,' Christine, my latest personal adviser, had said when I'd told her I was going self-employed. 'I'm so pleased for you. I was speaking to Joan at Job Club the other day and she told me how hard you'd been working down there. You've done really well.'

For the past four years I hadn't been the person they'd assumed I was, as each time I'd walked in to sign on I'd had to wear the mask of the persona I wanted them to see, and having to play that role had been a constant drain. As I walked out of the Job Centre, I had a strange feeling of being free at last.

It was two nights before Off The Peg and I was frazzled but fairly pleased with the way things were going. Cas and Stig had been doing repairs to the ramp, the sound system was ready to go, the stock was boxed and labelled, and the Pig had sorted a wagon big enough to transport the whole lot up to London.

I'd managed to persuade McTafferty to stump the cash up front, requesting the cheque be made out to The Castro Trading Company. Aware that this was going to be something of a swan song mission for Sewerside, Travis and I had called up the entire crew. We still hadn't told them of our impending fate, and I was wondering how we were going to break it to them. Unfortunately, one vital component would be missing. The Pig claimed he was too busy in his new role as entertainment manager at The Golden Shower and wouldn't be joining us. Glyn would run the sound system instead.

With such an extensive crew we were going to need a place big enough to accommodate us all, and there was no question of hotel rooms on the budget we had. Fortune smiled, however, as Stig had 'discovered' a forgotten uncle who happened to have a house near to the venue. He lived there alone and was always strapped for cash. 'He's a bit of a black sheep,' Stig had told me. His name was Bob and he wanted five quid per person per night. It sounded perfect.

The evening was wearing on and I was preparing to knock my working day on the head when the phone rang.

'Che?'

'Yes.'

'Terry.'

I had to think who it was for a moment. 'Oh. Hello.' Why was Bacon calling me?

'Listen. Can you meet me? It's quite important. Won't take long. I'm in the pub round the corner from your place.'

Bacon was already sitting at a table when I got there. The pub was local, the kind of place frequented by old men quietly drinking their pints. There was a domino game going on in the corner. I asked him if he wanted a drink.

'Shandy,' he said, 'I'm still working.'

I bought the drinks and pulled up a chair.

'This isn't a social call,' said Bacon. 'I called you down here because I've got something to tell you. There was a briefing tonight.' The first thought that popped into my head was that this had something to do with the Pig.

Bacon drew his eyes around the bar to make sure no one was listening. 'There's going to be a series of raids.' I gulped on my drink and felt the flutter of butterflies in my stomach. I could see where this was leading. The Pig was going to get busted.

'A tactical operations unit has been in the area for the past couple of days.'

The fucking Pig.

He hadn't heeded the warning in the yard.

He was about to get his trotters burnt.

He was about to get taken down...

'And your name's come out of the hat.'

The Pig was going down and…

'What?' I spluttered, suddenly choking on my thoughts.

'The Sewerside office is going to get busted,' said Bacon, without changing expression.

'Our office?'

He nodded. 'There's been a complaint made about you.'

'A complaint?'

'That you've been holding raves up there.'

'What raves?' I snarled.

'And selling drugs to school kids,' he furthered.

Raves and drugs to school kids? This was right out of the Daily Mail. Obviously I couldn't tell him it was company policy not to sell weed to under-18s…

He was reading my face for the truth and the fact that it was turning purple with rage probably convinced him. 'So that bit's not true either?'

'Course it's not fucking true!' I spat.

'Didn't think so,' he said, swilling the last of his shandy round the bottom of his glass.

'Any idea where this 'complaint' came from?'

'Someone in your building is all I know,' said Bacon.

Of course, who else could it have been but Lesnik? Perhaps he'd got cold feet over the building repairs blag. I was astounded. Did he really want us out so much that he was prepared to call the rozzers with a cock and bull story that painted us out to be Yardies? He'd sunk to new depths this time.

'Bastard!' I seethed.

'Look, I know you smoke weed, and I'll be honest with you, I don't really give a shit. But these are serious allegations and they'll be looked into. There's a new boss at regional headquarters who's looking to make a big impression. There's a big pre-Christmas bust campaign.'

'When's it happening?'

'I'm working on something else at the moment so I don't know details. All I know is they've got 30 warrants to execute, and I know they're doing 12 tomorrow. They're bringing in a dog unit too.'

I sat there absorbing the information he was telling me, my mind working overtime. 'Why are you telling me this?' I asked.

Bacon shrugged. 'I can see you're just trying to do something different, and I respect that. You might have some funny acquaintances but you could do without having this shit fall on your head unnecessarily. Let's just say the world isn't always as black and white as people take it for.'

Jesus, I thought, don't tell me you're one of the Menace's Grey Men?

I was about to push him further when there was a murmur from a corner table as the domino game reached its conclusion. 'Look, I've got to get back,' he said briskly. He stood up to leave.

'Thanks, Terry,' I said, 'I really appreciate it.'

He shrugged and shook the hand I offered him. 'Just keep your head down, yeah?'

I nodded.

'Oh, and you might want to tell your friend Archie to do the same,' he added on his way out.

Keep my head down? Jesus Christ. We had 12 ounces of weed sitting in the office that Travis had picked up to take to the OTP show. I called Travis immediately. He was still in the yard. I told him to stay put and picked up Cas before driving down there. Predictably, Travis's jaw went slack as I repeated what Bacon had told me. For the next three hours we swept the yard for incriminating evidence, operating under a cloud of paranoia, the sound of every passing car, every creak on the stairwell, enough to set our hearts pounding. It was past one before we were satisfied that the yard was clean. 'Give us a quarter of that weed,' I said to Travis before he went off to stash it in the woods.

'What for?'

'You'll see.'

He left in the van with Cas, and I stayed behind to do one last sweep. Besides, there was something else I had to do before I went home. I had to pay a visit to Sid-the-Dog, the Pykie Prince of Liddleton. I reached for my phone, and punched in Glyn's number. He told me Sid-the-Dog had just got out of prison again...

Chapter Twenty-one

December: Keep it Real

I hadn't slept much in the couple of nights since my meeting with Bacon and I was exhausted before we even left Devon. I didn't care if the coppers came crashing through the doors once we'd left for London, but if they came in before, the whole tactical withdrawal would be jeopardised. They were serious allegations that had been made against us, and although we'd been through the yard with a fine toothcomb there were still nasty niggles of doubt. After all, Travis was always 'losing' weed, and a paranoid search by eye was no substitute for a sniffer dog's nose.

I was also worried about the Pig. With the new kid on the way and Christmas coming up, he'd stepped up his nefarious business activities and, as usual, he was conducting them with all the subtlety of a boar with a hard-on. However, I knew that if I told him the truth he would only shrug it off in his usual manner and pretend it wasn't happening. I also knew that if I told him the whole truth he would blab it round town, and I owed it to Bacon not to let that happen.

I'd decided to approach him from a different angle. I called round his house the night before we left for London. His missus answered the door and waved me through to the kitchen where I found the Pig hunched over the table, a breadboard full of pharmaceuticals in

front of him. I'd told him that the OTP organisers had demanded the presence of a qualified soundman on site for insurance purposes. If the Pig didn't come then the deal would be off. For all his unorthodox ways it was the kind of official line the Pig could empathise with. He was reticent to begin with, but I hammered away at him.

'And what about this lot?' he demanded, motioning to the drugs on the table. 'I've got to pay for it by next week and I'm not going to do that in London, am I?'

'Are you kidding?' I feigned incredulity. 'Mate, we're going to a major fashion event and half the stand holders there wouldn't last the duration without the aid of their little mate charlie.' I saw a sudden sparkle in the Pig's eyes. 'You'll be able to make far more up there than you would on a weekend down here.'

The Pig was in.

We were taking two vehicles to London, the Pig's green army truck with the ramp and sound system inside, and the Sewerside van, which would transport me, Travis, Cas, the skaters and all our stock and stand stuff. We would be forming the advance party, and the rest of the crew would join us once we'd set up and the show opened. The wagon had been packed up the night before, and I'd set a 9am rendezvous at my house, seeing as our office was burning hotter by the day.

However, things hadn't quite gone according to plan. Overnight, the weight in the Pig's wagon had flattened two of the tyres and Travis had managed to lose the weed he'd buried the night of Bacon's revelation. It took him five skaters, three hours and a lot of dug holes before he found it. The 9 o'clock start was rolled back to 11, then one and finally three. Eventually we were on the road, but it wasn't until we'd crossed the county border that I was able to breathe a sigh of relief. Halfway up the motorway my adrenalin levels subsided and exhaustion finally overwhelmed me, allowing sleep at last. When I eventually woke, it was dark and we were being waved through a security checkpoint.

The venue was a huge hulk of a place, a purpose-built exhibition centre housing nine halls the size of aircraft hangers, five of which were set to be occupied by Off The Peg show. The organisers were expecting close to a quarter of a million punters through the doors over the next few days.

We arrived to find scenes of chaos. As usual show preparations were running behind schedule; hammers sounded like a chorus of woodpeckers and workmen barked demands amidst whining drills and the bleeps of reversing forklifts. The floor area marked for the skate ramp was still occupied by large contractors' lorries so we unloaded the wagon, stacked the equipment in a pile and said our goodbyes to Glyn who was driving the van back to Devon and returning in five days' time to pick it all up again. With the rest of us in the Sewerside van, we drove to Bob's place. He wasn't at home. He'd called to say he'd been held up and may not be back for the night. He had the keys with him, but it wouldn't be a problem as there was a broken window round the back we could get through.

To say that our accommodation was basic was putting it kindly. Bob's place had the musty smell of abandonment about it. The furniture looked like it had time-travelled from before the war and the white walls had a nicotine wash to them. A two-bar electric fire was the only source of heat and the table was buried under empty cans, mouldy mugs, ripped cigarettes, and the paraphernalia of class A drug taking. The skaters weren't happy. They'd been expecting something a little plusher. Even the Grubby was put out. He complained this was the worst squat he'd ever seen, and added that he'd seen a few.

'You don't even want to go into the kitchen, mate,' he said with disgust. 'Hotel-de-la-Rat, mate, this is.'

'It's not a squat. This place is more like a fucking crack house,' grumbled Cas.

'Come on, boys,' said Travis, like the scout master trying to raise dampened spirits, 'It's not that bad.'

'Yes it is, mate,' countered Ginger Gaz.

'I did say he was the black sheep,' shrugged Stig.

'It's got a TV,' said the Pig, plotting himself in an armchair. 'What more do you want?'

'There you go,' I said, but the others didn't look too convinced.

The rooms in the rest of the house were in various states of disrepair and a couple of them had doors hanging off their hinges. While nosing around, the Pig had become rather interested in a small room at the back of the house filled with assorted electrical junk. Meanwhile, our quarters were in the attic. Bob had sorted out a couple of stained mattresses that looked like they'd been hauled out of a skip. There were fresh vacuum tracks on the carpet, and a tub of flea powder on the sideboard.

Bob turned up later in the evening. A Brummie in his late 30s with a chin full of whiskers that matched the nicotine stains on his fingers, he was wearing tight black jeans, a beaten leather jacket and a pair of soiled tennis shoes that looked as though they'd been grafted onto his feet.

'Awright, chaps,' he said, giving us all a warm handshake. 'Sorry about the state of the place. It looked worse last week. Place got fookin' raided.' The Grubby gave me a told-you-so look. A couple of the skaters laughed. Cas, Travis and I didn't look at each other but we were obviously thinking the same thing. Out of the frying pan and into the fucking fire.

'I 'ad 36 plants that were two days off pickin'. Bastards kicked me door down and took the lot.'

'Ouch,' said Travis.

'Ouch isn't the fuckin' word for it,' he mused. 'They wanna pin it down as a 'skunk factory' – what a load of fucking toss eh? Ah well, these things 'appen. I'm gonna plead guilty and give it a 'for medical reasons' story line. Suffice to say though I'm not in a position to offer you boys a smoke. None of you's lot's got any, I s'pose?'

The others disappeared up to the attic with food they'd scored from the chippy up the road, while Travis, the Pig and I hung around to be polite. As he helped himself to Travis's weed, Bob explained that he'd run away from home at 16 to become a roadie for a band and had kept on going. His uncle had died a couple of years ago, leaving him the house, which he'd been living in since.

'It ain't bad,' he said, looking around him. 'Could do with a lick of paint an' that to make it a bit more homely. That's what the plants were gonna pay for. Do it up a bit. Maybe gerra couple o' lodgers in and get on the road again. I don't like stayin' still, me. Been workin' as a security guard for the past couple o' years, but I fookin' hate it. None of the glamour of workin' the road.'

He was soon ensconced in deep conversation with the Pig and the talk had degenerated into sound system specs that were too technical to hold any interest for me.

'Roight, seein' as you bastards ain't got no booze oop 'ere, I'd best be gettin' off down the pub,' said Bob eventually. 'Fancy a swift one, Archie?'

The Pig nodded and they both stood up to leave.

'Before you go, Bob,' I asked. 'What do you want to do about the money? Do you want me to pay by the day?'

'Don't you worry about that, pal. I can tell you're a good bunch of lads.' He tossed me a set of keys and got up to leave. Patting down his jacket and turned back to me. 'Actually, thinkin' about it, perhaps I will take a couple o' quid off ya now. Seem to be a bit short loike…'

After some food, a couple of beers and a few spliffs, the place no longer seemed so bad and as we lay in our sleeping bags, talk turned to the next day.

'A VIP area would be nice, eh?' said the Grubby, midnight snacking on half a saveloy he'd stashed for the occasion. Despite his grubby habits, he shared with the Pig a secret craving for the trappings of officialdom.

'How many VIPs do you know?' Travis asked.

'True, mate. But I've made a few of these up anyway, just in case, eh.'

He tossed over a couple of home-made VIP passes that he'd made and had laminated before coming up.

'Nice job, mate,' said Travis, suppressing a laugh.

The Grubby took it as a compliment and began distributing passes to all of us.

'What the fuck's this?' asked Stig, pulling off his headphones.

'Laminate, mate,' said the Grubby.

'What for?'

'Access to the ramp area, stall, graf wall. So we know who's supposed to be in the area. Skater identification, blah, blah, blah.'

'We know everyone who's supposed to be there,' derided Stig.

'You never know when you might need them, mate,' said the Grubby, with a sniff.

'They look gay,' said Little Johnny with a scowl.

'And what do you think you look with your green hair?' the Grubby shot back.

I should have fallen asleep at the click of a finger but, despite my fatigue, my mind wouldn't have any of it and I couldn't shut it down. I spent a restless night trying to count sheep, while listening to farting grubbies and suspicious scratching noises coming from behind the walls.

On Site: Day One

The girl with the clipboard could tell I wasn't from London. I had mud on my shoes. I wouldn't have thought twice about it, but it seemed to be the first thing she noticed. 'Oi can see you lot are country bwoys.' Her laugh was patronising, and her attempt at an accent was atrocious. 'Did ya come up here on a tractor?' She pronounced the 'or' as in 'saw'.

'I can see you've never been to the country,' I stabbed back.

'How come you haven't got a Cornish accent?' she asked, disappointed.

'Because I'm not from Cornwall,' I replied sarcastically.

She flicked her pen against the side of her clipboard and I could tell she didn't like me. I hadn't kissed the ground she walked on, and I saw her flirtatiousness for what it was – bullshit.

'Here are your passes,' she scowled. 'Sign here.'

We'd been at the exhibition centre since eight in the morning, and it was all hands on deck to get the ramp and the sound system set up in a day. Although there were few complications, setting up always took time. It was the same at all the big events we'd ever done. You couldn't just ask the organisers a question and get a straight answer. So it was that I was in the main site office waiting for the relevant person to come off the phone and tell me when the carpet fitters would be covering our area, so we could start building.

As I waited, I scanned the Off The Peg Show site map. The show was split into five zones that had been carefully branded. There was 'Grand Design', filled with stands selling faux haute culture, and 'Under Garm', which basically translated as knickers and bras. 'Casual Acquaintance' was stacked with smart and casual wear and 'Free 4 All' was a section entirely devoted to clothing the big, the fat, the tall and the very, very small. We were in the 'Lifestyle' zone, the ramp and sound system comprising the 'feature' around which all the stands selling street, extreme sports and active wear were clustered.

The Off The Peg Show concept was simple. Charge punters 20 quid to attend, stick on a few random 'features', such as fashion shows and free makeovers, and market the event as a treasure trove of fashion bargains. In reality, there were few bargains as every fashion business used OTP as the opportunity to dump its leftover stock on the market before the new season. Despite the sham of it all, punters were easily persuaded otherwise. All you had to do was mark your product up by 100%, stick up a sign saying 'Sale – 50% off marked price', and sure enough it wouldn't be long before the consumer instinct kicked into gear.

'Che.'

I turned round to see Brian McTafferty, who greeted me as if I was a long-lost friend. He was wearing black leather trousers and a tight fitting polo-neck beneath his sports jacket. A small pair of designer spectacles perched on his nose and his hair was an expansive fop that had been intentionally styled to look greasy.

'I'm so grateful you guys could help us out at such short notice,' he crooned. 'I'm really excited about the Lifestyle area. As I told you over the phone, this year OTP's all about keeping it real.' He meekly punched the air as he said it.

'I know,' I said. I'd seen the publicity – a drossy flyer featuring models dressed in garb appropriate to each zone. 'Lifestyle' had been illustrated with a collection of overly styled street kids, awkwardly wielding record bags, skateboards and upside-down spray cans.

'Everything OK?'

'Fine,' I replied. 'Just got a quick question. It seems like the rest of the show floor's been carpeted, and I was just wondering what's happening about our area, seeing as we're building the ramp now.'

'Executive decision,' he said waving his hand. 'Your area isn't getting any – we thought we'd leave it with a bare floor. It'll give the feature more of an 'urban' feel.'

'I see. I guess that's part of the "keep it real" theme?' I added, with more than a hint of sarcasm.

'Ahem. You've got it. Sorry, I should have come over to explain. Truth is, I've been swept off my feet trying to sort out the celebrity VIP bar.'

Another OTP tactic was to roll out B and C list celebrities, who would be contracted to wander the show, smile a lot and have their pictures taken with punters. Kind of reinforced the false sense of glamour.

'Listen,' Brian added, 'I've got to shoot off. I'm running around all over the place so if you can't find me, ask for Rob. He's my man on the floor when it comes to the Lifestyle section. If you've got a problem, just go through him. Anyway, good to see you again.' He shook my hand, and with a swish of his styled fop he was gone.

It had been a long day setting up and the night was wearing on. Around us, OTP was taking shape as stands were stocked and carpets were being laid. Inevitably, our stand was the last thing to go up and not for the first time, the garden gazebo and the stock arrangement inside it looked like it had fallen off the back of a lorry. I stood back and tried to look at it objectively, but no matter how it was rearranged it still looked like a Bedouin laundry, strapped as it was between the white walls and faux pine floors of the stands that flanked us on either side.

The gazebo was tacked onto the back of the skate ramp, which we'd screened off with fruit netting to contain flying boards. I'd got the ramp into the show by sending Brian blurred pictures that made it look tidy, professional and deceptively big. However, despite its ample dimensions, the ramp looked at best untidy, at worst an ugly carbuncle that rose out of the surrounding sea of smart red carpet like the run-aground hull of an old ship. As I watched the skaters testing it out, I noticed a nasty wobble too. Cas told me there was nothing we could do about it.

'I wouldn't worry about it,' said Stig, 'I've skated a lot worse. At least there's no bits of jagged metal sticking out.' Somehow his comments didn't put me at ease.

A couple of speaker stacks stood at one end (the Pig had brought 10k up with us) and we'd added a graffiti wall to the other where Travis was going to be live painting with a couple of local graf artists we'd called up. Amidst the chrome and carpet and ringed by eight-foot high security fencing, I couldn't help thinking that our area resembled a ghetto more and more. Oh well, I reasoned, the organisers had wanted an 'urban' feel to the feature. However, I reasoned again, they'd probably been thinking more London town than Sharptown…

On Site: Day Two

The first day of the show started off quietly. I wasn't complaining though. It gave us the opportunity to rearrange the stall and to smooth out any ramp and sound system hitches. I was also knackered. Events in exhibition centres were always hard work. It probably had something to do with the scale and the totally artificial environment of these places. Without realising, you walked miles just to-ing and fro-ing, while standing in one place was just as tiring. The huge banks of bright lights that panelled the ceiling were unforgiving in their constant glare, and the air you breathed was pumped in from outside and constantly circulated so that it had been inhaled by numerous others by the time it got to you. Once inside you were oblivious to whatever was happening on the outside and regardless of whether it was day or night, minus ten and snowing or 30 degrees and sunny, your environment always remained the same.

Shows worked on the same principal as Glastonbury in as it would spring up like a small town where the previous day there had been nothing, populated by exhibitors living out a kind of retail community existence for the duration of the event. Once you got your bearings, the show became a collection of neighbourhoods filled with faces you either knew from past shows or had become acquainted with this time round. I liked the camaraderie of these dos and the fact that beneath the 'show' umbrella thousands of little scenarios tended to unfold, running the gamut of emotions; stories of successes, disappointments, horrors, romances, sobs and smiles. And yet, deep down at the root of it all, the biggest story of all was that everyone in that place was motivated by the drive to make as much cash as they could in the short time available to them.

Once the show doors opened, GP (General Public) would add a new dynamic to the world of the exhibition centre, bringing with it a myriad of additional stories that unfolded during the day from school tripping kids caught on the rob, to middle-aged mums making over their images, or plain girls in the crowd getting spotted as the next face of the various model agencies patrolling the place.

Our interaction with the show organisers had so far been limited. With a production on this scale they were too busy to deal with anything other than immediate problems. Short of ramp side fatalities, they weren't interested in what we were up to. It was probably a mistake on their behalf. It gave the Sewerside virus time to breed.

We'd been doing our best to infiltrate the ground staff since we'd got there. The security guards, the sandwich sellers, the cleaners, the grunt workers on the ground crews – we always made a point of befriending them. These people, employed by the exhibition centre, worked a different show every week of the year. Technically, they may not have been in charge but to all intents and purposes they ran the place. Most exhibitors tended to treat them like shit (the show organisers were the worst. They'd hire the venue and swagger around acting like they owned the place). Give the venue staff a smile and a few friendly words, however, treat them with the respect they deserved, and these people could make your life a whole lot easier. We had two security personnel allocated to our zone and already they had been neutralised. One of them was an old boy, whose anecdotes I'd been feigning interest in since we'd arrived, and the other was a moonlighting student, who remembered us from Glastonbury and was already busy spending his wages on Travis's weed.

Our ranks had been swelled by the arrival of the London skate and graf posses. Travis and a couple of the graf boys were already marking out the piece they would be painting on the graffiti wall over the next few days. We'd given the Grubby the responsibility of overseeing the ramp. He'd bestowed himself with the title of 'Ramp Coordinator' and was already wearing one of his home-made laminates round his neck. Under the glare of overhead lights, the ramp area was looking increasingly untidy. Cross lengths of scaffold pole jutted out at awkward angles and the exposed timbers looked dull and termite-ridden. Where the top surface paint wasn't scratched and peeling it was flecked with grime and bits of mildew from being left in the damp of Stig's garage. The wobble was still there, and it seemed to be getting worse.

'Oh well,' Travis laughed when I pointed out my observations. 'They've paid us now, so it's too late. If they've got a problem, they can take it down themselves.'

The area beneath the ramp was also proving to be a magnet for deviant activity, boxed off as it was from the outside world. The

Grubby had started to complain that he was feeling like a club doorman, he was fielding so many requests from other exhibitors who were clamouring to make use of his 'VIP areas'. There was so much smoke coming out from beneath the ramp that the elderly security guard asked me if we had a dried ice machine under there.

It was lunchtime, and I had just had my first shot of 'sales medicine', a line of the Pig's charlie underneath the ramp. Cas had been holding the fort back at the stall and I returned to find him leaning against a rail.

'Ready for a livener?' I asked, discreetly handing over the bag with the powder in it.

'Back in a minute,' he said.

I took his place, leaning on the rail, nodding my head to the dub playing over the sound system, my gaze wandering over the succession of beautiful girls walking around the place. I had been charting the journey of a particularly striking redhead down the aisle when into my line of view appeared a face that was as familiar as the waddling gait.

No, I thought, it couldn't be? It was.

Heading straight for the stall was Glastonbury Nobit, and he was wearing a suit. Instinctively, I ducked down behind the rail and pretended to be busy shuffling through a file in the hope he hadn't spotted me, but it was too late.

'Che?'

I stood up. 'Robert,' I said, feigning surprise. 'What are you doing here?'

The kid still had the same awkward look about him, but something had changed, and it wasn't just the fact that he'd got rid of the spectacles. Behind him stood two girls in OTP T-shirts, one of them the clipboard holder who'd given me the dodgy West Country accent routine.

'It's Rob, actually,' he said with a sniff, and then the penny dropped.

'You're working here, aren't you?' I asked, my smile frozen.

'Correct. I'm the Lifestyle zone floor manager.' He pointed to the name tag pinned onto the front of his jacket, and adjusted his tie, 'and these are my assistants.' He nodded in the direction of the two girls. He looked puzzled. 'What are you lot doing here?' he asked, scanning his floor plan. 'It's supposed to be the Castro Trading Company.'

'That's us,' I said quickly.

He looked surprised, but not amused. 'Well, then, I suppose it's you I've got to see.'

'About what?'

'You've got yourself your first written warning,' he said smugly.

'You what?'

Nobit, for it was clear that the name still fitted, put his clipboard down and pulled an electronic device from a leather shoulder holster, holding it up so I could see the needle bouncing along a numbered scale in time to the sound system's bass line. 'This is a decibel meter. See that needle? It should be on 85 decibels. I've taken three readings from different positions. You're running at a hundred and two. That contravenes health and safety regulations and could get the whole show closed down.'

'Come on, Rob,' I replied, 'I thought OTP was all about keeping it real (I did that meek fist punch in the air thing). How are we supposed to run a sound system on those levels? It's not like the music's loud enough to cause offence.'

Nobit sucked in his cheeks, holstering his meter as if it was a semi-automatic pistol. 'Wrong!' he snapped. 'It's too loud. A hundred decibels is comparative to the sound of a pneumatic drill. Eight hours of that would be a serious risk to personal health. I don't think you realise how dangerous sound can be. Much louder, and there's a serious risk the bass frequency could cause spectators to involuntarily lose control of their bodily functions.' He delivered his facts in the monotonous drone of an automaton.

'That's a little bit sensationalist mate. Listen to the noise of the show.' I paused for effect. I had a point too. Umpteen thousands of people engaged in consumer activity at the same time was loud, even without the noise coming from the stages and fashion catwalks dotted around the venue. 'I hardly think we're pushing the levels that far.'

'We're not at Glastonbury now, Che,' he said, his tone patronising. He fixed me with an angry stare. 'Exhibitors have paid good money to be here, you know,' he added, handing me the written warning. 'One more and you'll have an abatement notice. If you fail to comply, it'll be breach of contract and we'll shut you down.'

'Come on, Robert. How about a verbal warning first?'

He shook his head. 'Sorry,' he said, but he wasn't sorry at all. 'I don't make the rules, I only enforce them.'

'Of course you do.' I wondered if he'd been dropping the same power trips as our landlord.

'I'm going to need you to have a word with your ramp engineer too. I've noted a few health and safety hazards for you to sort out,' he picked up his clipboard and handed me a piece of paper.

'Still into your coloured pens, I see.'

He ignored me. 'Just one last thing,' he smiled. 'I can smell cannabis.'

'You know, I thought I could smell it too,' I replied.

'I'll be keeping an eye on this area,' he sniffed.

'I'm glad we've got someone to watch out for us.'

'Right then,' he replied, unsure of what to say next. 'Obviously, I'm very busy, so I'll leave it with you to sort out.' He stepped backwards and right onto the foot of the Pig who'd wandered round the corner of the stand. Nobit turned round to apologise, only to shrink into his suit when he saw who it was.

'I can't believe he's working for this lot,' said the Pig once he'd gone.

'Oh, I can,' said Travis who'd turned up soon after. 'Daddy probably owns the company this time round.'

'Whatever, we're going to have to tread carefully,' I said. 'The kid's got a clipboard and a chip on his shoulder. Don't forget we ruined his college project.'

'Why don't I just go and fill him in?' Cas asked.

I laughed but he wasn't smiling. 'Not before we've sold out of stock.'

Cas nodded acknowledging the point.

'We'll have to play it by ear. Tell the rest of the boys. If he's spotted, they're to let Archie know, soon as. So long as those levels are legal by the time he gets his monitor rolling, we'll be OK.'

Seeing Nobit had been strange, but not altogether surprising. I suppose that after the past couple of months, it took a great deal to surprise me any more...

Bright lights, the hum of noise and the bustle and buzz of consumer consumption surrounded us. It was constant, like the floor of a casino that never stops, just a blur of noise and colour and money passing hands. Cloistered inside the artificial environment of the exhibition centre, the outside world, and thoughts of police busts, Lesnik, and the bankruptcy seemed a million miles away. Besides, I was on a mission to sell. Over the next three days, everything must go...

Late in the afternoon, Natty finally turned up along with Haze. Despite doctor's recommendations to rest after picking up an infection on his last DJ mission to Devon, he was intent on playing. 'Still weepin' a bit of pus,' he shrugged, pulling his trousers down in the middle of the stand to show me, 'but I'm not too bovvered about it.' He looked pale and still hadn't regained the weight he'd lost after the accident. 'I'll be honest though, bruv, I ain't felt this healthy for a long time. Knocked the drugs on the head an' that. Still drinking the brews,' he said, adding reflectively, 'Way I see it, I'd be mad not to. Two cans of lager on top of me painkillers an' I'm off me head. 'Aven't 'ad that sort of value for money since I was at school.'

I had little doubt that we were fouling up the Lifestyle zone, and every now and again I would spot Nobit's two assistants in huddled consultation on the other side of the security fence that separated the Sewerside ghetto from GP. I could tell that they were itching to say something, but they couldn't. As much as they wanted to reprimand us they were finding it very difficult to actually catch us doing anything. Also, word had spread and our area had taken on the status of a free-state within the boundaries of the show. In the darkened space below the ramp skaters swapped joints with giggling models and fashionistas, who chopped out lines on the bottoms of skateboards. It placed the organisers in a tricky position. They'd spent months with their tongues up the arses of half the people under there, people whose presence added weight to OTP's claims that it was cutting edge retail fashion. Having spent so long playing the 'cool' card to get these people in to OTP, the organisers could hardly send in the storm troopers to clear out the ghetto. I watched with glee as one of Nobit's assistants rolled her eyes as she saw the marketing manager of an internationally renowned jeans brand emerge from beneath the ramp, rubbing his nose.

With Natty on the microphone and Haze installed behind the decks, it was inevitable that the decibel levels were going to start climbing. However, thanks to our extensive network of lookouts Nobit's attempts to catch us out with the decibel meter were proving unsuccessful. At one point he was spotted hitting the side of his meter, unable to explain why the needle had stopped jumping. True to form, the ghetto had started to fizz with the certain je ne sais Sewerside and you could see the effect on the show floor as people gravitated in our direction. The aisles became filled with people watching the skating or cheering for Natty's freestyle rhymes on the mic. Of course, the whole thing was very tame compared to somewhere like Glastonbury, but it was enjoyable all the same, and as far as I and the rest of the crew were concerned, we were just fulfilling our mandate. Like the publicity said, we were keeping it real...

By the end of the day, my throat was gacky, my head ached and so did my feet. I'd been on the OTP sales floor for only a day but already it felt as though I'd done three shows back to back. We'd racked up eight hundred in sales and already we were running in profit.

To say that the Hotel de la Rat was cosy may have been going too far, but it had become something like home, and a welcome relief after so many hours spent inside the show. Bob drifted in and out, and always on to the pub, leaving us pretty much with the place to ourselves. Despite Travis and my attempts to pressgang the skaters into leaving their shoes outside the door at night, our little attic room was starting to hum with the smell of an animal's lair. That night, it was far too cold to have the window open but nevertheless I insisted that it was, and I slept as close to it as I could.

On Site: Day Three

Saturday brought in the crowds, the weekend shoppers who attacked the stands like blood-lusting sharks. Trade was brisk and Cas was proving himself to be a bit of a secret weapon on the retail front, sweet-talking his way into the purses and wallets of teenage girls and cash-rich parents, while the aroma of grubbiness was enough to draw in the blokes. Business was booming.

Unfortunately, things weren't going so smoothly as far as the ghetto was concerned. I didn't know what conversations the organisers had had the night before but the atmosphere had changed.

Our kindly security guards had been swapped for a gang of no-nonsense types, dressed in black bomber jackets and smart shoes. I later found out that they'd been drafted in from the 'celebrity protection unit' (which didn't say much for the quality of the celebrities). It was clear that they'd been ordered to keep us on a tight rein. One of them had been instructed to stand guard at the entrance to our compound, checking the credentials of those coming into the ramp area. Another was standing sentry behind the decks to ensure that the sound levels stayed fixed. Mid-morning, Travis turned up at the stand smarting. The graf artists had been ordered to stop the large mural they were working on.

The last straw came when Nobit turned up and proclaimed that

Health and Safety required that all skaters wear helmets and pads. When I told him that it was impossible (not only would I have had a grubby uprising on my hands, but what was I going to do, magic the equipment out of the air?), he left to consult with the powers that be.

'OK,' he said on his return. 'The skaters don't have to wear the safety equipment so long as there's only one skater on the ramp at a time.'

Before the morning had passed, two of the skaters that we'd brought in locally had been busted and thrown out for riding the ramp without official permission.

'What the fuck are ya doin'?' raged Haze.

'We're throwing them out for breaking the rules,' replied the no-nonsense security guard.

'For skating?'

'For skating in a restricted area.'

'Where do you fink you are? Fuckin' Disneyland? This is supposed to be the skate area!'

'Only inside the cage,' security growled. 'And if you don't shut it you'll be joining them.'

By now the authoritarian crackdown was having a noticeable effect on the Lifestyle zone. What had been a swinging little area the day before was now decidedly dull. With the human element curtailed, the ramp area was now muted, boring, and had all the atmosphere of a vandalised recreation ground.

I went to seek out McTafferty. I found him in the organiser's office. 'Ahem,' he said when I'd finished my diatribe. 'You've been doing a great job, Che, and the area looks fantastic, it really does, but we've got some complications.'

'Like what?'

'Well, there's a dog show starting in Hall 8 this weekend, and unfortunately Rob seems to think the bass levels in your area are a safety concern for the welfare of... ahem... you know, the dogs.'

'Is this some kind of a joke?'

'Well, ahem, I know it sounds like one, but this is the Rustcombe Corporation's first year running OTP and Rob thinks it's best not to rock the boat with the venue owners.'

'I thought Rob worked as your floor manager?'

'Mmmm. Slip of the tongue. He does. It's just that... Well, without going into details, we've been put under a bit of pressure and unfortunately my hands are tied.' He was suddenly looking very uncomfortable.

'Brian,' I said, 'you're not making any sense.'

'It's just that... There's a feeling that the feature might be a little too...' he paused searching for the right word, ...gritty for our corporate sponsors. Look, Che, I'd really appreciate it if you could help us out on this one. I know it's not a perfect situation but circumstances change, and if you could just try and see it from my position and believe me when I say there's nothing I can do.' A message came crackling over his walkie talkie. 'Look, I've got to go. Just try and work it out with Rob, OK?'

'Did Rob tell you he knew us from before?'

McTafferty looked puzzled. 'You know Rob?'

'Yeah. Worked with him at Glastonbury.'

'Oh right,' said McTafferty, trying to wrap the conversation up. 'I heard it was a successful one. Not a bad little gig for his first outing. Funny, he didn't mention you guys were working for him there.'

'Working for him?' I balked. 'We ran that fucking gig!'

McTafferty seemed surprised by my vehemence.

'Look, I'm not being funny,' I continued, 'but I've seen him in action. How the hell did he manage to get a job with you lot?'

'Ahem. We just thought he had the right credentials for the position,' he replied, but from his body language I could tell some of the truth was missing.

'The thing is, Brian, that whole Glastonbury episode kind of ended with a bit of acrimony. I don't want to bleat about it but I can't help feeling that Rob's being a bit over-zealous towards us on account of what happened there. I mean the kid's marching round our area like he's just rolled out of the Hitler Youth.'

'Look, Che, I'd love to stay and chat, but I really do have to go. You're just going to have to make do as best you can.'

I knew McTafferty was sweating by the way his leather trousers squeaked as he turned to leave the room.

'Is that it?' I called after him.

'Sorry, Che. It's the best I can do.'

'What the fuck happened to keeping it real?' I chided, aware that my raised voice had brought a hush over the organiser's office. 'You've sold this frigging show on the fact that you are, and yet we've got a one-man ramp, a half-finished graffiti wall, a sound system that's not much louder than a hair dryer, and you're telling me to do the best I can?'

McTafferty spun round and came marching back towards me. 'Come with me,' he said, grabbing my arm. He shepherded me into a small box office off to one side and checked the corridor before he closed the door. 'OK, Che, I'll level with you,' he said, his tone hushed. 'The truth is that Rob's a Rustcombe.'

I stared blankly. 'His name's Rustcombe?'

'No!' he snapped impatiently. 'His name's Rob, but he's a Rustcombe, as in Rustcombe Corporation. Rob Rustcombe. He's the son of the chairman, the boss, the head honcho who runs the whole show.'

Involuntarily, my mouth opened and my eyes grew wide.

'Why's Rob got a job? Because Rob can do whatever the fuck he wants to. His appointment had nothing to do with me and once the kid's learnt the ropes, the next job he'll have will probably be mine. So now do you understand? Believe me, I'm not happy about it, but what can I do? My hands really are tied, Che.'

Funny, I'd always thought of McTafferty as an arrogant prick, but now I felt sorry for him. Beneath the hair gel and the designer labels he was just another drone in the system.

'So do yourself a favour,' he continued. 'Just suck it up for the next couple of days, take the money, and try to keep out of his way, because believe me, Rob's got clout.'

I told Travis about Nobit's association and his reaction was predictable. We decided not to tell the others for fear of what they might do to him. We'd spent the best part of five months planning the tactical withdrawal and our priority at the OTP show was to sell as much stock as we could. There was a time to fight and a time to sit tight. Now was that time. As the day went on I just blanked out the crew protestations that were growing more vociferous, promising that by tomorrow I'd have sorted it out. By the time the show closed for the night we'd cleared three grand in takings and with one day left to shift all our remaining stock, our mission was on target. I should have been happy, but instead I felt like shit.

Back at the Hotel de la Rat, the talk was of rebellion, and my hollow arguments were doing nothing to dampen down the flames.

'I can't be arsed with this!' Natty huffed. 'There's people in there talking louder on the phone than I am on the mic.'

'It's fuckin' stupid, Che!' snorted Haze, who'd been hopping round the front room for the past ten minutes. 'I've been round that place and every sound system in there is louder than ours.'

'I've told you, Haze. If we take the piss on the sound, we'll be in breach of contract and they'll be able to sue our arses.'

'The boys aren't happy, mate,' waded in the Grubby. 'Team morale's low.' The three skaters nodded in unison.

'There's nothing I can do about the one skater at a time rule.' My head was starting to ache with all the shaking it had been doing.

'I don't mean that, mate,' the Grubby replied. 'It's not being able to smoke under the ramp that's really getting to them.'

'It's shit!' scowled Little Johnny. 'I'd rather be down the skate park in Liddleton.'

'Look, boys. Short of assassinating four security guards, there's not a lot we can do about it.'

'I hear what you say, but I don't fink it's the organisers at all,' said Haze. 'I fink it's ole Nobit the hobbit who's behind this.' How close he was to the truth. 'We should have tied 'im to that tree and beaten the fuck out of 'im at Glastonbury when we 'ad the chance.'

'I agree,' said Cas.

'What's going on, Che? What 'appened to the old Glastonbury spirit? What about the Street Olympics an' that? Why are we rollin' over like puppies an' lettin' these corporate wankers walk all over us? That ain't the Sewerside way.'

Something inside of me snapped. '"Glastonbury spirit"?' I roared, jumping up from my seat. 'Do you realise how much is at stake for us at this show? You boys might think we're styling it but the truth of it is we're hanging on by our fucking fingernails. All that free product you lot get – and I know there's not exactly mountains of it – all that gets paid for out of our pockets. You might think it's all a big laugh but if we get kicked out of this place our business is fucked. Good and proper fucked. We need this money.'

'The money? Don't give us that, Che,' Haze shot back. 'What about the crew? What about Sewerside?'

The other faces in the room nodded. Exasperated, I looked to Travis for support. He raised his eyebrows. It was only a gesture, but I'd known him long enough to know what it meant: Tell them the truth.

'All right,' I said, putting my hands up. I took a moment, a dramatic pause. 'We weren't going to say anything because we were working on a way to pull it off so nobody would be any the wiser.'

The faces around me looked blank.

'The truth of it is, boys,' I said with all the drama I could muster, 'is that Sewerside the clothing label is about to go bust.' I stepped back, and bowed my head in deference. I'd said it.

The reaction I got took me by surprise. 'Oh that,' said Haze casually. 'Fuckin' ell Che, I fought it was some'fing serious. We know about that.'

'You do?' I looked over to Travis, who looked as gobsmacked as I'm sure I did, and then to Cas, who suddenly seemed very interested in the frayed fabric on the rest of the armchair he was sitting in.

'No secrets round here, mate,' chimed the Grubby.

'That's an even better reason why we shouldn't let these fuckers roll us over,' cackled Natty. 'Come on, Che, if this is goin' to be the last shout, then let's at least go out with a bang. Give the corporates a kick up the arse to remember us by.'

There were mumbles of agreement from the crew. Flabbergasted at the breach in confidentiality, by my own brother too, and also feeling slightly sheepish that for all of our cloak and dagger manoeuvres it had been Travis and I who had been in the dark, I put my hands up.

'Like I said, if we take the piss, we'll be in breach of contract. We'll be sued for our fee, and probably more, and to be honest…'

'Listen, we're Sewerside, right?' declared Natty, jumping up and practically bundling me out of the way. 'So what if the business is going bust, but it's not like any of us are going anywhere. How many times have we been against the odds before? Jesus, if we can sling together an event in a field, we can sure as fuck pull something off here.'

'There is a way,' said the Pig suddenly. He'd been sitting quietly whilst the debate had been raging.

'Go on,' said Travis.

'That electrical equipment in that room at the back of the house, you know what it is?'

'Junk?' I offered.

'To the untrained eye,' retorted the Pig. 'Transmitters and receivers.'

'So?'

'So, every sound system in that place has got a radio microphone patched into it and all those radio mics work on a certain frequency, right?' He'd already lost me, but I listened on anyway. 'Now it wouldn't be unfeasible to tinker with those receivers so that they receive whatever sounds are coming from the transmitter. With me so far?' Most of the faces in the room remained blank. 'It's simple. If we could get receivers on each of those sound systems we could patch whatever sounds we wanted through the entire show. The key to pulling it off would be to find somewhere safe to transmit from.'

I shook my head dismissively. 'It's just all too A-Team,' I added in exasperation.

'No,' said the Pig shaking his head. 'Trust me. It's actually incredibly simple if you've got the kit to do it with. And that kit is lying around in Bob's backroom. Obviously at some point someone's going to work out what's going on and just unplug the sound systems, but it'll probably take them a bit of time to work it out.'

'The fucking Pig!' yelled Haze. 'I love ya!' He hopped over and planted a theatrical kiss on the Pig's forehead. 'He's a fuckin' genius,' he told the room. 'An' you're wrong, Che, it's not the A-Team, it's like that cowboy film with the bald geezer. What's it called?'

'The Magnificent Seven,' Travis and I chorused wearily.

'That's the one. Us boys against those corporate wankers. Come on, boys, what do you say?'

'I'm going to get some food,' I said, hoping that the conversation would have blown over by the time I got back. The day had run me ragged and the last thing I needed was an evening of science fiction fantasy. I didn't doubt that the Pig had the ability to do what he was proposing. Neither did I doubt the consequences if our tactical withdrawal, so perfectly planned up until now, got hijacked by a mutinous crew.

'I think I'm going to have a nervous breakdown,' I told Travis as we walked to the chip shop.

'I think I'll join you,' he replied.

We decided to go to the pub instead.

We returned to discover that, far from the conversation blowing over, the Pig's plan had already begun to hatch in our absence. Bob's front room resembled Guy Fawkes's pad on the night of November 4th. The Pig was sitting at the table, a frown frosted onto his forehead, rooting inside one of the receivers with a screwdriver. Beside him sat Bob, his chin resting on his palm.

'I was doin' a job for the MOD, security guard stuff loike,' he was explaining. 'All this stuff was in one of the lock ups. Bastards laid me off early so I thought fuck it and helped meself.' He paused to swig from a can of cider. 'I was gonna sell it on, but never really got round to it. Was lucky really, 'cos the coppers totally missed this lot when they busted me growin' operation... Fockin' perfect for what you boys want 'em for though.'

'Ah, there you boys are,' said Haze, as Travis and I entered the room. 'We've been making a few plans.' He nodded at the crude sketchings the Grubby was busy drawing. 'I fink you'll find we've got a bit of a going concern,' he said drawing on a cigarette. 'Looks like it could be a Sunday to remember.'

On Site: Day Four

I didn't quite know how Travis and I had let ourselves be talked into it. That's not strictly true. I knew exactly how. If this had been about a business that sold clothes then we would have pulled the plug on the hare-brained scheme there and then and sent everyone home. But it wasn't just about the business, and, of course, both of us knew that. It was about Sewerside. It was about the crew and the ties that bound us, and the deep down and dirty knowledge that Sewerside was never going to quietly swim off into the sunset...

We'd spent most of the night locked in war council laying down rough plans. Turnist had been contacted and was going to document the whole episode for Upshot magazine. If this was going to have any chance of working, I knew we'd need a bit of specialist help too. 'Ah, the call to the barricades, is it?' the Menace had asked when I'd placed the call.

It was the final day of the show and the place was heaving from the moment the doors opened. The dense crowds would hopefully provide the perfect cover for our operations. We had agreed that the morning should pass without incident, so as to lull the OTP storm troopers into a false sense of security. To all intents and purposes we were towing the organiser's line. Having consented to the conspiracy, against my better judgement, I busied myself with taking as much cash as I could before the shit started hitting the fan. However, beneath the smiles I wore for the punters, I was sick to the stomach with anticipation and dread.

I had just finished a sale when the Pig burst into the stand. 'Che,' he bubbled. 'You'll never fucking guess what's happened? I've just got off the phone from the missus. My place got busted this morning.'

I felt my heart leap into my mouth. I'd forgotten about the bust campaign.

'Four uniform, two plain clothes, and a sniffer dog. Can't believe it. Missus said they turned the place upside down.'

'But you didn't have anything there?'

'Did I fuck,' he snorted. 'Missus had a bit of hash that got thrown out the window and everything else is up noses in this place.' I breathed a sigh of relief. 'She says there's been busts all over town. Not local old bill. Some special unit from out the area.'

'Who else got done?' I probed.

'Don't know yet. She's going to call back later. Don't look so worried, mate,' he said, clocking the look on my face, 'I'm in the clear.'

I took a walk to find somewhere quiet to use the phone. I tried my place, but there was no answer. My thoughts wandered to Lesnik. I gave Felicity a call.

'How'd it go?' I asked, inquiring about the Party Porpoise 'outing'.

'Not very well. It was terrible, to tell you the truth.' She went on to explain that the event had been rumbled before the curtain had even risen. Never the subtlest of operators, Felicity had aroused the attention of Special Branch who'd suspected the Party Porpoise was affiliated to an anti-capitalism terrorist group. They'd busted the place and arrested her.

'How did that happen?'

'I have my suspicions,' she said. 'These beasts have a lot of powerful friends, but I'd rather not talk about it over the phone.'

'So nobody got outed?'

'No.'

'Was Lesnik there?' It was the only information I really needed to know.

'Who?'

'The person I put you onto.'

'I think he was. I'm sorry, Che. I feel like I've failed you. It breaks my heart to think that your lovely corner of the world may soon be underwater.'

I told her as sincerely as I could that it was OK, she'd done her best, and the struggle against the Seven Valleys Dam would go on.

I returned to the stand and caught up with Travis, who looked anxious and bored, all at the same time.

He was on decoy duty, DJ'ing behind the decks while Natty and Haze were off trying to find a suitable place to transmit from. Travis had heard about the busts, and was understandably pensive. I told him I had no news on the yard yet. No news, I presumed, was good news. Besides, in the light of what was about to come, a sniffer dog with a wagging tail had become the least of our worries.

Meanwhile, the Sewerside ghetto was empty, except for the Grubby and the non-spectacle of a lone skater going through the motions on the ramp. Spectators drifted past but didn't stop. Our ramp area had the desperate feel of a zoo cage with nothing for people to see inside but a mangy old bear sleeping.

As we talked my phone rang. It was Haze. They still hadn't found anywhere to transmit from and were running out of ideas.

'I think I might know a place,' said Travis. 'I've just been talking to one of the dancers from the main stage. She was going on about the VIP bar. They've got decks up there and a little sound system, apparently.'

Of course, McTafferty's VIP bar! It would be the last place they'd think of looking.

'I like the sound of that.'

'The only problem is you need a pass to get in there.'

'What kind of pass?'

'Just a shitty laminate with VIP written on it.'

'Oh,' I said, ready to dismiss the idea.

'In fact,' he added, with the dawn of realisation, 'not unlike one of the Grubby's laminates.'

'You're kidding me?' I laughed. My phone went. It was the Menace. He was outside and needed to be busted in. 'See if the Grubby's got any more,' I said before I left.

I didn't recognise the Menace to begin with. He was dressed as a maintenance worker in overalls and a false beard. He had a large toolbox in his hand. To limit the risk of association it was imperative that he never went near the ramp, so I took him to the nearest cafeteria to talk strategy.

'You've picked a fine corporation to pick on,' he said, nodding his approval. 'I like the irony of it all, what with Christmas coming up. This place has the smack of the merchants in the temple about it, so I suppose you could even say it's our Christian duty to bring it down. I'm going to enjoy this.' He smacked his lips with the anticipation.

I filled him in on the background and explained we needed a diversion, something to keep the organisers' attentions distracted. 'I get your drift,' he said, opening up his tool box. 'In my experience, the spread of misinformation serves most purposes. People are generally stupid. They like to be told what to do and if it looks official you'd be amazed at how compliant they'll be.' He shifted through a stack of stencils. 'I'm going to have a quick recce round the place and then I'll get to work. If you need to get hold of me, just text.' He finished his coffee. 'Right then,' he said with a grin, 'time for a bit of deconstruction.'

I picked up Natty and Haze and took them off to find the VIP bar. It was situated upstairs on one of the balconies, and through its smoked-glass windows there was a view of the show floor below. A surly bouncer stood on the door checking passes, but he didn't flinch when we flashed the Grubby's home-made laminates. As forgeries of a pass the Grubby didn't even know existed at the time he knocked them up, they were uncannily similar.

The VIP bar was the usual waste of trendy space. Corporate executives sipped drinks or spoke loudly into their mobile phones, and OTP interns fussed over the minor celebrities. The interior had been decked out in a Hawaiian theme, and the bar staff wore loud floral shirts. Natty, Haze and I stood at the bar sussing out the set up. There was a set of decks in the corner and a small speaker system, currently churning out laid back grooves for lounge lizards. It was perfect. The only thing we had to do was wangle ourselves a DJ slot. I turned to speak to Haze, only to clock McTafferty striding towards us.

'Che,' he said, laying a hand on my shoulder. 'What brings you up here?'

'Rob gave us a couple of passes,' I said with a quick flash of the Grubby's laminate.

McTafferty cracked one of his best shit-eating grins. 'Good for Rob,' he said. 'Yeah, why not. Can I get you guys a drink?' He called the bartender over. 'It's funny, I was just thinking about you guys. I don't suppose one of your DJs would fancy spinning some tunes up here this afternoon? I've had a cancellation, and I've got a set I need to fill.'

Sometimes, fate just has a habit of tying up the knots in loose ends.

'I think we can sort something out,' I smiled.

Things were clicking into place. There were four large stages, which hosted various fashion shows, as well as a number of smaller sound systems belonging to radio roadshows and the like. The skaters had been busy depositing the transmitters around the venue, in accordance to the Pig's instructions, and had taken to their task with relish. They'd even managed to place a transmitter on the Tannoy system being used in the dog show next door.

Meanwhile, the Menace's deconstruction was causing ripples of chaos within the exhibition centre. The corridors had become clogged with disgruntled punters queuing up for a handful of toilets on account of the rest having 'Out of Order' signs stencilled on their doors. Halls four and eight, according to the signs, had been temporarily closed for 'Emergency refurbishment', and cleaners throughout the venue were scratching their heads at the mounting rubbish in numerous 'Designated Litter' zones. The Menace had even managed to alter the OTP's centrepiece banner. 'Keep it Real!' now read 'Keep it: Steal!'

Now what you have to realise is that there were seventy thousand punters in the building as well as more than five thousand people (everyone from exhibitors to exhibition centre maintenance) working there. The OTP staff was perhaps 30-strong at most, which was ample so long as everything was running smoothly. The Menace's deconstruction had allowed us to test the OTP defences, and was indeed having the desired diversionary effect. Travis had tracked down his weed-smoking security guard who'd divulged that his walkie talkie had been crackling with a stream of relays indicating that things weren't running smoothly at all. The news was encouraging. In such a big venue it had taken the best part of two hours of liaison between the OTP and exhibition centre chains of command to work out that something was going on, and now it was all hands on deck to hunt out the perpetrator. Little did they know that the Menace, having hit hard, had already left the building.

With everything else going on, Cas's revelation that we were down to our last box of stock came as something of an anticlimax. Five days ago, the cash had been my number one priority, but now it somehow seemed irrelevant. Despite my initial reservations, I had become sucked into the grand plan and was now obsessed with the need to pull it off.

By 3 o'clock, everything had been set in place and the crew had gathered for a final pep talk. The Pig had been working with the transmitter to determine what frequencies the radio mics on the various sound systems were working on. Never the most technically minded I nodded my head as he explained the process involved, but he may as well have been speaking Swahili for all I understood.

We split up. Travis, Cas, and the skaters were assuming surveillance positions at various points in the venue, while the Pig and the Grubby held fort at the ghetto. Meanwhile, Natty, Haze and I were on our way to the VIP bar.

'I've worked a proper nice little set out,' Haze mused. 'I'm gonna take this lace on a little story. Start off slow with a few easy rollers – 'cause I know you like 'em, Che – an' just when they fink they know the ending, I'm gonna crank up the heat and it's all gonna go a little bit crazy...'

'What's that?' said the bouncer when we got to the VIP bar. He pointed at the transmitter Natty was carrying.

'That's my beat box, mate,' Natty replied, and he waved us through without batting an eyelid.

The decks were set up in an alcove, off to the side of the window that overlooked the show floor. While Natty and Haze set up the transmitter beneath it, I kept McTafferty occupied. While he turned to air kiss a willowy brunette who'd just tapped him on the shoulder, I took the opportunity to turn the volume down on the walkie talkie he'd placed on the table.

Natty and Haze had been given a one-hour slot on the decks. We planned to start transmitting after half an hour, timing it to coincide with the beginning of the many stage shows down on the show floor, that repeated their performances on the hour. Our collective objective was to hit hard, wreak chaos and then melt away before anyone could point the finger at us.

For half an hour the butterflies gnawed away at my stomach as we waited for the appointed time. Four o'clock. It took an eon to arrive but as the second hand hit the hour I gave the sign. Natty dropped to his knees and flicked the switch on the transmitter. We were on air.

Haze dropped his first tune of the live set and Natty put the mic to his lips.

'Ring, ring,' he rapped, drawing the words out for emphasis.

'Is that the school bell or the Sewerside t'ing?

Bling, bling, are you ready for some de-shopping...'

It wasn't long before my phone started ringing. It was Travis. 'We've got lift off,' he laughed. 'I've got 20 dancers on the Grand Design stage who are looking very confused.'

Stig was the next to call. 'I'm by the Loud FM stage. There's a large crowd trying to work out what's going on because the boy band on stage is singing, but all that's coming out is Natty's voice. You do know this is going out as a live national broadcast, don't you?'

I called Cas. 'Yes, mate,' he said, and I could hear the bass line of the tune Haze was playing rumbling in the background. 'The fashion show's gone pear-shaped. It's hilarious. The crowd don't know any better, and the models are doing their best, but there's chaos behind the scenes. They haven't got a clue what's happening.'

'Che.' I turned round. Haze had a devious grin on his face. 'Got Turnist on the phone. Would you believe it? He took a wrong turn and ended up in the Dog Show. Says the whole place is dog dancin'.'

I looked around at the VIPs lounging on sofas around me, chatting and nodding their heads to the tune coming out of the tiny speaker system in the VIP bar. I clocked McTafferty, and he flashed me a thumbs-up sign. 'Great tune,' he mouthed.

This was just too good to be true. I had to check the show floor out for myself. 'Keep your phones on, yeah?' I told the other two before I left. I couldn't help the huge grin on my face as I walked through the show. The butterflies had given way to a surge of adrenalin that had the hairs on the back of my neck standing up, as the exhibition centre resonated to the sound of our Sewerside offensive.

It was the delicious sound of chaos.

While the punters may have thought it was a little odd that they were hearing the same tune throughout the exhibition centre, they would have assumed that it was part of the show. However, the ground staff and the OTP organisation were only just coming to the realisation that the disruptions were not isolated to individual stages. However, in spite of the pandemonium backstage, the prevailing mentality was one of 'the show must go on', while they figured it all out, so the sound systems just carried on rolling.

As the minutes ticked by Haze, as predicted, had started to turn up the heat. I noticed the people around me subconsciously bobbing their heads to the rhythms that were becoming more frantic with each tune, stand holders jigging from one foot to the other as the music took control. I passed the Grand Design stage, where the professional smiles were starting to wear thin, the dancers doing their best to adapt their choreographed routines to the change in tempo.

As I arrived at the ghetto area, Stig called to say that the radio stage had finally pulled the plug. I sought out the Pig. 'Archie,' I said slapping him on the back, 'you really are a fucking genius!'

He brushed my compliment aside. 'Where the fuck have you been? I've just had Nobit over. We've been rumbled, mate. He knows it's us – or he thinks he does, anyway. Natty's hardly fucking subtle, is he?'

'So where's he gone?'

Suddenly, things weren't so rosy.

'He was trying to get hold of someone on the walkie talkie for ages. I think he's gone to look for him.'

Shit, he was after McTafferty.

'How long ago did he leave?' I barked.

'You just missed him.'

I called Natty, only to get his answer phone. I hung up and called Haze. 'Come on, come on,' I mumbled under my breath as the phone rang and rang.

'Hello…?'

'Haze, it's Che, you've got to get out of there…'

'…Hello?'

'Haze can you hear me?'

'…Hello? It's Haze, I'm not around so leave a message,' his answer phone message sounded back.

'Haze. Kill the transmission. They're onto us!' I barked.

I hung up, cursing, and before the Pig could even say another word I was running across the show floor, fighting my way through the crowds...

I reached the top of the stairs, pausing to catch my breath to flash my laminate to the bouncer on the door. I pushed through to see that Nobit was already in there, locked in intense discussion with Brian McTafferty. I saw them look up, Nobit pointing towards the decks, which I couldn't see from where I was standing, tucked away as they were in the little alcove. I could hear the tune playing over the speakers, some techno whirlygig of a tune that seemed totally out of character with the set Haze had been playing so far. I watched the two of them move towards the decks with purpose, and I knew it was too late, even as I strode on jelly legs after them.

I was halfway across the bar when I heard the needle jump and drag across the record, amplified over the speaker like a rip and a tear that scratched at the eardrums. VIP guests winced and instinctively put their hands to their ears. Over the horrible noise, I could McTafferty and Nobit arguing.

'There,' I heard McTafferty say. 'You've killed the music. Satisfied now?'

Nobit didn't answer immediately, perhaps aware that every head in the VIP bar was turned towards them, the bu-dump, bu-dump, bu-dump sound of the needle bouncing up and down on the record, relentless like the echo of approaching helicopter blades. I heard Nobit remonstrating with the DJ. 'Turn that off!' he snapped.

'Fuck you!' said the DJ. 'You knocked the needle off. You do it.'

I'd made it across the bar and turned towards the alcove where MacTafferty and Nobit stood with their backs to me, the latter remonstrating with the DJ. But it wasn't Natty and Haze who I saw behind the decks. In their place stood some skinny black dude with a face full of piercings and a red mohican. In an instant I turned on my heel and pretended to stare out the window, not believing my luck.

Haze must have picked up his message. The boys were gone.

I felt the relief sweep over my body as I stood staring through the smoked glass that gave a panoramic view of the show floor below.

And it was then that I was suddenly aware of something very peculiar happening, something so surreal that I had to double-take to be sure. My eyes were drawn to a figure on the show floor. A woman, dressed in a black miniskirt, her hair piled high, shopping bags in both hands, was spewing a thick stream of vomit onto a rail of clothes. And then, beside her, another woman in a pink puffer jacket, suddenly double over and puked into her shopping bag. On the corner of a stand, a security guard was yacking up over a small kid in a buggy.

As I watched, half-horrified, half-enthralled by what I was seeing, it seemed as if an invisible, repulsive wave was rolling over the show floor. Everywhere I looked, people were throwing up. Some were running towards the exits, their hands over their mouths. Others just puked where they stood, projecting streams of vomit onto the floor, into their bags, into their jackets, onto stands filled with clothes rails and bargain boxes, down the backs of the people in front of them.

The entire place, this fool's paradise of glitz and glamour, carpet and chrome, was suddenly disappearing under cascading rivers of puke, and the sight was so disgusting that I wanted to turn away but I couldn't. And then, from the corner of my eye, I saw the Sewerside ramp. In a moment of twisted reality, that blot on the corporate landscape seemed to be rising out of the ocean of vomit around it, pitching through the putrid sea like Noah's fucking ark...

Epilogue

What happened? I'm still not quite sure. Probably best to ask the Pig. It had something to do with frequencies, decibel levels and a freak pitch caused by the needle bumping up and down on the record. Magnified through the venue on all those different sound systems it had caused an involuntary and instantaneous bodily reaction within everybody on the show floor...

I'd had away the transmitter in the chaos that had ensued, and it was now residing at the bottom of the sea. The OTP organisation, mindful of its shareholders (and also, no doubt, of the role the chairman's son had played) had gone to great lengths to blame a 'freak electrical incident'.

We hadn't quite planned for the ending to be so dramatic, yet we really couldn't have planned it any better, and somehow Sewerside wouldn't have had it any other way...

After the Battle of Off The Peg, proceedings back in Devon had seemed somewhat dull by comparison. The yard had been busted in our absence, this much I discovered from Maddy who'd heard it from Bacon first-hand. They hadn't found anything, not on our floor anyway, but the sniffer dog had been rather interested in something inside Lesnik's office.

She didn't have to tell me the rest. I knew the dog had found a quarter of weed stashed in the bottom of Lesnik's desk. I knew this because I'd had it put there. It was the reason I'd been to see Sid-the-Dog the night before leaving for OTP. It had cost me a couple of hundred quid to get the job done, but the money had been well spent.

I'd given him a set of keys to by-pass the front door, and told him the night to do it on. I knew Lesnik wouldn't be there, because he'd be attending Felicity's Party Porpoise event. The alarm hadn't been a problem, Sid-the-Dog was after all an expert in such things. The weed had smelt pungent enough that I'd had to wrap it up in plastic to stop Lesnik from getting a whiff of it beforehand, but Sid-the-Dog had marked a scent anyway. Lesnik had been busted on the spot. He'd started ranting on about police harassment, and claimed they'd planted it. Nothing serious would happen to him. It was only quarter of an ounce after all. He'd probably get a slapped wrist and a fine, but in a small town like Liddleton, his reputation would never recover. The phrase living and dying by the sword came to mind...

As for the bankruptcy, it was a very ordinary day on which Travis and I took a trip to the courts with the bankruptcy papers; cold, damp, grey. The world didn't grind to a halt. It was just the same as it had been the day before. The girl behind the counter didn't seem concerned that Travis had to consult with me for most of the answers to the questions she asked him. She saw bankruptcy petitioners every day, and he was just another case number in her book, another pile of paperwork to be processed. The bailiffs turned up on behalf of the bank, but once everything had been done and dusted there was just the one box left for them to repossess. If you have nothing, you have nothing to lose after all. It still had 'Bargain Box' written on its side, but of course there were no bargains in there to be had. Just some freak or unique garments and a ubiquitous yellow T-shirt.

Still, it was a funny feeling being at the courts. It felt a bit like laying the Sewerside to rest in the quiet backroom of a crematorium. But I knew Sewerside would never really die. The name would live on as some subterranean myth, where the facts became so jumbled that it would become impossible to discern quite what the truth had ever been.

And as for the crew... Like Natty had said that night in the Hotel de la Rat, we weren't going anywhere. Like those guerrillas from the hills, we'd lie low and bide our time while our various talents got tweaked and honed. I was sure that one day, one of us would escape the bears through the cracks between the pavement stones, and when that time came I knew there'd be a hand reaching down to pull the rest of us up.

In the meantime, it was time to mutate.

Mutate, survive, move on...

Enjoyed this book?

Find out more about the author,
and a whole range of exciting titles at
<u>www.discoveredauthors.co.uk</u>

Discover our other imprints:

DA Diamonds traditional mainstream publishing

DA Revivals republishing out-of-print titles

Four O'Clock Press assisted publishing

Horizon Press business and corporate materials